4

A CHANNEL FOUR BOOK

ANIMAL SQUAD

UNDERCOVER

ON THE TRAIL WITH THE SPECIAL OPERATIONS UNIT OF THE RSPCA

PAUL BERRIFF WITH THE CO-OPERATION
OF THE RSPCA

Hodder & Stoughton

LONDON   SYDNEY   AUCKLAND

In association with Channel Four Television
Company Limited

British Library Cataloguing in Publication Data
Berriff, Paul
  Animal squad undercover: The book of the Channel 4 series.
  I. Title
639.9

  ISBN 0–340–57108–X

Published by Hodder and Stoughton,
a division of Hodder and Stoughton Ltd,
Mill Road, Dunton Green, Sevenoaks, Kent TN13 2YA
Editorial Office: 47 Bedford Square, London WC1B 3DP

Designed by Dixon & Judd, Hythe, Kent
Photoset by Selwood Systems, Midsomer Norton
Printed in Great Britain by Butler & Tanner Ltd, Frome and London.

CONTENTS

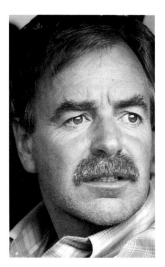

PAUL BERRIFF began work as a press photographer with the *Yorkshire Evening Post* and in 1967 joined BBC Television News as film cameraman. He has been making films for television ever since, winning the British Television News Film Award at the age of only twenty-two, and is now one of Britain's leading factual programme makers. He has won a number of awards including Documentary Award of the Year, Best British Film Award and the News Team Award. Among other citations, he has been presented with the Silver Medal for Bravery from the Royal Humane Society, and the Queen's Commendation for Brave Conduct. For many years, he has given his services to local coastguard stations and was a founder member of 'Humber Rescue', the River Humber Rescue Organisation. His previous books include *Rescue*, based on the BAFTA award-winning ITV series, and *Animal Squad* about the work of the uniformed RSPCA inspector, Sid Jenkins, televised on BBC 1. He collaborated with film director Werner Herzog in an apocalyptic documentary about the aftermath of the Gulf War in Kuwait, *Lessons of Darkness*, which received rapturous reviews from the national press.

PREFACE

During the summer of 1986 I produced the *Animal Squad* television series for BBC 1, which featured the day-to-day exploits of RSPCA Chief Inspector Sid Jenkins based in the Leeds office of the RSPCA inspectorate. While making the series, I came into contact with Chief Superintendent Frank Milner and his seven-man team of the Special Operations Unit based at the RSPCA's headquarters in Horsham. I knew nothing about the existence of the unit until I met them during a suspected dogfight raid on a farm in north Yorkshire.

For obvious reasons they were very wary about being filmed or photo-

graphed for television and newspapers. However, the work of this small undercover team intrigued me, as had Sid Jenkins when I first met him some twelve months earlier. If I could persuade the SOU to allow me into their secret world with my cameras then we would have a fascinating television documentary. I knew it would be difficult to induce them to 'reveal all' in front of a TV audience but with careful camera work we might be able to hide the identity of some of the team.

A few months after *Animal Squad* had been transmitted, I approached Frank Milner about my idea of a 'fly-on-the-wall' documentary about his department. Frank expressed an interest but pointed out that it might be difficult filming some of the team as anonymity was the key to the success of the unit. I explained that I didn't want to jeopardise the work of the Special Operations Unit but with some thoughtful planning we might be able to make a film that would eventually satisfy both of us.

It can take up to two years to plan, shoot and edit a documentary series. But first, as an independent producer, you have to sell the idea to a television broadcaster. During the winter of 1990 I visited Frank Milner at his office in Horsham and suggested, with his permission, that I send in a proposal to Channel 4. He agreed, and in April 1991 Peter Moore and John Willis of the Factual Programmes Department accepted the idea.

On Monday, 29 July 1991 my team, consisting of assistant producer Janice Kearns, cameraman Paul Kerrigan and sound recordist Keith Rodgerson, moved into Horsham and set up our office in the Special Operations Unit. For four months we lived with the SOU, monitoring their calls and following alongside them on their varied assignments both at home and abroad.

In the making of any television series more film is shot than is ultimately broadcast. Sadly, not all the cases we dealt with can be transmitted – there is just not enough airtime available. However, we have put this extra material into the book along with background information about the RSPCA, and how the frontline of the society operates. We hope it will give the reader the inside story of the Animal Squad Undercover team and, above all, help in some way the on-going fight to bring to justice those in our society who take pleasure in being cruel to animals.

PAUL BERRIFF

ACKNOWLEDGMENTS

This book has been written as a companion to the Channel 4 television series *Animal Squad Undercover*. It would not have been possible without the work of Amanda Aviss who researched and assisted with the material required to produce this insight into the work of the RSPCA.

Special thanks are due to the many people who co-operated in the production of the documentaries. Without the initial enthusiasm of RSPCA Chief Superintendent Frank Milner, the project would not have got off the ground. Thanks are owing also to all the members of the RSPCA's undercover team for letting me follow them on their varied assignments.

I am indebted also to assistance given from the various police forces and other authorities who allowed us to film the investigations featured. I would like to give a special thanks to Detective Sergeant Peter McCloy of the Durham Constabulary and Inspector Ken Reeves at Holloway Police Station, London for their co-operation.

I should like to single out the following for their special assistance with the creation of this book:

RSPCA Superintendent Don Balfour who read and amended the text to ensure the technical accuracy of this portrait of the Special Operations Unit;

RSPCA Chief Veterinary Officer David Wilkins who provided and checked historical and explanatory background material;

Dave Currey from the Environmental Investigation Agency who provided essential data for the chapter on the wild bird trade.

I am indebted to all the RSPCA staff who provided information and double-checked the content for accuracy. Special thanks to Michaela Miller, RSPCA Head of Publications, and Jerry Lloyd, Director of Public Relations, who steered this project through to a successful conclusion.

Thanks also to Caroline Evans who spent many hours transcribing the film sound track.

SOU Inspector Andy Foxcroft deserves a special mention as the photographer of many of the pictures featured in this book. Susanna Yager of Channel 4 Publishing and Celia Levett of Hodder & Stoughton must be thanked for their enthusiasm in backing this book.

And finally I would like to thank members of my film team, Janice Kearns, Keith Rodgerson and Paul Kerrigan, without whose professionalism and dedication the films could not have been made.

Campaigning for change

The RSPCA captured the headlines in 1991 through its high-profile campaigning image promoted by the Society's public relations division.

Into Europe

Intense media activity drew the nation's eyes to the live transport issue where thousands of British farm animals are transported for hours across Europe without adequate care for their welfare. The campaign prompted two million people to sign a petition against live transport; the petition was presented to the European Community Council of Ministers.

RSPCA revelations that many of the 300,000 British calves sent to the veal crates of France and Holland every year end up as meat back on British dinner tables prompted huge public response.

The RSPCA live transport campaign was featured widely on national radio and television and the issue was highlighted in programmes as diverse as BBC Radio Four's *The Archers* and Channel 4's *Check Out*.

In February the RSPCA found itself in the Gulf War zone and under the media spotlight in Jubail, Saudi Arabia. Television crews from around the world, co-ordinated by the Society's press office, converged on the emergency wildlife unit in Jubail set up by the RSPCA for long-term training of locals in specialist bird cleaning techniques.

Dangerous dogs bit into the headlines in 1991 after a series of attacks on both children and adults. And after the Government announced the Dangerous Dogs Act, centering upon pit bull terriers, the Society called once more for a registration scheme for all dogs.

Death in the air

The RSPCA highlighted the problems of the trade in wild-caught birds through a joint campaign with the Environmental Investigation Agency (EIA) and the Royal Society for the Protection of Birds (RSPB). A series of national newspaper advertisements drew attention to the fact that for every wild-caught bird that ends up in the pet shops three will have died en route from the jungles of South America, Asia and Africa to the pet shops of Europe. The campaign resulted in 48 airlines refusing to carry the birds by the end of 1991.

Public relations

Animal-friendly events with wide public appeal ranging from a 'cruelty-free' fashion ball to a celebrity-filled float at the Lord Mayor's Show in London were organised by the public relations division in 1991. In its first year, Bounce Scruffts

...n friends of the ...roup devoted ...ng animal ...thin the Asian ...y, was launched

...e Society received ...alls offering ...to the Perrycroft ...s after publicity ...nding the rescue.

It's not our advertising that should be banned. It's this.

On the campaign trail: RSPCA newspaper advertisements (right) and direct mail packs (below).

First, they stuff the parrot. Then it dies.

Above: Participants at Bounce Scruffts, the RSPCA's mongrel dog show.
Below: Animal World T-shirt competition winner 15-year-old Elinor Jeffries (centre) with celebrities Michaela Strachan and Jessica Muschamp.

– the RSPCA's rival to Crufts bu... dogs – attracted over 9,000 peop... 1,000 dogs to its two venues at R... Leeds, and the RSPCA's Sout... Centre, Potters Bar, London.

Through the letterbox

The RSPCA's direct mail pro... fund-raiser for the Society w... going out to specially selecte... month. The Gulf Oiled Birds... raised over £1 million m... successful pack of 1991. C... those mailed sent in a dona...

RSPCA fund-raising p... recognition through winn... leader awards for fund... national ECHO Awar... ECHO Awards are ... attracting entries from...

By the end of 1991 ... whelming response to ... supporters was at an ...

Field fund-raising

In 1991 more RSP... ordered goods fr... resale at their o... service to branch... variety of brand... to suit all ages an...

CHAPTER ONE

THE SPECIAL OPERATIONS UNIT

Uniformed inspectors are the most visible sign of the RSPCA's law enforcement work. These men and women – 287 of them stationed throughout England and Wales – are the RSPCA's 'fire-fighters', answering thousands of cruelty complaints every year. They ensure that the dozens of laws regulating the keeping of animals are being properly observed. And in the worst cases of abuse they obtain the evidence needed to bring offenders to court.

But there is another side to the RSPCA inspectorate's activities that is rarely seen: the work of the Special Operations Unit. The task of this 'plain-clothes' squad is to gather intelligence on the abuse and mistreatment of animals. Not from behind a desk, however. Often operating 'undercover' in order to mingle with suspects and pick up clues, the SOU officers are in the front line of the battle against cruelty, working closely with uniformed colleagues, the police, and other law-enforcement agencies.

The unit was set up in 1977 with four officers, to obtain information about the treatment of British animals shipped to continental slaughterhouses. Evidence that the trade was causing suffering was needed to underpin the RSPCA's campaign to ban the export of live animals. First-hand proof could only be gained by trailing the lorries carrying the animals. In its first year of operation the officers covered over 50,000 miles in Europe on long and arduous trails, obtaining graphic evidence that animals were being treated appallingly (chapter two provides more details).

The new unit was equally active at home, monitoring transit conditions within Britain. The squad staked out markets, livestock auctions and hauliers to see how the animals were handled and bring offences to light. Its members were also on call to deal with any national disaster, such as animals in distress as a result of oil pollution, blizzards, or floods. They could be drafted in to co-ordinate major rescues and boost the efforts of local inspectors in times of need, using their special incidents vehicle as a control base.

These 'flying squad' services were also in demand overseas. For example in 1980 Frank Milner, commander of the unit, went to Italy to help the animal rescue operation following a serious earthquake. SOU officers have been despatched to far-flung locations to monitor and report back on animal abuse. They have obtained information for campaigns against seal clubbing in Canada, the massacre of whales off Iceland, and the cruel traffic in horses from Greece to Italy for slaughter.

Although its first focus was transit offences, the unit's brief soon widened. Today SOU officers are used for any operation where extensive periods of surveillance are required, since hours of painstaking detective work are needed to expose illegal activities such as organised dogfighting or badger-baiting. To get a conviction they may have to infiltrate criminal circles or watch a target for weeks prior to a raid. The work is

The RSPCA continually campaigns to make registration of all dogs compulsory.

Evidence for dog registration is mounting up. We need your support now.

REGISTRATION, NOT EXTERMINATION

dirty and often dangerous and demands a special blend of patience, courage and dogged determination to nail those responsible for some of the worst forms of cruelty imaginable.

There are currently eight officers in the squad, all of whom had extensive experience as uniformed inspectors before being accepted for the Special Operations Unit. Chief Superintendent Frank Milner has been in charge of the unit for the last twelve years until his retirement at the end of 1991 when Superintendent Don Balfour took over. Two chief inspectors and five inspectors make up the complement.

On top of the gruelling seven months' training course that all RSPCA inspectors must pass, SOU officers have to acquire new, specialist skills. Perhaps most crucial is the ability to follow a target without detection; therefore officers are given an intensive course in basic surveillance to develop vital techniques. The officers also have to familiarise themselves with sophisticated communications and monitoring equipment which can prove invaluable, such as night-viewing equipment for a stakeout or concealed video cameras to record essential evidence.

A whole new range of animal welfare legislation must be absorbed, including complex European Community regulations as well as domestic laws. Cultivating informants or talking to suspects requires sophisticated interviewing techniques, while the ability to build good contacts with outside forces such as the police, customs and local authorities is a must. Advanced driving skills are useful too when so much time is spent on vehicle trails. 'Even the best drivers sometimes find they've overtaken the target and are following from in front,' joked Don.

A job specification for the ideal SOU officer would contain some unusual requirements. A cast-iron stomach for instance. The dreary hours speeding up and down motorways in pursuit of suspects yield few opportunities for haute cuisine. Plastic coffee and cold chips are a staple diet, makeshift snacks which must be snatched as the opportunity presents itself, for who can tell when the target will stop again? After a long trail, curry is the favoured fare as an antidote to bland motorway meals.

Chameleon-like qualities would be another attribute. SOU officers have to be able to blend in with their surroundings when on an enquiry, which means being unobtrusive. Waxed jackets and wellies work for market observations but not for a down-at-heel hang-out for dogfighters, where scruffy jeans and trainers would be the order of the day. Sometimes the camouflage works too well. A successful joint police/RSPCA dogfighting raid provided one such occasion, when the two officers who leapt into the pit to separate the fighting dogs found themselves at the end of a pump-action shotgun. An armed policeman taking part in the raid had confused them with the villains!

Those with a liking for privacy, a rare commodity on surveillance operations, would be unlikely to fit in. The unit's special incidents vehicle doubles as a control base when lengthy observations are needed and the officers have to spend prolonged periods together in a cramped space. Equally uncomfortable is the van with one-way windows used for undetected observation. But sometimes the best vantage-point calls for stronger nerves, as for instance when Inspector Andy Foxcroft spent several hours in connection with a dogfighting enquiry 200 feet up a gasometer in the company of a roosting falcon.

The ability to keep going on minimal sleep is another essential asset. On long trails the driver of the vehicle being tailed may snatch a quick sleep but no such luxury is allowed the SOU officers, who must remain alert at all times, ready to move when the driver wakes. One time, Don recalled, they were following a sheep transporter in France when they were almost caught out. 'It was 3.00 a.m. in the morning, sub-zero temperatures and freezing in the car. We were parked in a rest area while the driver we were following took a nap. We'd pulled on woollen hats and snuggled into sleeping-bags to try and keep warm. Suddenly he took off. We spent the next few miles in hot pursuit still encased in the sleeping-bags!'

A sense of humour and camaraderie marks out the Special Operations Unit inspectors. Each individual has particular strengths but it is as a team that they are most effective. They operate from the RSPCA's administrative headquarters in Horsham where they share a cramped office with Jane Smart, the unit's intelligence collator and back-up admin officer. Jane's dog Indy, a permanent resident in the office, cannot go unmentioned. This Jack Russell terrier has played his part in undercover operations too, providing useful 'cover' as a walker's dog on one mission to track down badger-baiters. In view of the cramped office conditions it is perhaps

fortunate that the inspectors spend most of their time on field operations.

The arrival of Paul Berriff and his film crew last summer filled the office to bursting point. Paul spent four months making a Channel 4 documentary on the unit, filming from August to November. The crew based themselves in Horsham, camping out in Chief Superintendent Milner's office during the day to ensure they were on hand to cover jobs as the calls came in. By night they were instantly contactable by mobile telephone. SOU officers agreed to allow themselves to be wired for sound so that Paul could achieve this unique 'fly on the wall' documentary of the unit's operations, tracking them from the jungles of Guyana to the back streets of British inner cities.

The chapters that follow uncover the hidden world of animal abuse exposed in the *Animal Squad Undercover* series. But first, here are the officers involved.

UNDERCOVER SQUAD UNCOVERED

CHIEF SUPERINTENDENT FRANK MILNER

Frank has thirty-seven years' experience in the RSPCA, joining in 1954 after a stint with the RAF and then the ambulance service. It was while working as an ambulance driver that he was first drawn to the RSPCA. Many elderly patients worried about leaving much loved pets at home when they had to go into hospital, so Frank would call in the local RSPCA inspector to help out. Favourably impressed by the charity's caring response, he eventually applied to become an inspector himself. Early postings to Woking, Bradford, Kettering, Bury and Manchester were followed by six years as travelling superintendent for the north of England.

Frank took over command of the Special Operations Unit in 1978 (it was called the Special Investigations and Operations Department in those days), since when he has been despatched to many far-flung locations to report back on animal abuse. In 1978 he joined Greenpeace campaigners aboard the *Rainbow Warrior* to prevent the annual seal cull in the Orkney Isles. He also sailed with Greenpeace from Iceland shadowing the Norwegian whalers. The information he brought back about the terrible cruelty inflicted by harpooning methods helped to rouse public opinion against whaling. He obtained a similar response after observing and reporting on the seal cull in Newfoundland. In 1981 Frank carried out a detailed enquiry into the transit of horses for slaughter between Greece and Italy. His findings were instrumental in persuading the Greek government to make improvements.

One incident in which he was involved combines the best and worst aspects of an inspector's job. A complaint led him to an address where he found a labrador nailed inside a garden shed. The dog had been there without food or water for three weeks, weighed only a quarter of its normal weight and was close to death. Frank considered putting it out of its misery straight away. He hesitated, then decided to take it home. The dog fought back to full health and remained with the Milner family, a much loved pet for many years. 'It took months but I eventually tracked down the owner responsible and brought him to justice.'

Frank, known as 'The Boss', retired just after filming finished on the *Animal Squad Undercover* series and now lives in Yorkshire with his wife Jean.

SUPERINTENDENT DON BALFOUR

Don took over as head of the Special Operations Unit at the beginning of 1992, thirty years after joining the RSPCA. Money was clearly not the

attraction in 1962 as he took a hefty cut in wages, dropping from £20 a week as a miner to a weekly take-home pay of just £7. But animal welfare was in the family tradition, or at least in that of his future wife. Watching her father, the RSPCA inspector for Wakefield, at work prompted Don to apply.

In those days inspectors were moved to different stations every seven years. Don served at King's Lynn, Liverpool and Sunderland before being posted to Newcastle as chief inspector. His calm temperament is invaluable in difficult situations, like the time he saved some ponies from a blazing stable, crawling through the smoke to reach the terrified animals and lead them to safety. In another dramatic rescue he was lowered into a gasometer trench to pluck to safety a dog that had fallen in. Despite being coated with tar the dog survived its ordeal.

After sixteen years with the uniformed inspectorate Don was keen to face a new challenge and joined the Special Operations Unit in 1979. He is now a veteran of more trails and stake-outs than he cares to count.

Asked for his best moment with the unit, Don responded with the successful raid at Dunscroft two years ago when twenty-one dogfighters were caught red-handed. His worst moment was when a cruelty case against a poultry processing unit accused of faulty slaughtering procedures was thrown out by the courts. The case, which alleged that hundreds of birds were being scalded to death, was dismissed due to a paperwork error by the magistrates' clerk.

Don predicts that the unit's work will increasingly focus on European issues. He welcomes plans to join forces with sister societies on the continent to form a European Task Force to tackle specific welfare problems within the Community.

Despite twelve years in the south of England Don is unmistakably still a Yorkshire man at heart. Known for his plain speaking and no-nonsense approach, he has carved himself a reputation for methodical and meticulous attention to detail. Those planning and deployment skills will be tested to the limit as he steers the Special Operations Unit through the challenges to come.

CHIEF INSPECTOR MIKE BUTCHER

When Mike joined the RSPCA in 1972 he exchanged one uniform for another. Pounding the beat as a policeman was followed by a spell with the Atomic Energy Authority as a security officer. Nowadays he works in plain clothes and is one of the unit's crack hands at 'deep cover', having successfully passed himself off as a number of different characters, some shady, in order to cultivate and chat up informants. When mixing with villains a few rough moments can be expected but physical intimidation from known criminals cannot be dismissed lightly. Yet Mike has a capacity to look unshaken even in the face of death threats.

This is Mike's second time in the Special Operations Unit. He first transferred to undercover operations in 1980 after seven years as the inspector for York and Alnwick, then two years later went back into uniform to take up the station of Harrogate. His most satisfying achievement as a uniformed inspector was bringing the first-ever successful prosecution against a travelling circus. Worst moment undercover was being threatened with a pump-action shotgun when police mistook him for a dogfighter.

Mike is a born investigator who enjoys the challenge of ferreting facts out of informants and following up leads. 'You need a lot of patience to build a case but when it all slots into place and you nail an offender it's a great feeling,' he explained. 'You just don't have the time needed to carry out lengthy investigations as a uniformed inspector.'

Even after years of exposure to animal abuse the capacity to be shocked by cruelty is undiminished, but officers have to remain detached. As one of the team investigating conditions in Spanish abattoirs Mike was sickened by the slaughtering methods he witnessed but carried on filming to get the evidence needed. Like Don he believes that the unit's work exposing cruelty on the continent is going to increase in importance.

Not a man cut out for paperwork and pen-pushing, Mike is happiest out on the streets 'mixing it' with some of the most unsavoury elements of society, seeking evidence of cruelty to animals wherever it occurs. 'Streetwise' sums him up best, a quality that has helped him to cope in the many risky situations that come with undercover operations.

The identity of many of the SOU officers must be protected to safeguard their anonymity in the field.

13

INSPECTOR BRYN PASS

Undercover officers assume a variety of 'disguises' in order to conceal their true occupation. One that comes easily to ex-art student Bryn is passing himself off as a painter – not the Michelangelo variety, of course, but a good old decorator. Scruffy overalls or paint-splashed jeans provide the perfect cover for hanging around to pick up information.

After leaving art college Bryn worked as a dog warden, which gave him first-hand experience of the callous way some people treat domestic animals. 'But even so, nothing really prepares you for your first serious cruelty case. That really hits you between the eyes.' His was that of a dog which had been starved and neglected, but the case had a happy outcome when the dog was rehomed. Joining the RSPCA in 1979, thirty-four-year-old Bryn's first posting to Great Yarmouth was followed by a spell at Oxford and then Bolton, where in one of his most distressing cases he found dead and dying animals throughout what he dubbed 'Death Farm'. The farmer was prosecuted and fined over £2,000.

Two years after he joined the Special Operations Unit in 1988, the first-ever prosecution for fox-baiting was brought, against a Londoner whose idea of a good day out was to drive into the countryside with four dogs and capture a fox for some later 'amusement'. The man took the fox home, locked it in a

shed, and set his dogs on the poor animal to rip it apart. He made the mistake of taking photographs of this 'sport', which were passed by someone at the processing laboratory to the SOU: as a result he was tracked down and prosecuted for cruelty to a 'captive' animal.

Bryn once pulled off an April Fool's prank with a serious message, based on the RSPCA's policy that all dogs should be licensed. He got the local paper to run a story that dog licence detector vans would be touring the neighbourhood and anybody tracked without a licence (less for black and white dogs, more for coloured!) would be in trouble. The post office was besieged by people applying for licences.

Like all his colleagues Bryn is as tough as nails when it comes to tackling cruelty.

Right: The man took the fox home, locked it in a shed and set his dogs on the poor animal to rip it apart.

INSPECTOR ANDY FOXCROFT

Andy's keen interest in photography has been put to good use during his time in the Special Operations Unit as the man behind the camera when photographic or video evidence is required to back up investigations.

Apart from a brief stint in retailing, thirty-three-year-old Andy has always worked in the animal welfare field, spending three years as an ambulance driver for the RSPCA's Putney Hospital before joining the inspectorate in 1980. His first posting was Bolton where he was involved in one of the most demanding rescues of his career when he saved the life of a horse that had fallen into a canal. Andy spent several hours, assisted by the Fire Brigade, trying to free the animal, wading into thick mud to keep the horse upright until it could be pulled to safety. Another memorable incident concerned turkey chicks en route from Canada to Spain on board a flight delayed by fog at Manchester airport. They were only a couple of days old and would die without food so Andy stayed up all night hand-feeding 6,000 chicks!

Bolton was followed by a posting to Richmond in Surrey before he transferred to the Special Operations Unit in 1986. Since then, like all his colleagues, Andy has worked on investigations into all sorts of sickening cruelty to animals both at home and abroad.

In his view one of the most barbaric spectacles was at the annual fiesta in Villanueva, Spain, where a donkey is paraded through the streets to the accompaniment of gunshots and fireworks. An SOU team had been despatched to collect information for the RSPCA's efforts to outlaw these fiestas. The donkey survived but in the course of its ordeal the terrified animal lost forty-two pounds in weight.

Andy's gentle charm disguises a steely resolve to catch the criminals responsible for atrocities like organised badger-baiting. He was delighted to be one of the SOU team responsible for catching badger-diggers recently on the Isle of Wight. The team watched in horror, from a concealed location, as the diggers pulled out a badger by its tail and hit it with a shovel. But there was rejoicing later when the people responsible, including two huntsmen, were brought to justice.

INSPECTOR ALAN GODDARD

Just two minutes with Alan Goddard prove why he has the reputation of being the joker of the unit. Joker in the best possible sense, for Alan's ready wit can lighten up even the tensest of operations. Asked why he joined the

15

RSPCA, he replied, 'I got the initials wrong and thought it was the RAC. I kept asking them throughout the seven-month training, "When are we going to start mending cars?"' But beneath the humour there's a deadly seriousness. Suspects on the end of Alan's razor-sharp interviewing techniques often find themselves tied up in knots and trapped into incriminating themselves and others.

Thirty-nine-year-old Alan joined the RSPCA in 1979 after working as a draughtsman and then joining the army. His military experience and rigorous training in surveillance techniques come in handy on undercover operations. On one occasion Alan spent the night out of doors dug into undergrowth, keeping observation on suspected badger-diggers. 'You know you're well concealed when they walk past inches away and even their dogs don't detect you!' he said. The dogs might not have got Alan but he got the baiters, who were successfully prosecuted.

He joined the Special Operations Unit in 1985 after five years as the uniformed inspector for Dartford. Since then Alan has been one of the key officers in forging the unit's close links with police forces up and down the country. He spent sixteen months attached to Lancashire CID looking into dog-fighting and helped them to obtain a number of dogfighting-related convictions. One noteworthy case was the first-ever prosecution under the Customs and Excise Act of an exporter shipping calves abroad without allowing them the statutory ten hours' rest required before transit to the continent.

Alan has been equally active monitoring the treatment of animals once they cross the Channel. During 1990's 'lamb wars', when unruly French farmers were attacking consignments of British sheep, Alan was trailing one of the lorries that got ambushed. When he and a colleague tried to prevent the attack on the sheep they incurred the wrath of an angry stick-wielding mob.

Their vehicle was damaged but they eventually escaped unharmed, as did the sheep.

Since filming the *Animal Squad Undercover* series Alan has been promoted and transferred back to the uniformed inspectorate as chief inspector for the Guildford area.

INSPECTOR TERRY SPAMER

Keep fit enthusiast Terry Spamer was a trainee diver in the Royal Navy before a keen interest in wildlife diverted him into animal welfare. He worked for the RSPCA Hull branch as an animal ambulance driver prior to joining the inspectorate in 1979. Terry believed in taking the job home with him. Injured badgers, deer, reptiles and other animals were all brought home to be nursed back to health, then returned to the wild.

A successful rescue is always one of the most rewarding moments in any inspector's career and Terry is no exception. The most memorable for him was that of a porpoise from the river in the centre of Doncaster. Dubbed Percy by the local media, the porpoise had been stranded for several weeks; it was coming under air-rifle fire from local thugs and was clearly dying. Various attempts to rescue it had failed, and plans were in hand for a mercy killing by captive bolt when Terry made a final attempt by boat. He succeeded in catch-

ing the porpoise by the tail and pulling it into the boat. A seventy-mile dash up the motorway to the nearest coastline ensued, complete with a siren-blaring police escort. En route the animal's pollution sores were soothed with lanolin and it was established that Percy was a female. It was therefore a hastily renamed Priscilla who was successfully returned to the sea.

Since joining the Special Operations Unit in 1989, Terry's most distressing case was one which involved casualty slaughter. Some hauliers specialise in removing sick or injured livestock. Animals in pain should be destroyed on site or moved by ambulance to the nearest abattoir, but one unscrupulous operator was transporting animals unfit to travel hundreds of miles in order to make more money. The SOU officers staked out the haulier to obtain the evidence needed for a prosecution. 'It was awful watching prolonged whipping of a lame cow to get it up a loading ramp instead of stepping in to stop the suffering immediately,' said Terry. But hasty intervention at that point would have brought the observation to light and sacrificed the chance of prosecuting those responsible.

Like all his colleagues Terry has been involved in many dogfighting-related incidents. One of the most satisfying was a joint operation with the police, in which they sledge-hammered their way into a remote cottage in Nidd to capture dogfighters in action. The dogs were still fighting in the cellar as they searched the house for the culprits. One was hiding in the wardrobe and another lying in bed, fully clothed, pretending to be asleep!

Since the *Animal Squad Undercover* series was filmed thirty-three-year-old Terry has been promoted to chief inspector.

INSPECTOR IAN GREEN

Thirty-three-year-old Ian Green is the newest recruit to the Special Operations Unit. His commitment to animals dates back to his schooldays when he spent weekends working as a volunteer in the RSPCA's Southridge Animal Home. As soon as he left school he got a job as a veterinary assistant at the charity's Harmsworth Hospital in London. After three years he had itchy feet and took off for Australia, where he spent a year doing, among other things, a stint on a sheep-shearing station. Back in Britain he rejoined the hospital as a night-shift ambulance driver until he was accepted for the inspectorate in 1984.

As the inspector for Bedford he had his fair share of cruelty prosecutions, including one that stands out in his memory: a case against a pig farmer who went abroad and abandoned his animals. The pigs were up to their hocks in faeces and dying of starvation when Ian came to the rescue. The irony was that the farmer was an 'ambassador' for the pig industry who regularly gave lectures on good husbandry techniques.

At Bedford there was the usual complement of trapped swans and injured animals to be rescued but a more unusual case involved some fox cubs that had fallen into a grain silo. It took half a day to dismantle the equipment and free the cubs.

Ian has plotted his career with the same cool efficiency he applies to tracking down villains in order to fulfil his 'ultimate ambition' of becoming one of the SOU team. 'It's the best job in the world – at the sharp end.'

A committed vegetarian, one of the worst assignments he has drawn since being with the unit must be the investigation of Spanish slaughterhouses, which revealed the inhumane methods of slaughter being used in EC-licensed Spanish abattoirs. He had to watch slaughtermen paralyse cattle and horses by stabbing them in the back of the neck with a four-inch blade called a *puntilla* (chapter 13 provides more details).

Ian enjoys the opportunities the job provides to work closely with other law-enforcement agencies. 'We have excellent access to the police and the help and assistance we get is second to none.' In its battle against escalating cruelty the Special Operations team needs all the help it can get.

JANE SMART

Any portrait of the staff of the Special Operations Unit would not be complete without mention of twenty-nine-year-old Jane Smart. Jane is the unit's admin assistant who types up the confidential reports, keeps the files and collates the intelligence on suspected offenders. She is often the first point of contact for anyone phoning the unit with important information. She is also 'agony aunt', tea-maker, memory prodder and a lot more besides.

Jane has been with the undercover unit for six years; one of her most gruelling duties is having to watch some of the videos of animal suffering that make their way into the unit. These have to be screened to try and pick out the participants at organised dogfights and other cruel events.

Indy, Jane's Jack Russell terrier who shares the office, has already been mentioned. This paragon of canine virtue has only one major fault – a tendency to attack the stuffed badger on display in the Inspectorate Training School upstairs. This is the only known incident of badger-baiting where the undercover investigators are prepared to look the other way!

BADGER-BAITING

Sadly, animal-baiting has yet to be consigned to history. Today badgers are probably the animal most at risk. In previous centuries badgers were often baited in bear or rat pits. The animal would be secured in a box and then terriers used to draw it out. Once the terrier got a grip the handler was supposed to loosen its hold by biting the dog on the tail or leg. Then the badger could be drawn again. Sometimes the badger's tail was nailed to the floor to prevent it from escaping and it would be baited until it died either from injuries or gangrene. Badger-baiting was a favourite 'sport' at top public schools like Eton and Winchester.

Despite strong laws to protect badgers the persecution of this most harmless of mammals continues.

The most common form of baiting consists of introducing terriers to a badger sett as part of a dig. Dogs are put down the setts to locate the 'quarry' then, guided by the dogs' barking, the owners dig down to the badger.

Part of the so-called 'excitement' comes from working the terriers. Below ground the badger at first attempts to retreat and dig through to a more inaccessible part of the sett. But when escape is frustrated it will turn and confront the dogs. Sometimes both badger and terrier may be suffocated below ground by the collapse of loose rocks and soil. The battle may rage for several hours and the dogs and badger can sustain terrible injuries.

Once a badger is exposed it is lifted by the tail and shaken to prevent it reaching up and biting its assailant. The animal may then be bagged so it can be baited later or reintroduced to the sett for the 'sport' to continue. Alternatively the unfortunate badger may be beaten senseless with spades or crowbars then thrown to the dogs as their reward.

168th Annual Report 1991
Royal Society for the Prevention of Cruelty to Animals

RSPCA

photo: Stuart Harrop

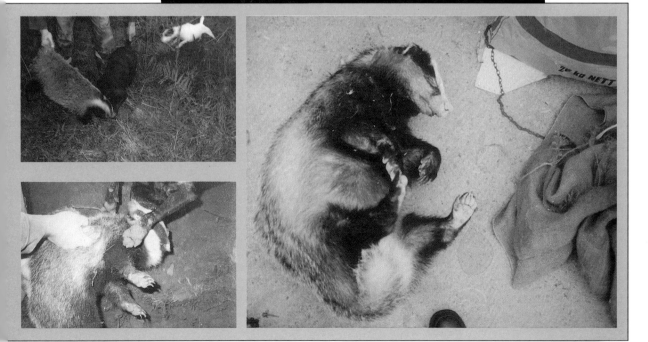

FRENCH BUR[N]

219 LAMBS

ALIVE IN LORR[Y]

by GARY MORGAN

[M]ORE than 200 [B]ritish lambs were [ro]asted alive in a [te]rrifying attack on [a] lorry by French [far]mers.

[T]he animals died [in] agony after a cal[lo]us gang of 30 [hoo]ded farmers set [the] truck ablaze.

[Th]e driver and his 14-[yea]r-old son were [trap]ped in their cabin [but] escaped death by [inch]es.

[Th]e attack is the most [savag]e yet in the French [farm]ers' campaign to stop [Britis]h imports

... of ...res-...bs, ...ere ...the

...ni-...ent ...ed ...o be destroyed.

The French govern-ment immediately con-demned the "appalli..."

with French agric[ultural] minister Henri [...] who promised an i[nvesti]gation.

A French police s[poke]man said: "It is terr[ible] that the man and h[is son] were trapped in the [burn]ing cab. It was a [cruel] and vicious ambush.

RSPCA chief veter[inary] officer David Wil[kins] said: "This barbaric [att]ack is an added horr[or to] the trade of live ani[mals] that is already unacc[epta]ble.

"It shows how vul[nera]ble innocent livestoc[k is.] We have launched a[n in]ternational investiga[tion] and we will take w[hat]ever action is necessar[y.]

A spokesman for

CHAPTER TWO

ON THE ROAD

F unny way to earn a living really. Chasing lorryloads of sheep all over the continent. Just what are those RSPCA inspectors looking for? The only way to answer that question is to step back in time, back even before the formation of the Special Operations Unit. Right back to the 1940s.

The cross-Channel trade in live animals built up after the Second World War, fuelled by a shortage of meat for the large number of American servicemen stationed in post-war Europe. The military wanted beef, large quan-

tities of it. It had to be slaughtered in European abattoirs under rigorous American supervision, since British slaughterhouses, frankly, were not up to their standards. The trade thrived. British exporters got a high price for their animals. The continental buyers benefited too. It kept their slaughterhouses busy and there was an extra bonus: by buying the whole animal, not just a carcase, they got the by-products as well. Hides and offal were valuable commodities.

The RSPCA watched the growth of

Above: Monitoring quickly established that British sheep were again travelling long distances without rest, food or water.

Left: Don Balfour inspects a shipment of calves at Calais Docks.
photo: Peter Nicholls, *Today*

21

The Minimum Value Orders currently protect Dartmoor ponies like these (pictured here with RSPCA Chief Inspector Tony Booth) from being exported for slaughter.

the trade with horror. At the start of the century the society had worked hard to end the cruelty of the cross-Channel horse trade, which had been particularly terrible. Old, worn-out horses were shipped to the continent for butchery. Many were in such a dreadful state that the Veterinary College of Brussels used to send its students to Antwerp to study the horses arriving. There they could see every known ailment. However, vigorous campaigning had eventually stopped the traffic. Legislation, called Minimum Value Orders, was introduced, stating that no equine below a certain monetary value could be shipped abroad.

But the measure applied only to horses and ponies. There was nothing to protect other farm animals, and it was feared that the post-war trade was causing considerable suffering. Pressure from the RSPCA played a part in obtaining a special government enquiry into the matter. A sub-committee of the Board of Trade was set up under Lord Balfour in 1957, with a brief to investigate the trade. This committee produced four main recommendations which became known as the Balfour Assurances. These were as follows:

– *all animals must be fed and watered during transit;*
– *no animal should have to travel more than 100 kilometres from where it was disembarked to a slaughterhouse;*
– *animals should be killed humanely either by captive bolt pistol or electric pre-stunning;*
– *no animal sent from Britain to one continental country should be re-exported to another.*

These recommendations were not the all-out ban the RSPCA would have liked. The society wanted a carcase-only trade. However, they were better than nothing.

Britain, Holland, Belgium, West Germany, and later Italy signed these assurances, which came into force in 1964. France only signed the assurances with reference to cattle. The British government therefore refused to issue export licences for sheep to go to France.

Still unhappy, the RSPCA decided to see for itself if the assurances were working and from time to time sent representatives to the continent to follow consignments through to their destinations. No substantial evidence of wrongdoing was obtained until 1970. That year the RSPCA stepped up its investigations and despatched Superintendent Ronald Butfield and Deputy Chief Veterinary Officer Phillip Brown to Belgium in October. They discovered beyond doubt that the Balfour Assurances were being broken. They brought back evidence of calves travelling over 100 kilometres to slaughterhouses and confirmed that animals were being re-exported across borders. Most distressing of all was the evidence they obtained of barbaric slaughterhouse conditions.

However, the government was reluctant to legislate against the trade. Cynics suggested the reason was that it did not want to offend foreign governments at precisely the moment it was trying to negotiate favourable terms of entry into the Common Market.

It was clear more data was needed to spur the government into action. Over the next two years RSPCA officials made many more trips to Europe. Sheep were traced from England to Ostend and through Belgium into France to abattoirs as far away as Marseille. Inspection of the abattoirs importing British sheep through the Belgian 'back door' included one at Sisteron in Provence. There Phillip Brown witnessed a gruesome spectacle: 420 English sheep slaughtered inhumanely, their throats slit while still fully conscious. An abattoir worker pinned the terrified animals down to keep them still during this ghastly procedure.

Despite the information accumulated the Ministry of Agriculture still hesitated. The RSPCA, therefore, swung into action with a massive publicity campaign in the winter of 1972. The aim of the SELFA campaign (Stop the Export of Live Food Animals) was to mobilise public opinion in favour of a Private Member's Bill to restrict the trade.

The events that followed underlined the might of the media. A BBC *Midweek* camera team accompanied Butfield on a routine observation trip. It was January 1973 and bitterly cold. They picked up and trailed a British consignment of

British calves are often shipped to Holland for fattening in Dutch veal crates. The veal may then be re-exported back into the UK for consumption.

photo: Peter Nicholls, *Today*

sheep from Belgium, across the French frontier, down to a slaughterhouse in Provence. The journey took two and a half days, much of the time in blizzard conditions. Not once were the sheep offered food or water. The crew was barred from entering the abattoir but there was every reason to fear for the fate of the animals inside. It was the Sisteron slaughterhouse. Shortly before the BBC was due to transmit this graphic film the government caved in: it announced a temporary ban on the issue of export licences for sheep.

But that wasn't the end of the matter. The RSPCA had concentrated its fact-finding on the plight of sheep. The trade in cattle continued. The government would not extend the ban without further arm-twisting. Once again the same tactics were employed, the RSPCA embarking on more observations to gain further proof that the Balfour Assurances were not working. Media and public backing grew.

In July the Labour Opposition decided to use one of its allocated Supply Days to push through a debate on the export of live food animals. When it came to the vote twenty-three Conservatives rebelled against a three-line whip and voted with the Opposition. Defeated by 285 votes to 265, the next day the government announced a ban on all further exports. If the story had ended there the Special Operations Unit might never have come into being.

The hard-fought battle proved to be only a temporary victory, however. The government set up a committee of enquiry, under the chairmanship of Lord O'Brien of Lothbury, to look into the whole trade. The committee made many recommendations, principal among them the need for EEC legislation to provide safeguards. Common European welfare regulations for both transport and slaughter should be implemented throughout the Community. Without even waiting for such arrangements to be established the government lifted the ban. Trade resumed in January 1975. The RSPCA resumed its investigations.

Monitoring quickly established that British sheep were again travelling long

Sheep being unloaded from a transporter at a lairage (a place for temporary rest).

distances without rest, food or water. It was at this time of renewed vigilance that the idea of forming a special task force to carry out these lengthy investigations was first conceived, since it was increasingly difficult to spare officers from other duties. At the end of 1976 Chief Superintendent Ron Butfield was appointed to head the new Special Investigations Unit (SIU), the forerunner of today's Special Operations Unit.

The evidence the inspectors obtained enabled the RSPCA to reactivate the SELFA campaign and submit a powerful case for a ban to the Ministry of Agriculture. But the politicians ignored the pleas for an end to the trade. Over the next decade SOU officers mounted dozens more investigations, returning time and again with proof that conditions overseas fell well below accepted UK standards. Full reports were submitted each time to the British government. But there was little headway in winning improvements.

In 1985 the society submitted a detailed complaint to the European Commission documenting shortcomings in the implementation of the EEC Directive on Transport. The complaint was upheld. Britain and France were rapped over the knuckles, the former for failing to implement the directive properly and the latter for failing to enforce it. But even this had minimal impact on the trade.

The advent of a 'free market' in 1992 changed all the rules. It was no longer feasible for the RSPCA to press for a ban on exports. Once frontiers go there will be no such thing as 'exports' between member countries of the European Community. New transport regulations that will supersede all domestic legislation are scheduled to come into force at the end of 1992. It is important to ensure these lay down the highest possible standards for regulating the movement of animals.

For that reason the RSPCA launched a new transport campaign at the start of the decade. The campaign was given added urgency by the impending threat to British equines. The Minimum Value Orders preventing the live export of horses for slaughter could be interpreted as a 'restraint' on trade and might be swept away in the move towards a 'free market'. The campaign had four principal aims:

– *eight-hour limit on journey time for any animal going for slaughter;*
– *certification of drivers and vehicles;*
– *strict enforcement of the laws by a properly trained inspectorate;*
– *Britain to be allowed to retain its Minimum Value Orders.*

Once again SOU officers were in the front line trailing consignments of British animals and accumulating material in support of the campaign. History repeated itself. Evidence piled up of marathon journeys without feeding or watering. Suspicion grew that animals were being illegally re-exported across frontiers. This time the 'back-door' route was between France and Spain. Spain could not import directly from Britain since the British government refused to issue export licences for consignments to Spain, on the ground that the Spanish had failed properly to implement and enforce the EC Directive on Slaughter.

In 1990 SOU officers gained access to Spanish slaughterhouses and filmed conditions which confirmed their worst fears: animals slaughtered in barbaric conditions. Pigs killed without proper stunning. Horses stabbed with short-handled daggers to render them unconscious. Goats strung up by their hind legs and slaughtered fully conscious. The RSPCA submitted an official complaint to the European Commission. The complaint was upheld.

The society subsequently hit the headlines with a series of controversial advertisements. One showed the conditions inside Spanish slaughterhouses, while another depicted a dead horse on a

butcher's hook. The Advertising Standards Authority took offence and banned it. But the RSPCA would not be silenced. Working with sister organisations throughout Europe it mobilised public opinion. Over two million people signed a petition calling for tough regulations. The European Parliament backed the campaign. The Council of Agricultural Ministers, responsible for finalising the shape of the new transport regulations, have, at the time of writing, still to decide on maximum journey times for slaughter animals, feeding and watering times and rest periods.

SOU inspectors are still mounting trails and, as the next chapter shows, still coming back with evidence of horrific long-distance journeys. That evidence is more important than ever. The Council of Ministers are reported to be lukewarm to the idea of setting maximum journey times for slaughter animals. Yet as SOU trails have shown it is the long-distance journeys that cause so much suffering. Underlining it all is the futility of the trade. The animals are going to be killed at journey's end, so why send them live in the first place? The rigours of the journey result in weight loss, possible damage to the animals and consequent deterioration in meat quality. So why not just send them as carcases? The answer lies in a complex system of premiums which mean that the dealers can charge higher prices for fresh 'home-killed' meat, thus ensuring increased profit for the middlemen.

One of the biggest fears is that the situation will deteriorate since Britain currently has much tougher legislation than its continental counterparts. Animals must be fed and watered after twelve hours in transit, a condition that can only be waived if the journey can be completed in under fifteen hours. Furthermore, if the animals are being 'exported', they must be rested in a lairage for at least ten hours, and fed and watered before the start of the journey. They must also pass a vet-erinary examination to confirm they are fit to travel.

One of the biggest frustrations of SOU officers is having to witness long journey times which would have resulted in prosecutions had they taken place on British soil. Under existing European legislation animals only have to be fed and watered after twenty-four hours in transit or a 'reasonable time' thereafter. Even this unacceptable twenty-four-hour limit is routinely ignored and the leeway provided by the phrase 'reasonable time' is of course open to interpretation and abuse.

Current European legislation also imposes a requirement for veterinary checks at frontiers. It may only be paid rudimentary lip-service (as the next chapter shows), but at least a mechanism exists for detecting animals unfit to travel. The abolition of frontiers will sweep away all the frontier checks and lairage requirements, although veterinary inspections will still be required before the start of journeys from one member state to another and those expected to last longer than twenty-four hours. For long journeys hauliers will have to submit an itinerary of planned 'staging-posts' for feeding and watering but there will be no compulsion to complete the journey within a specified time limit. The next check will be on arrival at the destination.

It is all too easy to falsify documentation; to claim a stop was made to feed and water even when one was not. As currently favoured by ministers the proposed new regulations are inadequate and open to abuse.

That is why the SOU's trails, revealing rife malpractice and abuse, are so important. One encouraging sign that the message might be getting through came as a result of the trail featured in the next chapter. A report of the trail was brought to the attention of the member state governments shortly before the Agriculture Ministers met in Luxembourg on 21 October 1991 to decide on the new legislation. They

decided to postpone any decision and in the interim called for a further report from the Commission on the question of maximum journey times and welfare standards for animals in transit.

So chasing lorryloads of sheep is not a pointless exercise. It is the only way to get the evidence that could persuade Eurocrats to bring in a better deal for slaughter animals.

Imagine being locked in a rush hour tube carriage for 36 hours.

All around you people are collapsing from thirst, hunger and exhaustion. There'd be urine and faeces all over the floor.

Now imagine the train's travelling at 100 mph, but there's nowhere to sit and nothing to hold on to. You'd be thrown about, crushed and trampled. If you're frail or weak you might not survive.

Now imagine there are 600 people crammed in there with you. That's five times more than the worst rush hour crowd.

Aren't you glad you're not a lamb being transported across Europe?

PLEASE HELP THE RSPCA FIGHT THE NEEDLESS TRANSPORT OF LIVE ANIMALS. PHONE 0800 400 478

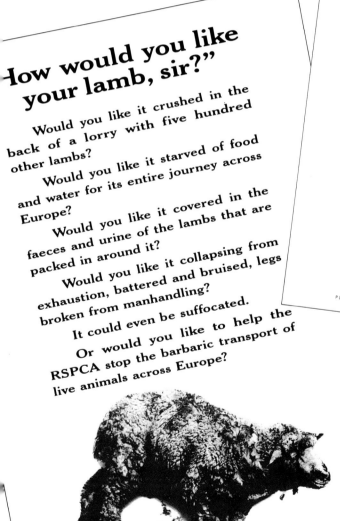

"How would you like your lamb, sir?"

Would you like it crushed in the back of a lorry with five hundred other lambs?

Would you like it starved of food and water for its entire journey across Europe?

Would you like it covered in the faeces and urine of the lambs that are packed in around it?

Would you like it collapsing from exhaustion, battered and bruised, legs broken from manhandling?

It could even be suffocated.

Or would you like to help the RSPCA stop the barbaric transport of live animals across Europe?

PLEASE HELP THE RSPCA FIGHT THE NEEDLESS TRANSPORT OF LIVE ANIMALS. PHONE 0800 400 478

The RSPCA mounted a hard-hitting campaign on the issue of live food animals for export.

port-
m.
nister
ople
to end
rtation.
use of
u need to
use of
or ask at

npaigning
as you
CA,
3YY.

and save
uffering.

LIVE TRANSPORTATION

...MARE

FA04 5.92

RSPCA

Case Number: SO/1891

Investigating Team: Chief Superintendent Frank Milner; Superintendent Don Balfour; Inspector Alan Goddard; Inspector Terry Spamer

C H A P T E R   T H R E E

THE ITALIAN JOB

At Calais, the film team await the arrival of the Dover–Calais ferry from their observation point in the café.

TUESDAY, 17 SEPTEMBER 1991

It was hot, the sun was shining, and the sky was a glorious blue. Perfect weather for an autumn break as the four RSPCA undercover officers arrived at Calais Ferryport. First stop was the Avis car rental desk, where they hired two cars with French registration plates: a black Audi and a silver Renault. Next stop was the terminal café.

However this was no pleasure trip. They were there to monitor the lorry-loads of British sheep that pass through the port every day en route to continental abattoirs. The café provides one of the best vantage-points to observe vehicles streaming off the ferries.

Numerous livestock vehicles came and went. But they were waiting for one particular consignment. Intelligence indicated that some British sheep were on their way, possibly bound for a slaughterhouse in Italy. If the information was correct a gruelling journey lay ahead.

The team's task was to monitor the trip and see if European regulations on the transportation of animals, which require that all animals must be fed and watered after twenty-four hours in transit, were being obeyed. If, as the team suspected, the rules were being flouted the evidence would be timely. European ministers were due to discuss new transport regulations, and the RSPCA was trying to persuade them of the need for tougher controls and enforcement.

Don chewed on a cigar as the team pored over maps, trying to work out the route their quarry might take. Then they split up to patrol the freight compound to investigate which of the many parked lorries might be waiting for a transfer of sheep. Anybody spotting the Englishmen as they ducked and weaved in between the vehicles would have wondered what on earth was going on. It looked like an elaborate game of hide-and-seek. But it was important to keep out of sight of the drivers. No point in alerting them they were under watch.

British transporters often only bring the animals as far as Calais then transfer them on to larger continental carriers. The SOU officers were anticipating one of these 'back-to-back' transfers. Before leaving Dover the sheep must spend at least ten hours resting in a lairage. They are then inspected by a vet and certified fit to travel. The loading has to be supervised by a local authority officer to ensure it is done correctly. 'Two hours later they arrive here and then they're shoved on to a French lorry. It makes a mockery of the system,' said Don.

It was a long hot day and by late afternoon there was still no sign of their target vehicle. The officers were clearly disappointed. Then a call came through on Frank's mobile phone from RSPCA headquarters. The sheep would be coming tomorrow, in two loads, and probably all the way from Scotland. 'Right,' said Frank grimly, 'we'll be waiting for them.'

Sheep lorries unloading 'back to back' in the lorry park at Calais; each has a capacity for 800 sheep.

WEDNESDAY, 18 SEPTEMBER

The team were back on observation duty early in the morning. The day ticked by and still nothing arrived matching the description. In the café one of a group of football supporters wandered over, intrigued by the team's intense surveillance of the traffic below.

'What have we got here?' he demanded.

'We're lorry-spotters,' replied Alan promptly.

'What, you come over here regular and spot lorries?' persisted the football fan.

'Yeah, it's a hobby,' said Alan. 'The bottom's gone right out of train-spotting.'

The mystified fan wandered back to his friends to report on this curious new hobby of lorry-spotting.

18.45 hours

At last the weary hours of waiting were rewarded. At 18.45 a red Volvo lorry, matching the description, drove off the P & O ferry and headed towards a large Belgian transporter parked in the customs compound. The empty Belgian vehicle, with its three main decks and a fourth suspended between the wheels, had already been identified as a likely candidate for a 'back-to-back'. The British lorry backed up and immediately started offloading sheep.

Out of sight Alan monitored the transfer and drew out a two-way radio to report back to his waiting colleagues. 'Right, I've just seen the vehicle transfer all his sheep and his load has taken up the entire bottom deck. I would expect him to fill the other two decks before he moves off.'

The team settled down for a further wait.

20.15 hours

At 20.15 another P & O ferry berthed. An articulated livestock vehicle carrying more British sheep disembarked. By now it was dark and the port was quiet after the bustle of the day. The radio crackled again. 'It looks like we're in business. The other vehicle is backing up now and I would suspect this load of sheep will be added to the previous load,' said Alan. Sure enough the new arrivals were herded along the ramps to fill up the top decks of the Belgian wagon, which Alan estimated now held some 800 sheep. The transfer was completed in under an hour.

As the team assembled for a last-minute briefing in the shadow of the lorries, ready for a quick getaway, the sodium floodlights threw an eerie glow over the port.

An undercover eye view. Sheep lorries of this type have a fourth compartment just inches from the wheels. Animals may spend agonising journeys cramped in one position, their legs pressed against the wheel arch for twenty-four hours or more.

31

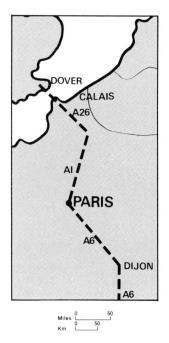

Miles 0 50
Km 0 50

21.02 hours

It was starting to rain heavily as the Belgian lorry driver started his engine and nosed towards the customs check. Ten minutes later the lights of the ferryport were receding into the distance as the driver took the autoroute heading towards Paris. The trail was on. Alan and Frank were in the lead car with Terry and Don tucked in behind. There was a third car in the convoy: Paul Berriff and the camera crew. The Belgian driver, meanwhile, seemed oblivious to the three cars in pursuit.

The sheep had already been on the go for many hours. First the journey down from Scotland, then the crossing in the bowels of the ferry. But the worst was still to come. If the intelligence was correct there were over 1,000 miles to go before they would reach their final destination in southern Italy.

The first few miles were simple. The flat countryside of the Pas de Calais is ideal tailing country, where it is easy to hang well back without fear of losing the quarry. The problems come with hilly terrain. 'You have to remember to slow down on the hills otherwise you'll suddenly find yourself right on top of

the target,' explained Frank. Trails are a cat and mouse operation, ducking and weaving through the traffic, always trying to keep out of sight. French number plates mean the pursuers don't stand out as much as they would in British cars, but even so if a driver sees the same vehicle behind him for too long he might get suspicious.

Throughout the night the Belgian driver made frequent stops. The team took it in turns to keep watch but not once did he check on the condition of the sheep. At an Esso service station between Paris and Lyon, Don sneaked up to snatch a quick look at the sheep, but it was impossible to see the condition of the animals packed in the centre, which would be suffering the most. The stench of ammonia was overwhelming. He could hear the shuffling of hooves as they jostled for position: if any collapsed from exhaustion it would be difficult to regain their footing.

This was always the most frustrating part of the job. Powerless to relieve the suffering of the animals, they had to concentrate on gaining the evidence to show that the transit regulations were being broken.

Negotiating roadworks at Macon in France, the Audi undercover car sticks close to the sheep lorry on its 1,700-kilometre journey across Europe to Italy.

THURSDAY, 19 SEPTEMBER

As dawn broke the team were bleary-eyed. During the night there had been a few anxious moments when one or other of the pursuing cars briefly lost touch. And there had been a terrifying near miss as the cars weaved in and out of the traffic on the *périphérique* around Paris. Nevertheless, they had managed to stay together and keep the Belgian vehicle in their sights.

Mist steamed off the fields, signalling another hot day ahead. As the morning wore on the Belgian driver stripped down to a singlet to keep cool. But for the sheep there was no respite. They were condemned to spend many more hours jammed together aboard the swaying vehicle.

10.02 hours

The temperature climbed and it became clear that the Belgian vehicle was suffering from mechanical problems. The journey was slow and laboured, adding to the ordeal of the animals on board. Just after 10.00 a.m. the driver pulled the vehicle into a service area, got out, and jacked up the cab. The engine had overheated. The halt was a godsend: an opportunity to grab a cool drink and bolt down a roll. No such luck for the sheep. The driver didn't even spare them a glance.

It was the first time the observers had a good opportunity to study their quarry. He was a burly man with a walrus moustache and dark hair, lank with sweat. Nestling in a thick clump of chest hair was a silver St Christopher – the patron saint of travellers. At that moment the sheep could have done with some divine assistance.

Shortly before noon the lorry was ready to move on again and the convoy headed towards the Mont Blanc Tunnel. The Alps towered overhead, their snowy caps a stark contrast to the sweltering temperature inside the tunnel.

15.00 hours

The Belgian vehicle crossed the border

between France and Italy at 3.00 p.m., eighteen hours and 940 kilometres after leaving Calais. Next stop was the freight customs compound at Aosta. As the vehicles inched their way down into the valley where Aosta lay, it looked as if they were heading into a storm: the sky was heavy and overcast and a strong, gritty wind was blowing. But the storm was nothing more than the haze of pollution that hung over the town.

The customs compound was packed with heavy freight vehicles. The noise, dust, petrol fumes and humidity conjured up an image of Dante's inferno. The Belgian parked in the area reserved for livestock vehicles and made his way to the drivers' café, from which issued a deafening babble of foreign languages.

But at least the driver could slake his hunger and thirst. Outside the sheep remained cooped up on the lorry. There were pens nearby that could have been used to unload the animals and provide food and water. It was just a simple matter of dropping the tailgate. But the pens remained empty. A dead pig lay on

Chief Superintendent Frank Milner (left) and Inspector Alan Goddard monitor the progress of the sheep lorry near the Mont Blanc Tunnel in the Alps.

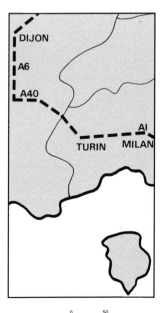

The Customs checkpoint at Aosta as seen by the undercover team hidden in the undergrowth.

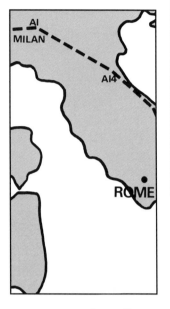

the ground – a casualty from one of the many livestock wagons that had passed through the compound earlier in the day.

Three hours later, after a wash and a rest, the driver was ready to move off again. Dusk was falling as he drove slowly past the veterinary inspection point. The inspection was a mockery. An indifferent-looking official gave the vehicle a cursory glance and waved it on.

In the dark the endless hours and kilometres slipped by, their progress signposted by the exits for Turin, Milan, Parma and Bologna.

FRIDAY, 20 SEPTEMBER, 01.05 HOURS

It was just after 1.00 a.m. when the driver pulled into a rest area, and quickly settled down for a sleep in his cab. The sheep had now been in transit for over twenty-eight hours without food or water.

Once again the RSPCA investigators took it in turns to keep watch. Taking advantage of the driver's nap they snatched another look at the sheep. By now the stench was terrible. Those that could be seen, by peering through the slats, looked shell-shocked, too exhausted even to jockey for position. It was impossible to gauge how many casualties there might be on board.

05.09 hours

As dawn broke, the driver emerged for the last leg of the journey south along the Adriatic coast, and just after 9.00 a.m. the convoy trundled into the bustling village of Pianella, near Pescara. The roads were congested. Suddenly a school bus pulled out in front of the lead car, blocking the route. They were cut off from the Belgian lorry which was rapidly disappearing from view. It would be unbearable to lose the trail now after thirty-six hours in pursuit. Frank leaned over and thumped the horn. After much cursing and waving, the bus at last moved forward. The drivers in the three following cars accelerated furiously and caught up just as the Belgian vehicle pulled in to 'The Sons of Leonardo' slaughterhouse.

The Belgian driver was still in his cab when the three cars drove into the yard. His jaw dropped and he did a double-take as he spotted the investigators. Throughout the long journey not once had he registered that he was being followed.

An Italian strode over to see what the RSPCA officers wanted. Frank enquired if he was the boss, flashed his ID card, and asked to watch the unloading. At first there was no objection. Then more officials came out, among them a nattily dressed gent with sunglasses and slicked-back hair who

Left: The three-decker transporter approaches the village of Pianella. During their forty-four-hour journey, the animals had not been fed or watered once.

Centre: The 'Sons of Leonardo' slaughterhouse ejects the film crew.

Bottom: After leaving the Pianella abattoir, Superintendent Don Balfour regroups the undercover team.

looked as if he had stepped straight off the set of *The Godfather*. What authorisation did the investigators have to stay and watch? The atmosphere grew menacing. They had no right to be there, insisted the Italians.

Frank repeated that they were from the English Society for the Protection of Animals. The sheep were from Scotland, not England, responded an Italian official. Therefore, he concluded triumphantly, English inspectors had no grounds for any interest in the animals. They must leave immediately.

As the debate continued Frank grabbed the opportunity to ask the driver a few questions. Had he stopped at all, en route, to feed or water the sheep?

The driver claimed that he had. One stop at the lairage in Bourges, just south of Paris, to rest the animals and, oh yes, he'd also fed and watered them at Aosta.

Shortly after this exchange the RSPCA officers and film crew were escorted off the premises. The gates of the abattoir were clanged shut behind them and firmly padlocked. Nobody would be allowed to witness the condition of the sheep after their nightmare journey.

A quick calculation showed the sheep had spent over forty-three hours in transit since leaving the lairage at Dover and had travelled 1,767 kilometres

across France and Italy to this foreign slaughterhouse. There was no doubt that many of the animals would be in an appalling state. Some might even have died en route. Locked out, the inspectors could only speculate as to why, if nothing was wrong, it was necessary to bar observers from watching the unloading.

Don had spotted a café on their way up the hill to the abattoir. At least they could have some coffee and unwind on its terrace after the long journey. Later, hot and sticky, they made their way down to the coast and plunged gratefully into the sea, delighted to be able to wash away the grime of the journey. For the sheep the only release now would be the oblivion provided by the slaughterman's knife.

That night the team stayed at a small hotel on the shore, anxious to get a good night's sleep before undertaking the long haul back to Britain. During the night Berriff was woken by the sound of piano music and a haunting melody drifting across the night air. It was the words of the 'Police' hit: 'Every breath you take I'll be watching you and you'll be watching me . . .' It seemed to sum up the trip: waiting and watching but powerless to intervene.

Back in England the officers typed up their trail reports. Enquiries revealed that the sheep came from a Scottish exporter and had been shipped by an English agent. The documentation had been falsified: the animals had never stopped at the points indicated.

A week later RSPCA officers mounted another trail from Calais, this time accompanied by a reporter from a radio programme. They picked up a vehicle from the same Belgian haulage company. Another marathon journey, lasting forty-seven hours, ended at the same slaughterhouse near Pescara. Again the driver had not realised he was being followed. Again it was the same exporter. Again no food or water was provided for the sheep throughout the journey.

This time the RSPCA officers managed to witness part of the unloading. The wagon was parked just eighteen inches from a pile of bloody sheepskins covered in flies. 'They'll be able to smell death,' said the inspector watching. The sheep spilled off the ramps in a daze. Clumsy and stiff-legged, they staggered towards the feeding troughs and attacked the hay with a vengeance. The inspectors saw at least two dead sheep pulled out of the first deck to be unloaded. Then the management intervened and threw them off the premises. But the inspectors had already seen enough.

Alerted by the RSPCA, the Ministry of Agriculture reacted swiftly and launched a full investigation. Agriculture Minister David Maclean immediately suspended export licences for the exporter and agent.

The trail reports were also brought to the attention of the European Agriculture Ministers. On 21 October 1991 they met in Luxembourg to decide on the shape of the new transport directive. The RSPCA's evidence of suffering caused by long-distance transportation had some effect: the ministers called for a further report on the issue of maximum journey times and welfare standards for animals in transit. That report must be submitted by July 1992. In the interim the RSPCA will continue to monitor the traffic. 'The drivers never know when we'll show up,' said Frank. 'Just the mere threat of us being around may help to keep them on their toes.'

CHAPTER FOUR

A DANGEROUS ASSIGNMENT

WEDNESDAY, 13 NOVEMBER 1991, 18.00 HOURS

Don Balfour sat across the table from Peter Vingerling, Farm Animals Expert for the Dutch Animal Welfare Society, in a meeting room at the Dutch society's offices in Hilversum, near Amsterdam. Don was seeking information that would help with an undercover trail the RSPCA officers planned to mount the next day.

The objective was to follow a consignment of Dutch pigs to obtain more evidence for the RSPCA's transport campaign which so far had concentrated on the plight of British sheep en route to continental abattoirs. But the RSPCA was convinced sheep weren't the only animals getting a raw deal. It was vital to show the European Council of Ministers that animals of all types, and from all countries, were suffering as a result of gruelling, long-distance journeys to slaughterhouses.

Holland exports around 2.5 million pigs a year, over 650,000 of them to Italy. That involves many hours in transit and it was a safe bet that this long haul was causing much suffering. But the only way to obtain the hard evidence needed was to follow one of the consignments.

The RSPCA had worked closely with its Dutch counterpart on many issues and the two men had built up a good rapport. Vingerling promised to help by assigning an inspector to meet them the next day at the border post where the lorries must complete a customs check before departure. The Dutch inspectors

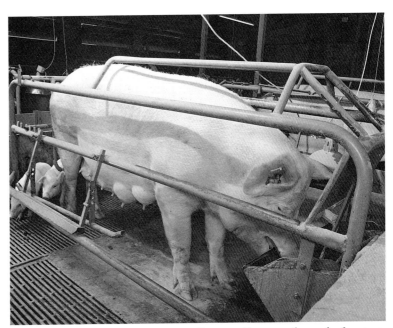

have the same rights as police officers and could, therefore, inspect the customs clearance documents of the drivers. That way they could spot the intended destination and tip off the SOU as to which consignments were worth following.

'If you pick up a consignment bound for Italy you can expect it to go via the Aosta crossing,' advised Vingerling. There had been a strike by customs officers earlier that week and Vingerling warned there could be chaos at the crossing point.

But at least with cooler weather the journey would be better than during the summer months when it can be hell for heat-sensitive animals like pigs. Pigs drink at least fifteen to twenty times a

Every year thousands of sows are confined in farrowing crates like this to give birth and raise their litters. The sows are closely confined to limit movement and prevent them from trampling on the piglets. This confinement is extremely distressing to the sows at a time when the animal is particularly vulnerable to stress.

37

day. The transit lorries should be fitted with 'self-service' watering nipples so the pigs can quench their thirst but they are often packed in so densely that some are unable to reach the water.

'I bet that you'll see no proper feeding or drinking stops during the journey,' predicted Vingerling.

THURSDAY, 14 NOVEMBER

It was raining heavily and the car windows kept steaming up. The team had been waiting in the lorry park at the Dutch border post of Breda monitoring the traffic since 8.00 a.m. It was now midday. Three cars were ready to pick up the trail when the Dutch inspector, Ynse Kwast, gave them the go-ahead.

The party included the Berriff camera team, the three undercover officers, and a freelance journalist, Jemima Harrison, who was hoping to get some good copy for a feature on the RSPCA's 'routine' investigative work. In the event this trip would provide more 'action' than anybody could have anticipated. Ynse, dressed for the weather in flat cap and waterproof waxed jacket, reported back at regular intervals. So far, nothing bound for Italy had turned up.

The three cars were in contact with each other by personal radios. 'When we get the call we'll have to be ready to go in a flash,' warned Don. Once the formalities are completed the drivers waste no time. But for now all they could do was watch and wait.

Don Balfour identifies the transporter carrying the pigs bound for Italy.

En route, Alan Goddard tracks the pig transporter through heavy traffic.

Some of the party were grabbing a quick snack in the transport café when Ynse came striding over. He had picked out a consignment. He leaned into Don's car and showed him a piece of paper with the destination.

Don's heart sank. It was Pianella. They had followed a consignment of sheep there the previous month and had had a very poor reception. Somehow Don doubted the abattoir would put out a welcoming party. Little did he suspect just how hostile the staff would be.

There was a rush to empty bladders before the start of the trail – nobody knew when the next stop would be – and then a frantic scramble for the cars.

13.10 hours

Alan and Don were in the lead car as they swung out of the border crossing just after 1.00 p.m. in pursuit of the quarry, a large green and silver articu-lated livestock lorry with the letter V painted on the tailgate. Alan strained to read the registration plate but there was so much muck and spray from the filthy weather that at first it was hard to distinguish.

At last he made out the letters and radioed back to the following cars. But there was no response. The radios only had a limited range. Could they have got separated and lost contact already? There was palpable relief when Terry's voice finally came over the radio. The other cars had caught up, and they settled down into the rhythm of a routine trail.

As they sped through the flat country-side, following the signs for Brussels, the weather brightened up briefly, casting a watery sunshine over the autumn leaves, a glorious mix of red, russet and gold. Alan flicked through a large road atlas of Europe trying to plot their likely route.

39

As a precaution, near the Luxembourg border Terry took over in the lead. There were two drivers with the Dutch lorry which therefore doubled the chance of their being spotted.

16.15 hours

Dusk was falling as they drew into the customs area at the Belgian/French border. The lorry drivers went in search of a cup of tea, while their pursuers parked discreetly so as not to attract attention. But they weren't quite discreet enough. Some alert customs officers spotted Terry, Jemima, and sound engineer Keith Rodgerson lingering in the lorry park.

The three were hauled in for questioning, not helped by the language barrier as they desperately tried to allay the officers' suspicions. Jemima spoke the best French and took on the tricky task of explaining that they were chasing pig lorries. As the nail-biting minutes ticked by their main fear was that the lorry drivers would emerge and take off without them. The customs officers laboriously took down passport details – no doubt they wanted to run a thorough check on these crazy foreigners.

Finally they were through and the three escaped, weak with relief to see the lorry still there. 'I went hot and cold trying to get the sentence construction right round the word *cochon*,' said Jemima. 'I knew calling a French customs official a pig probably wasn't the best way to ensure a speedy getaway!'

18.00 hours

It was dark when they set off again and raining heavily once more. The lorry travelled just over 100 kilometres, then stopped in a Total service area between Metz and Nancy, evidently a popular gathering point for Dutch lorry drivers. The two went off with some colleagues to play arcade games.

No rest or recreation, however, for the pigs. Alan stole over to the lorry for a quick peep. There were over 200 pigs on board. Pigs from different social groups don't take kindly to mixing with 'rivals'. Crammed into a confined space trouble was inevitable and every so often the silence was shattered by squeals as one pig attacked another.

21.21 hours

The drivers took off in convoy with another truck. The long haul through the night was only broken by one refuelling stop and a short break just after 3.00 a.m. On the approach to the Alps thick snow was piled up on both sides of the road. The winter scene, with sleepy villages muffled under a blanket of snow, was picturesque but bad news for the pigs. The cold added to their ordeal. They weren't free-range animals used to climatic variations but had been intensively reared and until now had spent their lives in a controlled environment with constant temperatures. The temperature shot up again as they travelled through the fifteen-mile-long Mont Blanc Tunnel. It was just after 6.00 a.m. when they arrived at the Aosta Autoport.

The Italians are notoriously slow with paperwork, and as usual there was a long wait before the customs formalities were completed. Dozens of other pig lorries were also parked. The team took it in turns to watch or grab a few minutes' sleep. One of the drivers went for a coffee; the other remained in the cab, probably also trying to get a little sleep.

Alan went to snatch another look at the pigs. They were quiet now – numbed by the journey.

FRIDAY, 15 NOVEMBER, 10.15 HOURS

Four hours later they were back en route. It had started to rain again heavily and visibility was down to about fifty yards, but the lorry was cracking along at a speed of around eighty mph.

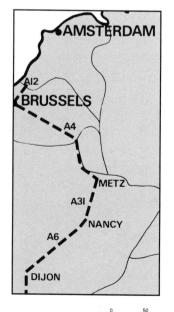

The pigs had little protection from the driving rain and spray.

The monotony of the journey was only broken by a brief moment of panic just before Bologna when the lorry pulled into a service station to refuel. The cars followed suit and were still filling up when the target pulled away. It took some high-speed driving to regain contact.

As they drew nearer to their destination Don's thoughts turned to what lay ahead. The abattoir management would have realised that the supply of Scottish sheep had been cut off as a result of the reports filed by the investigators after the last trail. Drily he said, 'We're going to be about as welcome as a turd in a swimming pool.'

The rush hour was in full swing when they pulled off the autoroute and drove into Pescara. In the resulting traffic chaos the lead car lost contact with the lorry so, trusting to luck, they took the route they had followed before to the village of Pianella and spotted the pig lorry, on the horizon, just before entering the village. It must, as they had suspected all along, be bound for the slaughterhouse they already knew. The RSPCA team parked at the entrance to the lane leading down to the slaughterhouse and waited for the others to catch up.

18.23 hours

They pulled up shortly after, having been delayed at the autoroute exit finding the correct currency for the tolls. It was getting dark and difficult to see. Don, Alan and Terry got out and walked down the lane towards the slaughterhouse, followed by the film crew.

But when they reached the abattoir the lorry was nowhere to be seen. The yard was quiet. They could hear a few sheep coughing but no sign of the pigs. Disappointment swept over them all. They had driven for over thirty hours and nearly 2,000 kilometres and at the last moment lost the quarry. But how? Where else could the lorry have gone?

Dejectedly, they made their way back to the cars. Then, as if in answer to their prayers, a pig lorry thundered round the corner. It even had the same signwriting as their original quarry – a large V on the tailgate.

They leapt back into the cars and set off in pursuit. On the other side of the village the lorry forked right into a narrow twisting lane. As they followed the lane round hairpin bends they spotted a blockhouse-type building perched on top of a hill. Enormous lettering on the roof spelled out the words Salumificio Di Leonardo. It was a salami processing plant.

19.05 hours

All three cars pulled to a halt outside the slaughterhouse gates. Don and Alan went ahead to check that the target lorry had arrived. It was there. They introduced themselves to one of the drivers and showed their identification. Terry waited by the gates. In the meantime Berriff made his way to the end of the yard where the pigs were unloading and started filming.

Don and Alan joined him to watch the last few animals coming off the lorry. They noticed that many of the pigs were badly marked with cuts and gashes. Not surprisingly, after a journey in excess of thirty hours without food or water, they looked the worse for wear.

Suddenly an excitable Italian appeared, ranting and raving, and pointing furiously at the camera. The men decided to beat a hasty retreat and started edging towards the gates. The Italian was joined by others, including some Dutch drivers. They didn't like the filming. Not one bit. They grabbed Berriff and roughly manhandled him into the weighbridge office where they demanded his film. He tried desperately to protect the camera but these men meant business. They kneed him in the testicles and back and forced him into an armlock.

Don, Alan and Terry intervened, trying to calm the men and pull Paul

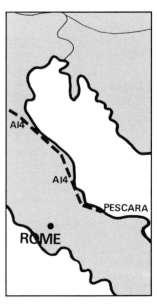

Sound recordist, Keith Rodgerson, at action stations.

free. Images of bloody cleavers and meat-hooks flashed through their minds at the sinister appearance of the slaughterhouse caps worn by some of the men. The camera was wrenched away and the film ripped out. Paul managed to push his way free, but in the struggle Keith Rodgerson was attacked with an electric stunning prod.

Outside the gates Jemima and assistant producer Janice Kearns waited anxiously in the parked cars. They had heard the scuffle inside and were horrified when several men hurtled out and lunged towards the cars. One was wearing a balaclava, another brandishing an electric prod.

Jemima decided not to hang around and ask questions. She gunned the engine and took off, but in her panic to escape drove over the edge of a steep bank, whereupon the car took off like something out of the *Dukes of Hazzard*. It crash-landed with an enormous bang, blowing out all four tyres, and ground to a halt. Petrified, Jemima leapt out and scrabbled her way up the bank to conceal herself in an olive grove.

A couple of minutes later Berriff's Volvo came shooting down the lane. Janice had stayed put long enough to pick up Paul. At the sight of Jemima's battered car, she slammed on the brakes.

'I'm up here,' shouted Jemima scrambling down the bank to the safety of the Volvo. 'As I raced for the car a powerful searchlight panned down from the top of the abattoir,' she recalled afterwards. 'I braced myself for the bullet in the back that tiredness, terror, and an overworked imagination had convinced me was imminent!'

The Volvo was also in poor shape. In her haste to get away, Janice had hit some rocks and ripped out the sump. Gingerly they drove back to the main road and waited for the others to regroup.

In the meantime Don, Alan, Terry and Keith had escaped from the slaughterhouse to discover only one remaining

car. They jumped in and drove off smartly, but came to a halt when they saw Jemima's abandoned car. Keith got out, found the keys still in the ignition, and started it up. In the darkness they had not noticed the buckled wheels. That car was going nowhere. Don and Keith worked furiously to change the front tyre, anxious in case the angry slaughtermen might pursue them down the hill. Two tyres later the car was movable – but only just – and they nursed it back to the rendezvous.

There, they exchanged accounts of what had happened in the mêlée back at the slaughterhouse. It seemed a miracle they had all escaped without serious injury.

A breakdown lorry was called to recover the two damaged cars; then they took taxis to a seafront hotel in Pescara where they could unwind. But, exhausted by the drive and drained by their ordeal at the slaughterhouse, they still had to face the return drive to England the next day.

Had it been worth while? Berriff had lost the film for his programme. They had wrecked two cars. And they had come within inches of being made into sausagemeat themselves.

The answer was yes. They returned with the proof they needed to try and persuade European ministers to change the law. The pigs had travelled 1,810 kilometres across Europe through atrocious weather conditions just to end up as salami. The journey from Breda to Pianella had taken thirty hours twenty-five minutes. But the pigs' ordeal had been even longer. There was no way of knowing how many hours they had already spent on the lorry before the RSPCA took up the trail at the border. And Vingerling's prediction was right: not once were the animals offered food or water.

The RSPCA would fight on with its campaign to end this needless torture.

THE DOGS OF WAR

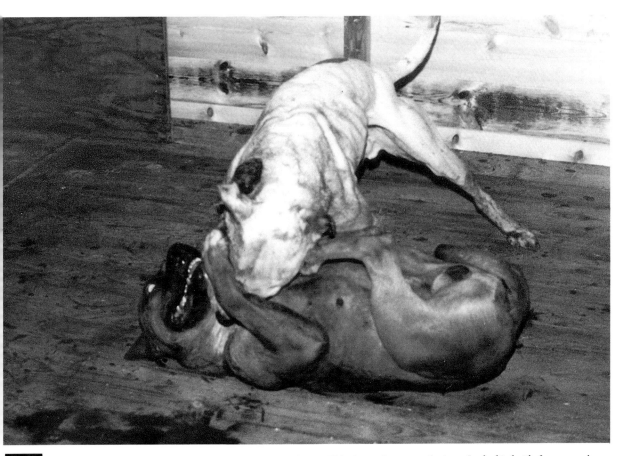

Two trained killers are tearing each other to pieces. Blood drips from their jaws and is spattered over the whitewashed walls of the pit in which they are fighting. They have been locked in battle for over an hour, urged on by the bloodlust of the spectators betting on the outcome.

Despite the frenzied yelps of the crowd the combatants themselves are chillingly silent. This brutal spectacle is organised dogfighting, a 'sport' which has attracted a seedy following from the criminal underworld, where stakes are high with big money to be won for the 'champions'.

Dogfighting is illegal under the 1911 Protection of Animals Act. The penalties for causing, organising, promoting, or merely attending a dogfight

Locked in battle for over an hour, urged on by the bloodlust of the spectators betting on the outcome.

43

The dogs of war

IN normal times, Man Bites Dog is a story — and Dog Bites Man is not. But these are abnormal times, as particular dogs are involved in attacks on men, women and children: culminating this weekend with the savaging of a six-year-old girl by a pit bull terrier. Suddenly the news wires seem full of pit bull terriers, Japanese Tosas and rottweilers unleashed.

There is, of course, a danger of hysteria. There is always that risk when an especially awful case focuses concern and generates supporting tales of similar incidents which would never routinely be filed. But the tragedy of Rucksana Khan and, in lesser degree, of many like her, is one to pause over. Some dogs are bred by man to be vicious, to attack automatically, to kill or be killed. They are not, and never

Baker to a

Madeleine Bunting

KENNETH Baker, the Home Secretary, is considering banning two breeds of dogs specifically bred for fighting, the US pit bull terrier and the Japanese Tosa.

A ban on specific breeds could mean destroying existing animals. There are up to 30,000 pit bull terriers in the country and one Tosa, imported earlier this year by an owner who hopes to import a mate for breeding.

Mr Baker is responding to public pressure that has intensified since six-year-old Ruck-

so-called pets," he said on the eve of the federation's annual conference in Bournemouth.

"Ban all these vicious dogs," he said. "They should be stopped from breeding. Those people that have them should be forced to put a muzzle on them at all times."

Mr Baker is considering other controls on dangerous dogs, including a criminal charge against owners who do not control their dogs.

Because the dog which savaged Rucksana was killed, the police said they could not charge the owner. If the dog had not been destroyed, a charge of keeping a dangerous dog might have been

were increased in 1988, and participants now face maximum fines of up to £2,000 and/or six months in prison. Yet the fight game flourishes. The Special Operations Unit reckons there is probably a fight going on somewhere in Britain every week.

Although popular in Britain last century it was thought dogfighting had been stamped out – consigned to the history books like bear-baiting, bull-fighting, and other relics of a cruel past. Then rumours surfaced, in the late 1970s, that it was on its way back. There were reports of organised fights in the West Country. But intensive investigations turned up nothing. However it was known to thrive in some parts of America, particularly the southern states. And it was from here that the dog most closely associated with dogfighting was to come.

While other breeds, including Staffordshire and English bull terriers, have been used for fighting, it is a 'sport' reigned over by the American pit bull terrier. Opinions as to its origins differ. Some breed historians believe the pit

bull terrier's ancestry can be traced back to ancient times. They claim that dogs resembling the pit bull type are depicted fighting large prey in early Egyptian paintings dating from 3000 BC. These same mastiff-type dogs crop up again in Chaucer's time, when they were used to hunt deer and lions, and there are references in Middle English writings decrying these 'engines of destruction'.

Other theorists suggest that the breed developed from cross-breeding bull dogs and terriers at some point in the last century. Bull dogs were large, long-legged animals, weighing eighty to ninety pounds, bred for their ferocity and used for bull-running and baiting. They were pitted against staked bulls which they would attack by grabbing the bull's vulnerable spot – the tender nose or lip – and once they got a grip nothing would make them relinquish it. An oft-cited horror story concerned a bull-baiter determined to demonstrate the courage of his bitch. Seizing an axe he hacked off her feet one by one. Throughout this ordeal the dog never loosened her grip on the bull.

yal Infirmary.
.o were at her
.heir voices to
an. Nishad Ali
vife, Julie, said
.ad almost died.
a 33-year-old
"If dogs are
s they shouldn't
. up to the Gov-
.ange the law.
lo something to
the dogs down.
ay daughter, it
meone else's

3-month-old boy,
w, was taken to
Birmingham for
r being bitten by
bull terrier.
yesterday dis-
ls on dangerous

July. Over the weekend he said he opposed a ban because it would be difficult to implement in the case of cross-breeds such as the pit bull terrier. But yesterday he appeared to have changed his mind. He said he was quite prepared to see a ban on certain fighting dogs and on certain breeds muzzled in public.

He said: "We want to make it an offence to allow any dog to be out of control in a public place, and this should be backed with a heavy fine." But he ruled out bringing back dog registration.

Roy Hattersley, the shadow home secretary, accused the Government of dithering. He said the case for banning certain breeds was overwhelming.

tration and importation bans on certain breeds. Registration would pay for an effective dog warden scheme and third party insurance should be necessary to register.

It also proposed the neutering of dangerous dogs to curb their aggression. "Pit bull terriers have killed over 30 people in the US. It is only a matter of time before someone is killed in this country," said Tim Wass, RSPCA senior inspector.

The Kennel Club opposes registration and bans but agrees that owners should have to take out compulsory third party insurance. "If courts imposed some hefty fines, owners would be more responsible about buying dangerous breeds and controlling them," said Bill

The Blue Cross and the Canine Crisis Council both argue that dangerous breeds should be muzzled in public places and the Blue Cross supports the ban on the breeding of pit bull terriers.

The RSPCA believes the increase in serious attacks, put at 180 over the last 18 months, is evidence of a growing illegal dog fighting business.

It estimated there were about 50 organised dog fighting syndicates in the country, 15 of them based in London.

Eighty-five people were convicted of dog fighting last year, the largest number in 200 years, Mr Wass said.

"We're losing the battle against dog fighting because we can't get a search warrant or

If the dogs fell they would be trampled underfoot by the enraged bull. Victory came when the weakened bull eventually lowered its head to the ground and collapsed.

The terriers were small, agile dogs used for 'ratting', a popular poor man's sport strongly sponsored by the licensed trade, in which the dogs competed to kill the largest number of rats in the shortest time in a specially constructed pit.

Cross-breeding these terriers with the heavier bull dogs, with the aim of producing a more compact dog that could be easily handled, hidden, and ate less, resulted in the American pit bull terrier. It was brought to America by English and Irish settlers. At first it was used as a 'catch' dog to round up cattle, but before long it was being cultivated for its fighting prowess.

Whatever the truth of the various theories, what is beyond dispute is that today's pit bull terrier is a 'mean machine', purpose-bred for its ferocity, legendary strength, and the quality fighters prize above all else: 'gameness'.

In a nutshell that means never quitting. These dogs have been reared and trained to fight and die in the pit. They relish the challenge of taking on an opponent regardless of size. Hanging on, no matter how battered or bloodied, impervious to the pain.

The fight-bred pit bull terrier is profoundly different in temperament from other dogs. It is subjected to a punishing training regime to prepare it for the murderous events ahead. Treadmills are a favoured training device. This is a continuous belt on which the animal is exercised for prolonged periods with the aim of building stamina. Sometimes the dog is yoked to a turnmill with meat, or even live bait, suspended just beyond reach. The animals will pound round in circles for hours on end trying to reach the prey. The flirtpole is another piece of equipment used to condition pit bull terriers and develop agility. A tyre, animal hide or something similar is suspended from a rope. The dogs are encouraged to jump up and grab the 'target'. They will hang on, shaking it vigorously, in an exercise calculated to

45

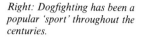
Right: Dogfighting has been a popular 'sport' throughout the centuries.

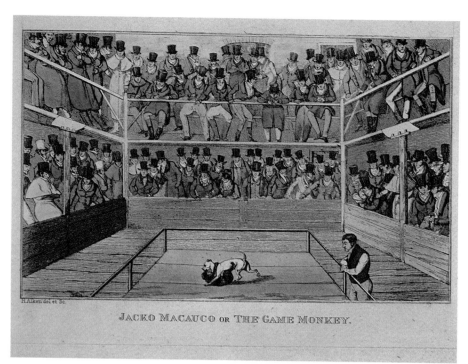

JACKO MACAUCO or THE GAME MONKEY.

develop the strength of those awesome jaws, powerful enough to break bones.

One of the most startling differences between these dogs and other fighting animals is the lack of threat display. Most animals rely heavily on threatening behaviour. Bared teeth, raised hair to produce an illusion of larger size, and aggressive growling are 'watch out' signals designed to intimidate an adversary. The pit bull terrier gets straight down to business. It rarely bares its teeth, raises its hackles, or growls. It goes straight for the kill.

Small wonder that with this sort of training regime the dogs are often psychotic. In fact the tragedy for the breed is the way it has been developed: as ever, not so much bad dogs as bad owners. Indeed many reputable owners insist the dogs are affectionate and make loyal companions, and there may well be individuals that would not hurt the proverbial fly. But sadly the breed as a whole is now suspect, corrupted for criminal purposes. The fighting tendencies have become so deeply engrained that pit bulls cannot be risked as a family pet.

So when the RSPCA first heard of moves, at the start of the 1980s, to import American pit bull terriers, alarm bells started ringing. The Kennel Club had refused to recognise what is in effect a cross-breed. That ruled out the possibility of making money from pedigree breeding or showing. Yet 'fanciers' were still prepared to shell out a small fortune to buy, ship and quarantine the dogs to get them into Britain. Why? It didn't take a genius to work out the attraction of the animals: dogfighting could be the only plausible motive.

The RSPCA asked the government not to let them in. Sadly it turned down the request for an import ban. Within a decade the number of American pit bull terriers shot up from nought to 10,000 plus. And the problems accelerated too. How the government must regret that initial refusal. By 1991 it had to concede the need to deal with the dogs.

The spur was a series of attacks by pit bull terriers. Although APBTs were not the only dogs involved in attacks on humans, their capacity for inflicting horrific injuries sealed their fate. The daughter of a pit bull owner on Canvey Island was nearly scalped by the family 'pet', which only let go after being beaten unconscious. A Lincoln baker was disfigured for life when he was attacked early one morning on his way home from work. His face was literally torn to shreds by two pit bulls that had escaped from their enclosure. A Portsmouth man had his testicles ripped off when attempting to intervene in an assault by a pit bull owner on a woman.

IN THE PIT

Many people regard bull-fighting as a peculiarly continental atrocity. They might, therefore, be surprised to learn of Britain's own record with regard to torturing bulls. Over the centuries animals possessing strong fighting instincts have always been regarded as good sport. The bull proved no exception.

The ancient custom of bull-baiting had the full weight of the law behind it and was reputed to tenderise the meat, making it more digestible. Butchers could be prosecuted if they failed to bait the animal before slaughter. Indeed fines were still being imposed for this offence in Stuart times. As with so many other blood sports baiting enjoyed royal patronage. In Tudor times bears, rather than bulls, were the favourite victim. The famous bear gardens at Bankside, capable of holding up to 1,000 spectators, were built by Henry VIII.

The bears were usually tethered by chains and pitted against enormous mastiff dogs and might have to fight off up to six dogs at a time. The Puritans, however, made determined efforts to wipe out baiting. They tried to kill all the bears. It was said they were motivated not by a desire to prevent pain to the animals but a determination to prevent the pleasure it gave spectators.

Although they failed to suppress baiting entirely it gradually declined. No longer fashionable with the upper classes, baiting earned a reputation as a vulgar entertainment fit only for the masses. Bears were too expensive for poorer people and gradually bulls took their place as the favourite victim, fighting against specially bred dogs.

The phrase 'lying doggo' originates from bull-baiting. The bull rarely attacked a prone target and the dogs would sometimes lie still, picking a suitable moment to launch another attack. As with other blood sports betting was much in evidence. The owner of a winning dog could pick up a purse of several guineas.

Nothing was more disappointing to the rowdy supporters than a bull unwilling to fight. In those cases every effort would be made to enrage the animal, perhaps by lighting fires, exploding gunpowder or shoving pepper up its nostrils. If that failed there were other options. The horns could be cut off, ears cropped, tail wrenched, or acid applied to the wounds. These tortures could be relied on to galvanise the bull into providing good 'sport'.

The final straw was the attack on a Bradford schoolgirl. Seven-year-old Rukhsana Khan was torn apart by a pit bull off its leash. The savaging left her with eight fractured ribs, severe muscle damage and a lacerated, collapsed lung. She needed more than eighty stitches.

The public was shocked and appalled by these attacks. The pit bull terrier was branded public enemy number one and pressure grew for controls. The government responded by announcing a mass extermination plan in which all American pit bull terriers would be destroyed. There was an outcry. Home Office Minister Kenneth Baker scaled down his plans and rushed through the Dangerous Dogs legislation.

This measure, which took full effect on 1 December 1991, is intended to phase out fighting dogs. It is now illegal in Britain to own, breed, or keep specified breeds. Top of the list of banned dogs is the pit bull terrier. Also listed are the Japanese tosa, Fila Braziliera, and Dogo Argentino. Existing owners have to apply for an exemption to keep their dog and had to comply with a battery of controls including compulsory neutering, micro-chipping, tattooing and insurance. They are also required to keep their dogs muzzled and leashed at all times in a public place. Failure to comply could result in a fine of up to £2,000 and/or six months in prison.

It is pointless to talk of shutting the stable door after the horse had bolted. The RSPCA is still trying to eradicate the dogfighting menace.

The fights can be held anywhere. Isolated barns, industrial units or warehouses are favourite locations. The more remote the venue the easier it is to post lookouts to spot strangers and impending trouble. But fights can just as easily take place in back alleys, pub cellars, and even the living room, garage or kitchen of a 'respectable' home.

To preserve secrecy the precise venue for an organised dogfight may not be announced until the last moment. The participants will assemble at a given rendezvous and only if the coast seems clear proceed to the fight. That cuts down on the risk of informants tipping off the authorities. It also makes it frustratingly difficult to pull off a successful raid.

The pit, usually about fifteen feet square, where the dogs fight, may be specially constructed and precisely marked out. Or it could be a makeshift assembly fencing off part of a room. Carpeting is often used to afford a grip for the dogs and prevent slipping. One suspected pit was the empty swimming pool of a wealthy 'fan', where telltale blood splashes could be quickly hosed away. Another was in the changing rooms of a junior school: the school caretaker was involved.

A referee is usually appointed to ensure 'fair play'. He keeps the purse the winning dog owner will collect, which can be substantial and, in addition, large sums change hands in side bets. The contests are often videoed. There is a lucrative market for these tapes with punters who enjoy the 'spectacle' but not the risk of attending.

The procedure adopted is very similar to a boxing match. The dogs are weighed beforehand to check they have 'come in' at the agreed weight and are evenly matched. They are also washed

Bottom: Dogfighters carry their own First Aid kit of ointments and drugs, often illegally obtained, to patch up their dogs after a fight and to avoid having to take them to a vet.

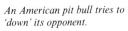

An American pit bull tries to 'down' its opponent.

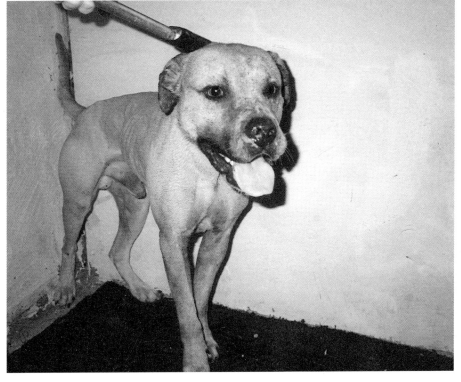

After a fight has been broken up, RSPCA Inspectors use heavy-duty graspers to restrain the dogs and keep them apart.

49

American pit bull terriers have been purpose-bred for their ferocity, legendary strength and the quality fighters prize above all else – 'gameness'. In a nutshell, that means never quitting.

down before the start of a bout to make sure they are 'clean'. Owners, determined to win at all costs, have been known to coat their dogs in poisonous substances. Corners are assigned and the handlers will normally have a helper there, who stands by with bucket and sponge. On the instruction 'Release your dogs' the fight is on. There is no time limit for these contests – some go on for hours.

The referee is usually assisted by an official time-keeper to keep a record of the number of 'scratches' and 'turns'. He also counts down the time between rounds and the period of time allowed for the dogs to make a scratch. A 'scratch' is the way the dog demonstrates its gameness. A line is drawn, either across the centre of the pit, or diagonally across each dog's corner. This is the scratch line. The dogs take it in turn to make a scratch by going across the pit into the other dog's 'territory' and attacking.

When a dog is 'scratching', the oppos-

ing dog is held just inside its scratch line. The attacking dog must not be pushed towards the defender by the handler. If a dog fails to engage with its opponent within an allotted time the other dog is declared the winner. This is literally the origin of the saying 'not coming up to scratch'.

Although spectators rowdily cheer on the dogs they must not be touched during the fight unless one turns away. In that case the referee will shout, 'Turn – pick up your dogs.' The animals are then returned to their respective corners and sponged down. After a specified period the referee will restart the fight. The dog that turned first must cross the scratch line and attack its opponent. If it fails to do so the other dog is declared the winner.

A handler can concede the fight, at any time, by picking up his dog. A dog can be picked up and still regarded as a 'game' loser.

The dogs go for any part of each other's anatomy – nose, leg, jaw or

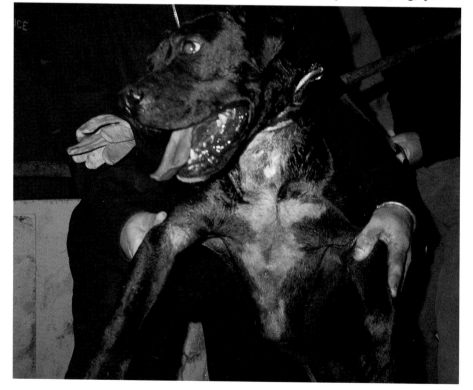

throat and once they've got a grip hang on with ferocious staying power.

Cropped ears are one of the give-away signs of dogfighting-related activities, amputated so that once in the pit an opponent will have less to grip onto. Puncture marks and scarring are other telltale clues. Once they are locked in combat the only way to separate the dogs is with chisel-shaped 'breaking sticks', made out of hard wood. The stick is worked into the dog's mouth, behind the eye-teeth, then rocked to and fro to prise the jaws apart.

Both dogs, even the 'victor', are likely to sustain terrible injuries in the course of a fight. Shock, caused by dehydration and loss of blood (inevitable in a sustained and bloody contest), is the greatest killer. For obvious reasons the fighters are reluctant to seek veterinary treatment and many carry their own illegally obtained drugs to administer emergency first-aid.

The clandestine nature of dogfighting makes it hard to root out. Dogfighters take extraordinary precautions and catching them in the act is as difficult as busting drug-runners. Sometimes the two go hand-in-hand.

The first breakthrough in detection came in 1985. In May of that year the Special Operations Unit caught a number of dogfighters red-handed. The resulting court case was the first successful prosecution for dogfighting this century.

The officers had staked out an isolated barn in the Home Counties just north of London, acting on a tip-off. Surveillance revealed a car parked directly across a track to the barn to obstruct access. A lone man was stationed in a nearby field, apparently on lookout duty. They radioed for police assistance. Three officers then worked their way round behind the barn and concealed themselves in the nearby woods. The remaining RSPCA officers, joined by the police, approached the barn directly along the track.

As expected, the 'lookout' man raised

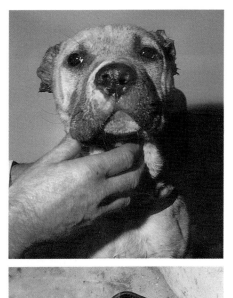

Top: Cropped ears are one of the giveaway signs of dogfighting.

Centre: Once locked in combat, the only way to separate the dogs is with chisel-shaped breaking sticks.

Bottom: After a fight is raided, the 'purse' is left behind against the blood-spattered walls of the pit.

the alarm. About fifteen men emerged from the barn and fled towards the woods where the RSPCA investigators were lying in wait. In the ensuing mêlée five men were arrested.

Two bull terriers were found locked in combat, both severely injured and covered in blood. A vet was summoned immediately.

A search of the shed revealed a dog-fighting pit with blood-smeared walls and floor, and dogfighting equipment scattered around. As the search continued a man was discovered hiding underneath the shed. He had video equipment, including a videotape, which proved to be a horrific record of the interrupted fight. Four vehicles parked near the barn were found to contain incriminating evidence. Also present were two badly scarred fighting dogs obviously due to have fought later that day.

Interrogation of the arrested men led eventually to seven more men being charged with offences. In all eleven people were prosecuted and convicted. Three received prison sentences of two months, one was placed in youth custody for three months, while the remainder received substantial fines.

Both the dogs caught fighting needed intensive care. One, a Staffordshire bull terrier, was beyond recovery, and was humanely destroyed.

Since that initial success SOU officers have mounted dozens of investigations and raids. By December 1991 the RSPCA had obtained a total of 193 dog-fighting-related convictions. The SOU officers are quick to pay tribute to the help they receive from uniformed colleagues. They also work closely with the serious crime squads of police forces up and down the country.

Typical of the military precision that goes into planning a successful 'bust' was a recent case in Scotland, where intelligence indicated a fight was scheduled at an isolated farmhouse near Fife. The Special Operations Unit tipped off colleagues in the Scottish Society for

the Prevention of Cruelty to Animals (SSPCA) and the local police force. Together they mounted a spectacular joint operation, codenamed 'Trojan Horse', for reasons that will become apparent.

The farmhouse was staked out and observation confirmed it would be difficult to make a surprise raid since a long drive led up to the farm buildings and the dogfighters would have plenty of time to escape if they spotted the authorities approaching. The officers hit upon the idea of concealing themselves in a horse transporter, which could drive up to the farmhouse without attracting undue attention.

So, on a sunny Sunday morning in May four SOU officers, four SSPCA officers, and about eighty police officers found themselves packed into a horse box approaching the farmhouse. All were kitted out in police overalls and protective helmets to aid identification as they swooped on the fighters. Many of the people expected to attend the fight were known criminals – some with a record for armed robbery and other

violent offences. There might be guns on the premises.

Hearts sank as on the first approach towards the drive they saw people milling around outside the farm buildings. Perhaps the fight was already over. 'It turned out later that the fighters were having a breather in between bouts,' explained Chief Inspector Mike Butcher.

The horse box drove on, then thirty minutes later returned for another sortie. Four back-up vehicles lay in support. This time they turned into the drive and headed purposefully towards the farm. The officers rushed out of the horse box and into the buildings where they caught the fighters red-handed, completely taken by surprise. Stake money of £1,000, in used notes, was scattered around the pit. Thirty-four men were arrested.

Inspectors Bryn Pass and Terry Spamer leapt into the pit to part the fighting dogs. The two pit bull terriers, plus two others that had already fought earlier in the day, were badly injured and all were later humanely destroyed.

The premises were searched and in addition to dogfighting-related equipment, like breaking sticks and treadmills, they found drugs and guns – amphetamines and three shotguns. Some of the 'spectators' had travelled miles to attend the fight, from as far afield as the North-East, Lancashire and the Midlands. One man had been arrested on two previous occasions in similar operations.

In a series of follow-up house raids in Newcastle and Sunderland five more fighting dogs were seized. Operation 'Trojan Horse' had gone like clockwork. Thirty-four convictions were obtained in the resulting prosecution, the first of its kind in Scotland.

Of course not all operations are so spectacularly successful. There have been many abortive raids and tip-offs that come to nothing. Penetrating the close-knit world of the dogfighting 'mafia' is fraught with difficulties.

But the Special Operations Unit will not let up in its fight against the horrors of dogfighting. There are hopes that the new Dangerous Dogs legislation, including its register, may help the officers in their task. (The RSPCA is in favour of compulsory registration for *all* dogs.) Eventually pit bull terriers

Left: Police and RSPCA support vehicles gather prior to a raid on an illegal dogfight.

Below: The officers hit upon the idea of concealing themselves in a horse transporter.

Right: Many dogs die immediately from their injuries or later through shock.

could be phased out. But nobody is expecting overnight results. 'There are enough criminals and enough stock to sustain the fight game for many years to come,' predicted Frank Milner.

The following chapters show some of the SOU's recent investigations into this shadowy underworld.

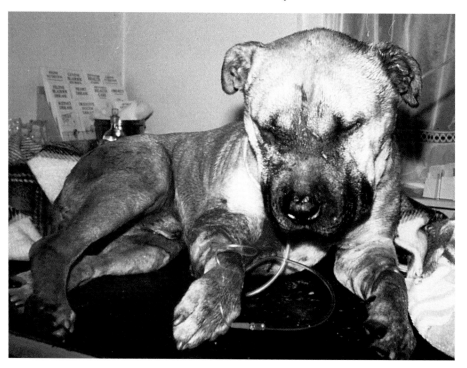

C H A P T E R   S I X

MUZZLING THE 'DEVIL DOGS'

19 AUGUST 1991

The SOU office received information from their uniformed colleagues in Lancashire that a 'weight-pulling contest' was going to be held in Wigan on the following Sunday.

These contests started about five years ago and are held every few weeks in the summer in almost every area of Britain. Staffordshire and pit bull owners test the pulling power of their dogs by allowing them to drag a trolley piled high with breeze blocks. The dogs have one minute to pull weights of up to 3,000 pounds over a distance of fifteen feet. If a dog keeps winning he can be worth thousands of pounds in stud fees. Chief Superintendent Frank Milner and his team have spotted several convicted dogfighters at these events.

However this meeting, which was to take place at a cricket ground in Wigan on Bank Holiday Sunday, was to be different from previous meetings which the SOU had attended. This was to be the first event held since the new Dangerous Dogs Act had come into force seven days earlier.

The Dangerous Dogs Act had been rushed through Parliament in response to a massive public outcry following a spate of vicious attacks by pit bull terriers. On 12 August 1991 it became law and amongst its provisions were several which would have a direct bearing on the planned weight-pulling contest and which would, in effect, test how it would work in practice. These provisions were:

The dogs have one minute to pull weights of up to 3,000 pounds.

... *to prohibit persons from having in their possession or custody dogs belonging to types bred for fighting; to impose restrictions in respect of such dogs pending the coming into force of the prohibition; to enable restrictions to be imposed in relation to other types of dog which present a serious danger to the public; to make further provision for securing that dogs are kept under proper control; and for connected purposes.*

Section 1
(1) This section applies to:
 (a) any dog of the type known as the pit bull terrier;
 (b) any dog of the type known as the Japanese tosa; and
 (c) any dog of any type designated for the purpose of this section by an order

of the Secretary of State, being a type appearing to him to be bred for fighting or to have the characteristics of a type bred for that purpose.

Section 2
(2) No person shall:
(a) breed, or breed from, a dog to which this section applies;
(b) sell or exchange such a dog or offer, advertise or expose such a dog for sale or exchange;
(c) make or offer to make a gift of such a dog or advertise or expose such a dog as a gift;
(d) allow such a dog of which he is the owner or of which he is for the time being in charge to be in a public place without being muzzled and kept on a lead; or
(e) abandon such a dog of which he is the owner or, being the owner or for the time being in charge of such a dog, allow it to stray.

Section 7
(1) In this Act:
(a) references to a dog being muzzled are to its being securely fitted with a muzzle sufficient to prevent it biting any person; and
(b) references to its being kept on a lead are to its being securely held on a lead by a person who is not less than sixteen years old.

20 AUGUST 1991

Frank Milner walked into the office of Richard Davies, head of the RSPCA inspectorate, clutching the typed notes about the impending weight-pull show. He had just spoken with the Home Office about the legality of the event, which would be occurring in a public place, and told Richard: 'As far as the Home Office is concerned it will be a public place and therefore all dogs must be muzzled and on leads.'

The two men discussed the possibility

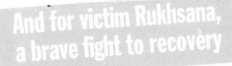

And for victim Rukhsana, a brave fight to recovery

How the Mail reported the latest attack yesterday

A MUZZLE ON THE PIT BULLS

TOUGH new laws are on the way to end the menace of the pit bull terrier,

By CHRISTOPHER BELL
Political Reporter

ment acted swiftly in the wake of the horrific weekend attack which almost killed six-year-old Rukhsana Khan.

Girl savaged by pit bull is scarred for life says surgeon

By Tim Butcher and Robert Shrimsley

THE six-year-old girl savaged by a pit bull terrier will be scarred for life and is almost certain to need plastic surgery to repair the terrible damage, a surgeon said last night.

Rucksana Khan spent the night in intensive care at Bradford Royal Infirmary, but there was no longer any threat to her life. Her condition was stable and she was expected to be moved to a ward today.

Mr Sabaratnan Sabaratnam, who spent two hours in the operating theatre rebuilding the girl's rib cage, said Rucksana's injuries were the worst of their kind he had

refused to name the owner of the dog — a 21-year-old pregnant woman — saying it was against force policy.

The dog's attack left Rucksana with 20 to 25 bites on her back, some of them causing deep muscle damage.

But her facial injuries were not as bad as they had looked and would mend, Mr Sabaratnam said.

Despite her appalling injuries Rucksana had been extremely brave. "She asked if she could go downstairs to watch the morning cartoons on TV. She was more bothered about missing those than anything else," he said.

"She is a very brave girl,

blood she was lucky not to die'

of a dog fitted with a muzzle attempting to pull a large weight. This would inhibit the animal's ability to pant, causing it some distress and therefore its owner would be subject to Section 1 of the Protection of Animals Act 1911 (causing unnecessary suffering to an animal).

22 AUGUST 1991, 10.00 HOURS

Frank Milner had spent most of the night thinking how he and his team would tackle the problem of hundreds of unmuzzled pit bull terriers parading around the cricket field in Wigan. But, to his relief, his worries eased somewhat when he made his first telephone call of the day. Inspector Jewitt of the Lancashire police told him the organisers of the event had phoned in to say that because of the recent press coverage, fewer dogs would be at the show and those dogs present would be fitted with muzzles and on leads.

The police were intent on keeping a low profile but Frank persuaded the inspector that even though fewer dogs were expected there should be a police

presence alongside the uniformed RSPCA officers who would be attending. He further suggested that the local RSPCA chief inspector would drop into the Wigan police office to meet the police sergeant who would be dealing with arrangements for the Sunday meeting. The RSPCA officer would also pass on advice to the police on the kind of scenario they could expect at a weight-pull and who was likely to be present.

14.00 hours

RSPCA Chief Inspector Frank Franzmann, who had volunteered to assist Frank Milner with plain-clothes observation at Sunday's weight-pull, arrived at the SOU office. Formerly on the staff of the SOU, Franzmann was now in charge of the uniformed inspectorate covering the south coast of England. He had offered his services because he was not known amongst the dogfighters and therefore would cause no suspicion at the forthcoming event.

Don Balfour and Frank Milner briefed him on the location and arrangements made with the police. Don told him that a vet had been asked to be on stand-by for the day and would be available at the cricket ground during the afternoon, should one be needed. The three men discussed the new Dangerous Dogs Act and how it would take a test case to determine how the Act would work.

25 AUGUST 1991, 08.30 HOURS

Frank Franzmann and Frank Milner had travelled north up the M6 to Lancashire the previous evening. They emerged from the motel at Charnock Richard, refreshed but somewhat apprehensive at what might lie in store for them at the Wigan cricket ground.

10.00 hours

On their arrival at Wigan police station both men were met by Sergeant Bamber who was to be the co-ordinating police officer for the day. He led the two men deep into the bowels of the station to

where a group of officers was waiting, along with three uniformed RSPCA men, in the briefing room. (It is always customary for a detailed briefing to take place before any joint operation with the police and RSPCA.)

Sergeant Bamber welcomed everyone, set out the scenario, and the location of the weight-pull, then went on to discuss the legislation in the new Dangerous Dogs Act. 'Very briefly,' he said, 'your part in this today will, first of all, be to prevent any breach of the peace and second, to take action that is necessary under the new legislation. You may be required to take action when you see an unmuzzled dog. If there are three to four hundred people there, and the dog is in the middle of the cricket pitch, there's going to be some aggro. So it's a matter of using common sense. Wait until the opportune moment, get hold of the owner and report him. If that's impossible, don't worry about it; with the help of these

Sergeant Bamber briefs the team.

Chief Inspector Frank Franzmann at the police briefing.

gentlemen here,' he said, nodding towards the group of five RSPCA officers, 'we hope to identify them at a later date, and maybe then we can take proceedings by summons.'

Sergeant Bamber discussed who might be present and the extension granted to the drink licence. He then pointed out Frank Franzmann as the RSPCA undercover officer who would not be known to those people attending the event, and who would be mingling with the crowd.

Frank Milner then instructed the police officers on weight-pulling events and the effects a muzzle would have on a dog dragging a fully loaded cart. He also asked the officers to look out for scarred dogs that could have been in a recent fight. 'If you see any just slip my men the word and they'll have a quiet look.'

The team brought the briefing to a close and headed for the yard at the rear of the police station where a riot van was waiting to take everyone on a reconnaissance of the area.

12.30 hours

The police van crept slowly into the housing estate adjacent to the cricket ground. Sergeant Bamber, seated in the front passenger seat, was giving a running commentary, like a tour guide, on the geography of the area surrounding the venue. The houses on the estate were all detached and expensive-looking, their occupants probably unaware that only a few yards away the first arrivals were gathering with their 'Devil Dogs' that for the past few months had been making national news headlines virtually every week.

Sergeant Bamber told the driver to stop. The riot van pulled up alongside a narrow passageway that ran between two of the detached houses and led to a brick archway housing a ten-foot wrought-iron gate which opened directly onto the cricket ground. It was suggested that it might become an escape route for both parties – for dog owners who wanted to avoid detection and for the RSPCA and police, should they need to get out in a hurry. Through the one-way windows in the van, Frank

Franzmann could just make out the first signs of activity on the other side of the gate.

The police van moved off, turned right along a main road for a few yards then turned right again through the car park of the cricket ground beside the main entrance. The police sergeant instructed the driver not to stop but to turn around and head back out. This gave enough time for the van's occupants to have a glimpse at the twenty or so people already there, and for them to register the police van. Surprisingly, only one pit bull could be seen. On the way out one of the police officers remarked that none of the dozen cars already there had local number plates. They drove the few miles back to Wigan police station where the team split into groups before returning to the cricket ground. The uniformed RSPCA officers, each accompanied by a police officer, drove off in white RSPCA vans but Frank Franzmann, dressed in jeans and light blue bomber jacket, left the police station in his car. Frank Milner followed in his Cavalier.

13.00 hours

Frank Franzmann had parked in the housing estate next to the back gate that led to the cricket field, but instead of going through he decided to walk round the block to the main entrance and pay the £2 admission fee. There were only about fifty people and twenty dogs present in the ground. According to the official programme the day's events started at 11.30 a.m., so this would probably be the total size of the crowd. Certainly the number had fallen well short of the 300–400 that were expected. About half the dogs present were wearing muzzles and being held on various lengths of leads by their owners. The other half were on leads but not muzzled.

The three uniformed RSPCA officers, with their police escorts, walked purposefully through the small gathering. The owners, with their dogs, had gath-

ered in one corner of the cricket ground. Frank Franzmann was concerned at what certainly now looked like police and RSPCA overkill, especially with such a small crowd which had been watching the officers' every move. He walked to a coin-box telephone in the bar which overlooked the venue and contacted the police operations room suggesting they radio their officers, and the uniformed RSPCA men, asking them to leave the immediate area. Within a few minutes the RSPCA undercover inspector was on his own.

The small gathering seemed to relax now that the arm of the law had disappeared and before long a sketchy programme of events began. Because of the poor turnout it was obvious there would be no weight-pulling; instead, the organisers were busy putting the few dogs

IT'S horrifying that th British Veterinary Asso ciation and the RSPC are leading moves t block the Government's ba on killer dogs.

The BVA spokesman who de scribed the ban as "as a knee jerk reaction" must surely have seen the pictures of poor little Rucksana Khan – and know some- thing of the orgy of savage mayhem caused by vicious dogs which only exist for use in dog-fighting.

These organisations should be made to realise that human beings come first. We will protect our

present through 'conformation' where each dog is judged for size, shape and movement – exactly like any other dog show. While this was going on Franzmann, holding his pint of lager, began to mingle with the spectators, hoping to pick up information on anything connected with dogfighting.

The first two onlookers that he spoke to indicated that since the introduction of the Dangerous Dogs Act, pit bull owners were being invited to join the newly formed Endangered Dog Association. The EDA was set up by a group of 'concerned working dog fanciers' who objected to one specific breed of dog being 'wiped out'. Their aims were to fight the Dangerous Dogs Act and, if possible, modify the legislation by taking a test case to the European Court.

By now Frank Milner, who had been keeping a low profile, watching events from a distance, appeared for a quick look. Immediately he set foot into the cricket ground he was met by a barrage of foul language from a group of dog owners sitting together near the conformation arena. In their eyes, Chief Superintendent Frank Milner and his team of undercover officers had done more to track down and eradicate dogfighting than anyone else. His high media profile had made Frank Milner known to every dogfighter in the country. He stood puffing on his pipe for a few minutes and listening to the abuse before quietly walking back through the entrance.

Meanwhile Franzmann had moved across to the steps leading up to the pavilion. There he struck up a dis-

troy these devil dogs

alling on
t a move
censes to

stopping
to the
ardy, Bir-

by pit
to defy
-nment

law calling for the destruction of their dogs shows what sort of people they are.

They are unmoved by the savage attacks on children by animals bred to kill. They put animals before our kids. If they persist in their defiance they must be

jailed – to protect us from them. – L. Gordon, Romford.

● THE action of the 11 responsible owners of pit bulls, rottweilers and crossbreds in Bradford, who have asked for their animals to be destroyed, puts to shame the outrageous gang who vow to keep their dogs whatever the law says. More should fol-

● THE decision to kill all pit bull terriers is as shocking as the threat to animals at London Zoo. To wipe out an entire breed because of a few irresponsible owners is the most stupid and inhumane act since King Herod's slaughter of the innocents. – Douglas Mcpherson, Raynes Park

cussion with a spectator from south Yorkshire who was praising a vet he knew who had obvious connections with the dogfighting fraternity. Frank listened intently to some intriguing stories before being rewarded with the name of the town where the vet practised.

By now it was nearly 2.00 p.m. and the fifty or so spectators were beginning to thin out quite rapidly. For them the day had been a disaster. It was obvious to Frank Franzmann and his colleagues that the new legislation had made its mark in the first week of coming into being. As the undercover officer turned to take his empty glass back to the bar, the organiser of the event walked past, turned to Frank and remarked this would be the last event of its kind. Frank Franzmann nodded in agreement, placed the empty glass on the bar and left the cricket ground grinning hugely.

EVENING STANDARD

Riot gear officers round up all illegal pit bulls

by Geraint Smith

POLICE in riot gear have seized every illegal pit bull terrier in Luton in a co-ordinated series of dawn raids.

The 13 dogs, including two puppies, are now on death row awaiting court orders for their destruction.

They are being held at a secret address until a court passes sentence.

In the five-day operation police marksmen accompanied a team of a dozen officers, two RSPCA chief inspectors and two dog wardens in case any of the dogs broke free.

The team included officers wearing helmets, leg protectors and carrying riot shields. Police dog handlers were kept in reserve.

"Pit bulls are aggressive and dangerous animals," said Pc David Hurn, who set up the operation. "They are only about 90lb but could rip your arms off. Safety was paramount throughout the operation."

The object of the operation was to seize every dog bought or bred for fighting, he said.

Sergeant Debbie Simpson, who led the raids, said: "If one of these dogs had got hold of an officer then that officer's police career would be over. It is as simple as that."

Most of the dogs were scarred from fighting, say the police, and are believed to be the major part of a dog-fighting ring.

"These are fighting dogs. They are not pets," said Pc Hurn.

"Since the Dangerous Dogs Act came into force in August last year we have worked hard..."

had been planned for four weeks. Under the cover of a news blackout it began at 6.30am on Sunday and continued until this morning.

Police with summons and search warrants entered the houses, the riot teams leading the way. The RSPCA and dog wardens took charge of the pitbulls once they were secure.

Only two dogs are believed to have been missed in the operation. They and their owners disappeared on Sunday before the squad arrived.

Superintendent Ralph Miller declared Operation Blue "a huge success".

"These dogs are a menace. There was ample opportunity for these people to become lawful owners and they chose not to," he said.

The operation had forestalled any possibility of more children being mauled, he said.

The names of those dogs seized include Hagler, Tyson and Samson.

At one address raided today, and alleged to be that of the dogfight ringleader, police seized diaries and phone-number books as well as more than 20 videos believed to feature dogfighting.

Following a series of horrific attacks by the animals on adults and children, the Dangerous Dogs Act 1991 made it illegal to keep any pitbull terrier-type dog unless it was neutered...

CHAPTER SEVEN

A RABIES TIME BOMB

Suddenly spotting one of the Berriff camera crew, Daglish turned violent.

THURSDAY, 11 APRIL 1991

During the night of Thursday, 11 April, an American pit bull terrier, called Jenny, was stolen from the Prospect Kennels near Harrogate. The thief broke into the kennels and cut through a padlocked chain to get to the dog, which had arrived at the kennels just six weeks earlier. She had been imported from Florida and was scheduled to spend six months in quarantine. This quarantine is obligatory for all animals coming into the country to ensure they

63

UNDERCOVER

Detective Sergeant Peter McCloy of the Durham constabulary who led the joint police/RSPCA raid.

are rabies-free. Bringing a dog into Britain is not cheap. The kennelling bills alone work out at around £800. Add on transportation and other costs and it quickly becomes an expensive business.

The person importing the dog had given an address in Whitehaven. But when attempts were made to initiate enquiries through the owner, the name and address turned out to be false. Notification of the theft filtered through to the RSPCA's Special Operations Unit. They checked their files to see if they could throw any light on the incident but there were no obvious leads.

Several weeks later they got a call. An informant claimed to know where Jenny was. A raid was set up with the police, but the information was false and there was no sign of the dog. The trail went cold. But the file remained open. Then the SOU investigators got another tip-off. Durham police force also got a call. The person named as possibly having the dog in his possession lived in Meadowfield, a suburb of Durham. The SOU undercover team hoped it would be a question of third time lucky. The police and RSPCA joined forces for another raid.

TUESDAY, 30 JULY

Superintendent Don Balfour and Chief Inspector Mike Butcher travelled up to Durham, their 300-mile journey dogged by accidents and diversions. They arrived late and hurriedly made their way to Durham police headquarters, which is housed in a Victorian building next door to the jail.

16.00 hours

In a crowded room the pre-raid briefing got under way. The investigation was being jointly handled by Detective Sergeant Peter McCloy and Mike Butcher. McCloy warned that the suspect had in his possession three American pit bull terriers, one of which was believed to be Jenny although she was no longer being called by that name. The officers present included two police dog handlers and

two uniformed RSPCA inspectors who would provide back-up if the dogs turned nasty. There were also a detective constable, a police intelligence officer and Mr Adamson, an officer from the local authority. The owner of the quarantine kennels had been called in too and listened intently as McCloy provided a description of the pit bull terrier.

'The dog we are going to search for today goes by the name of Wilma. It's described as being dangerous, having been trained for dogfighting,' said McCloy. 'Wilma is believed to be a thirty-eight-pound bitch with red colouring and possibly scarring to one of its rear legs. Obvious risks are evident as a result of Wilma not completing a period of quarantine and extreme caution should be exercised by anyone coming into contact with this dog.'

McCloy gave the name of the twenty-nine-year-old suspect – Scott Daglish. He warned that one of the other dogs suspected of being in Daglish's possession, a chocolate-coloured APBT, could recently have been involved in organised dogfighting. 'It will in fact be showing wounds as a result of this fight. It's our intention to gain entry to identify the stolen dog.' McCloy explained

Dog badly injured in fight

Ban for bull terrier owner

AN American pit bull terrier was found "mauled" and "chewed up" during a raid on a house near Durham.

RSPCA inspectors, police and public protection officials came across the badly injured dog while searching for an imported pit bull bitch which had been stolen from quarantine.

They found the bitch and also came across Bolio, a three-year-old pit bull dog which was carrying bite marks and scars.

Durham magistrates heard

By BRUCE UNWIN

...unds were later ...those ...ere was no suggestion ...the theft.

no veterinary care had been given, the suffering would have been increased.

...mitigat-

that if the animal proved to be Jenny then all three dogs would be seized because of the risk of 'contamination' from contact with a dog that had not completed quarantine and therefore posed a rabies risk. The local authority officer, Mr Adamson, would attempt to gain entry under powers conferred by the relevant legislation. If that failed the police would execute a search warrant issued in respect of the suspected theft of the dog from the kennels.

Reading from a brief, McCloy assigned everybody's role and responsibilities during the raid. Officers would cover both the front and the rear of the premises in order to frustrate any attempt by Daglish to escape or to set the dogs free. 'We will communicate with each other once the operation is in progress by personal radio.'

The briefing broke up and everyone hurried to Meadowfield police station, which was close to the suspect's house. They would wait there for confirmation that Daglish was at home.

It was known that he always took the dogs for an early evening walk. The plan was to catch him at home before this daily promenade. No sense, however, forewarning him. He might be alerted if

he spotted the kennel's quarantine van cruising the vicinity, therefore the kennel owner had been left behind at headquarters. He would be sent for, with the van, once the dogs were secured. He had got to know the dog during its time in his kennels and was confident he would recognise it again.

The convoy of vehicles pulled into the Meadowfield station and the officers reassembled. The RSPCA inspectors checked the restraining equipment that might be needed if the dogs were belligerent. Then they ran through the details of the raid one more time. Mike Butcher passed round photographs of the dog they were seeking, taken at the kennels shortly before the dog was stolen.

The officers studied them intently. This was an animal that might, for all anybody knew, be carrying rabies.

'What happens if we get in and the stolen dog isn't there?' asked someone.

Mike responded, 'If we find a dog we think we can get a ticket on, i.e. a cruelty case –' he began.

'Have you got powers of seizure?' interrupted McCloy.

Don grimaced and said, 'You can't leave an animal in a suffering condition.'

65

Two RSPCA uniformed inspectors standing by with graspers.

'If he tries to resist in any way we'll execute the search warrant, arrest him and rely on the PACE laws,' decided McCloy. (The Police and Criminal Evidence Act (PACE) 1984 provides authority for the police to enter and search premises in certain circumstances.)

A telephone shrilled in the room next door and McCloy strode away to answer it. Silence fell as everybody strained to hear if this was the go-ahead. It was a false alarm. The tension built up. The phone rang again and McCloy snatched up the grey handset. The officers next door heard him say, 'Right . . . okay . . . smashing.' He swept back in like an express train. Firmly tapping the truncheon into his left hand he announced, 'Right – it's on! He's in there now. He's going out very, very shortly.'

The others hastily gulped down the tea they had been nursing and followed him out of the station.

17.45 hours

Frederick Street North, where a red and green 'For Sale' sign marked the terraced house that was their quarry, was just a few hundred yards away. Some made their way on foot, others by van. In the street running parallel at the back of the house the police dog handlers stationed themselves at the rear of the premises. The RSPCA uniformed officers joined them, nervously fingering the graspers that might be needed to restrain the dogs.

Adamson and McCloy walked up to the front door, Don and Mike following in their footsteps. McCloy gave Adamson a final briefing: 'You just go up and tell him who you are and your reason for being here.'

The hand-held radio crackled. 'The dogs are in the back,' reported one of the police officers from the rear of the house.

'Roger,' responded the receiving officer.

Adamson rapped on the door sharply three times. Seconds later the door was opened by a woman.

'Is Mr Daglish available, please? Could I have a word with him? The name is Adamson,' said the local authority officer.

'Just one moment,' replied the woman as she tried to shut the door.

McCloy moved quickly, wedging his foot between the door and the frame. 'Can we just come in for a minute, please?' he demanded, stepping smartly inside. Immediately he came face to face with the suspect, a stocky man, about five feet six inches in height, dressed casually in blue jeans and a grey sweatshirt. McCloy flashed his ID and said, 'Scott, I'm Peter McCloy. This is a chap from the council. He wants to have a word with you.'

The other officers followed him over the threshold into a narrow front room. The curtains had been pulled and as they entered, the sound of frenzied dog-barking filtered into the darkened room.

'What's happening today?' asked Daglish in a Geordie accent.

Adamson explained the purpose of the visit: 'I'm an authorised officer under the Animal Health Act. I've reason to believe you have a stolen dog on the premises and I would like to have a look at it, please.'

Daglish showed no surprise at this accusation and led them through the kitchen into the back yard. The concreted yard was secured like a fortress with six-foot-high fencing and brick walls. A brown velour three-piece suite sagged against a side wall, providing an incongruous contrast to the stark compound opposite which contained kennels and dog runs. There were two pit bull terriers inside the wire compound. A third APBT was chained to a wooden pillar sunk in concrete in the middle of the yard.

'Where did you get the dogs from, Scott?' asked McCloy.

'I've had them from all over the place,' replied Daglish. The dogs continued to bark furiously. 'Hold on, stand back just in case because there's a lot of people about,' he warned. Dog faeces were scattered over the yard. 'Shit!' he exclaimed appropriately as he trod in some.

The dog chained to the pillar was tan-coloured and looked suspiciously like the pictures of Jenny.

'What are the dogs' names?' asked Adamson.

'Wilma,' replied Daglish, gesturing towards the chained dog, 'Spooky,' pointing at a tan-coloured dog inside the compound, 'and Bolio.'

Don and Mike studied Bolio with interest. This dog was the chocolate-coloured pit bull thought to have been involved in organised dogfighting. Even from a distance it was easy to see that the animal was very scarred. Spooky seemed relatively docile. The bitch was heavily pregnant – probably about a week away from whelping.

As the police handlers cautiously entered the yard, the dogs' barking rose to a new crescendo and Scott's patience snapped.

'Who are these people here?' he demanded.

'Can we just go through where all the

Above: Wilma and Spooky in the yard.

Left: When Daglish angrily protested, the film crew is forced to retreat to a neighbour's wall.

dogs come from,' persisted Mike calmly.

'Are any of them imported?' added Don.

'No, no,' said Daglish, shaking his head emphatically. A brief flicker of hesitation and then he changed his story. 'Oh, sorry – that one over there,' pointing at Bolio.

Later investigations would establish

67

that Bolio had been brought in from Holland over a year earlier. The dog had been quarantined at the same kennels from which Wilma had been stolen.

'Have you registered any of them?' enquired Don.

'No,' said Daglish. Suddenly spotting one of the Berriff camera crew he turned violent.

'They're making a programme about the work of the RSPCA,' explained one of the police officers.

'Well I want them out, off my property,' exploded Daglish.

The camera crew retreated to a neighbour's wall and continued to film.

'Scott, I'm going to have to caution you,' said McCloy. He read him his rights and explained, 'I am arresting you on suspicion of theft of a pit bull terrier. All right? We'll go down to Durham city police station.'

McCloy escorted Daglish back inside the house while Mike Butcher flicked through the photographs again. Was Wilma really Jenny?

Sounds of a dispute came from the house. The woman could be heard crying. Suddenly Daglish burst out of the back gate, and lunged for one of the camera crew. 'I'll break your jaw,' he screamed as a police officer moved forward to restrain him.

By now several neighbours, alerted by the commotion coming from the house, had drifted onto the street for a better view of the proceedings, and stood around smoking and speculating about the row.

18.15 hours
As a police officer escorted Daglish away McCloy comforted the tearful woman. 'Don't get yourself upset. He's not going to be long, pet.'

One of the dog handlers bent down to stroke Wilma. The dog was wearing a two-inch-wide leather collar, attached to the chain securing the dog by a heavy-duty climbing clip. The chain was the thickness of a ship's anchor cable.

Wilma was thin, her ribcage clearly visible. But by now Don and Mike were more concerned about the condition of Bolio.

Bolio's face was a patchwork quilt of scar tissue. The RSPCA investigators were anxious to get the dog examined by a veterinary surgeon who could confirm if the injuries had been sustained as a result of dogfighting. The officers waited for the kennel owner to arrive with the quarantine van. He would know best if Wilma was the stolen dog.

Once the kennel owner arrived he ran a practised eye over Wilma and announced his certainty that it was the dog in question. 'She's lost a lot of weight,' he observed.

The kennel owner's identification was enough for McCloy, who was taking no chances with three dogs that were a potential rabies risk. He ordered all three to be seized.

As the three dogs were loaded into secure carrying cages the remaining officers embarked on a thorough search of the premises. Inside a shed in the back yard they found a first-aid kit, some steroid tablets and two breaking sticks. Some weighing scales, of the type used to weigh dogs before a match to ensure they have 'come in' at the agreed weight, were also found. All the items were methodically listed and bagged for removal.

Inside the house there was a large collection of pit bull magazines, books and photographs. An address book made interesting reading: many of the names it contained were familiar to the SOU officers for suspected involvement in dogfighting.

'What sort of penalties do you get for dogfighting, then?' asked one of the police officers conversationally.

'Six months,' replied Mike.

The policeman looked surprised. 'Is that it? It's nowt, is it?' he remarked.

By the time the dogs were driven away, the curious crowd watching had swelled to about thirty people, for whom the raid had broken the tedium of a muggy, overcast evening. Little did they know they had been living in the vicinity of a potential rabies time bomb.

19.00 hours

Back at Durham police station the officers reassembled for a debriefing.

'Well, it came good at the end of the day,' began McCloy. He leaned back in his swivel chair and continued, 'Three dogs seized and the one we were looking for has been positively identified by the kennel owner as being the one stolen from the kennels.'

'Anything of interest in the property seized?'

'In the cupboard at the top of the stairs we found an American dog registration certificate relating to a dog called Wilma,' said Don.

There was little doubt that Wilma had been imported from America. But there was no trace of any quarantine documents or import certificate. These would be handed over once a dog has completed its quarantine.

'There's a letter you might find interesting to read,' continued Don. The letter had been with the other documents. He read from it:

'She [Wilma] is almost back to her normal colour but her coat is still a bit dull from the dye we used. We are finding it hard to get her matched up but we do have Bolio fixed . . . Bolio is a good one, he heals quickly. Billy told me yesterday that he saw Tyson the other day and he still can't get up and walk . . . I refereed a match the other day between two thirty-three-pound Staffs. It was good to watch, very fast for the whole time. An hour and seven minutes . . . At the moment his [Bolio's] face is a mess and Spooky looks as though she is going to have a litter of Great Danes.'

McCloy listened thoughtfully. 'Very interesting, that letter,' he concluded when Don finished reading.

The sooner Bolio could be examined by a vet the better. Don and Mike would arrange this for the following day. The briefing broke up.

WEDNESDAY, 31 JULY, 10.00 HOURS

Don and Mike arrived at the kennels where the dogs had been secured. A veterinary surgeon had been asked to meet them there to inspect the dogs and give a professional opinion.

Don gently lifted Bolio on to the examination table. 'He's a very pleasant friendly dog at the moment,' he observed. 'But things would almost certainly change if you put him in a dog-fight situation.'

The vet gently ran his hands over the network of scar tissue that criss-crossed Bolio's face. The animal was a pathetic sight, and must have been badly injured to produce that degree of scarring. 'He's well scarred about his face with some quite deep lacerations around his eyes,' pronounced the vet. The untreated facial wounds had produced a nasty case of conjunctivitis. 'Judging by the amount of discharge the dog clearly hasn't received any treatment,' was the vet's next comment.

He started to examine the body and remarked, 'These wounds that we see on the legs are very, very typical of dog-bite wounds. I think anybody who has seen a fight, even between poodles, will realise that they bite each other on the front legs and shoulders. He's been involved in a fairly substantial dogfight.'

Bolio remained placid throughout the examination. He wagged his tail and tried to lick Don when he asked, 'How long do you think it's been since those wounds were inflicted?'

The vet paused to calculate and volunteered between three to five weeks earlier.

'So, it's nothing that could have been caused by a chance domestic encounter?' persisted Don.

'Oh, there's no way you could have that sort of injury caused in, I think, any other way except a major fight,' responded the vet.

Bolio grew restless. Don patted the dog reassuringly and asked, 'Would you be able to go so far, do you think, to say how long that fight might have gone on? Could it have been more than ten minutes?'

It was usually a difficult question to answer with certainty. It would depend on various factors like how evenly the dogs had been matched. But the vet didn't hesitate. 'Oh yes, obviously. I would have thought an absolute minimum of ten minutes and probably twenty or thirty. Or maybe even longer depending on who had the upper hand.'

This was the veterinary confirmation Don and Mike needed. They now had the backing needed to proceed with a cruelty charge.

Don thanked the vet for his examination and Bolio was led back to the kennels.

14.00 hours

Don and Mike arrived at Knaresborough police station where Daglish had been brought for questioning. (The Knaresborough force were now handling the investigation because the theft took place on their patch). Detective Constable Sean Bollon was in charge of the enquiry. The SOU officers knew Bollon well as they had worked together earlier in the year on a successful dog-fighting bust.

Daglish had already been questioned by Bollon when the SOU officers arrived. 'He's not disputing that Jenny is the dog stolen from the kennels,' advised Bollon. However Daglish was denying any role in the theft. He said that he had bought the dog a few weeks earlier from somebody he had met casually in a pub in Birmingham. There was no evidence so far to link Daglish directly with the kennels break-in.

'What I intend to do, Don, is to bail him to leave the police station today and to come back in about six weeks' time. That will enable us to make further enquiries into the theft aspect,' said Bollon.

'We're quite interested in the scarred pit bull terrier that was found in his possession,' said Don. He told Bollon that they had veterinary confirmation that the injuries were consistent with an organised dogfight.

Daglish had already denied this. He claimed that Bolio had been injured

One of the dog handlers bent down to stroke Wilma.

after a domestic scrap with Spooky, the third dog in his possession, who was expecting puppies. Yet there wasn't a mark on Spooky. All the officers were sceptical that it could have been such a one-sided encounter that Spooky got off scot-free while Bolio was savaged.

'We'd like to speak to him about Bolio while he's still here at the police station if that's possible,' said Don. They were also anxious to question him about the reference to dyeing Wilma in the letter they had found. Bollon gave them the go-ahead.

But it proved an unrewarding exercise. Daglish stuck rigidly to his story even though he was unable to provide a name or address for the person who had sold him the dog.

How had the American dog registration certificate come into his possession, asked the SOU officers? The envelope had an American postmark and it had been sent directly to his home. Daglish said he wrote to the breeder in the States and asked for it, having got his name from the Birmingham contact. He claimed he had no quarantine documents simply because he had not thought to ask for them, while the letter he dismissed as a fantasy, all made up for his own amusement.

Over the next few weeks further enquiries proved equally fruitless. There was no evidence to link Daglish with the crime. No fingerprints at the kennels ... nothing of any substance. However, the RSPCA would still proceed with its cruelty investigation.

THURSDAY, 3 OCTOBER

The RSPCA's legal department had decided that Daglish's failure to obtain veterinary treatment for Bolio's injuries, no matter how they were sustained, was enough to justify a cruelty charge.

Mike Butcher travelled to Durham to serve the summons on Daglish. The charge read: 'Between 1 May 1991 and 4 July 1991 you did cause unnecessary suffering by unreasonably omitting to

Above: Bolio, the pit bull terrier, was found with severe scars. RSPCA officers and a veterinary surgeon estimated the dog had been in a fight some two to three weeks earlier.

Below: A medicine box found during the search of Daglish's home.

Don Balfour gently lifts Bolio onto the examination table for a veterinary inspection.

provide the said animal with proper and necessary care and attention.'

In the interim Bolio and Spooky had been returned to Daglish. Once it had been established beyond doubt that they were rabies-free there were no further grounds for denying Daglish possession of his dogs.

But Jenny/Wilma was stolen property. Daglish had no more right to the dog than anybody else. In the absence of a legal owner the dog was retained and later put down on veterinary advice. The new Dangerous Dogs legislation made it illegal to rehome the dog.

5 FEBRUARY 1992

After several delays the case was finally heard by Durham Magistrates. The court was told how Bolio had been found with 'massive' bite injuries after RSPCA and police officers raided Daglish's home in search of an imported pit bull terrier (Jenny/Wilma) stolen from quarantine kennels.

The court heard how the officers had found the stolen dog at Daglish's home but prosecutor Michael Moreland stated: 'I say at the outset there are absolutely no suggestions the defendant was involved in the theft of the dog. He told investigators he bought it from a man in Birmingham and that cannot be challenged. But it was the condition of Bolio that was noted.'

The accusation against Daglish was that he had caused the dog unnecessary suffering by not taking it to a vet after he discovered its injuries. A report from the veterinary surgeon who had examined Bolio was read to the court:

'I am unreservedly of the opinion that the dog [Bolio] had been involved in at least one major dogfight prior to my examination, and was quite seriously injured. The dog was caused a great deal of unnecessary suffering.' The statement added that if no veterinary treatment had been given, the dog's suffering would have been increased.

Daglish pleaded guilty to the charge

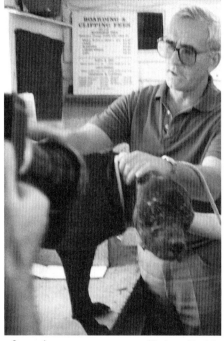

of causing unnecessary suffering. In his defence it was stated that he had kept dogs for several years and had always looked after them. It was claimed that Bolio's injuries were caused by being bitten by the pregnant bitch, Spooky. The defence maintained that Daglish had cleaned the wounds, put on anti-septic powder and ointment, and thought not a great deal more could have been done. Daglish maintained throughout the case that the injuries were caused in play and vehemently denied that he was involved in dog-fighting.

Daglish was banned from keeping any animal for six years, fined £150 and ordered to pay £250 costs plus £52.75 in veterinary fees.

CHAPTER EIGHT

FIGHT TO THE DEATH

This case has yet to come to court and for legal reasons the names of those involved have been changed.

SATURDAY, 31 AUGUST 1991, 15.30 HOURS

The five-month-old white and tan pit bull terrier was a pathetic sight. It was very shocked, in a collapsed state, and badly wounded. Adrienne Murphy was the vet on duty when the dog was carried in to one of the RSPCA's hospitals one hot summer afternoon. She examined the dog immediately and found numerous lacerations and puncture marks. For the next three hours she battled to save its life but it failed to respond to intensive treatment. At about 6.30 p.m. the animal's condition deteriorated. It had diarrhoea, was vomiting blood, and in deep shock. It died on the operating table.

The owner, an unemployed twenty-year-old called Kostas Papadopoulos, brought her in for treatment, saying she had been involved in a scrap in the park. He claimed he had been exercising

RSPCA vet Adrienne Murphy examines the dying pit bull terrier brought in by its owner.

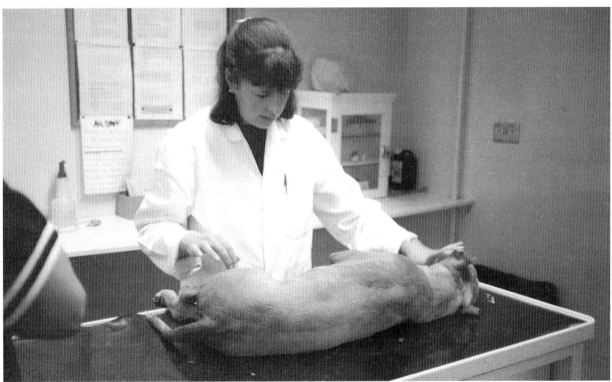

Inspector Jon Storey

the dog, off the leash, when another dog, which he described as a rottweiler/alsatian cross, attacked. Papadopoulos said he tried to protect his dog, Sally, by fending off the other dog with sticks. It eventually let go. He could see Sally was in a bad way so he rushed her to the RSPCA hospital.

Adrienne Murphy was immediately suspicious about the nature of the wounds. In a statement prepared later she noted: 'In my professional opinion the injuries were inconsistent with those caused by a rottweiler or other domesticated dog as was alleged by the owner. I would have to conclude that these injuries were the result of a fight with another American pit bull terrier. The animal had been caused considerable unnecessary suffering.'

Murphy called in the RSPCA inspectorate. Uniformed Inspector John Bowe attended and took a series of still photographs to record the dog's condition. Bowe, like Murphy, thought the dog's severe injuries had possibly come from a dogfight, and he alerted the Special Operations Unit. Papadopoulos was already known to the undercover officers for suspected involvement in dogfighting. The Special Operations Unit decided to request police assistance for a raid on his home.

WEDNESDAY, 4 SEPTEMBER, 05.30 HOURS

It was a very early start for the RSPCA officers assigned to the case. They met at the hospital to run through the battle plan.

Ian Green explained what they were hoping to achieve: 'The object this morning is to go to Papadopoulos's address, wake him up nice and early, get him arrested and bring him back for interview. We'll do a thorough search of his house and see what else we can find.'

The RSPCA uniformed inspectors who would be helping, Jon Storey and John Bowe, listened attentively, as did

Alan Goddard. They knew that Papadopoulos had other dogs, but not how many, or whether they were kept at the house. Ian added that there would be police dog handlers on stand-by to help out if needed.

The meeting broke up and hastily they made their way to Holloway police station to assemble for a pre-raid briefing with the police officers who would be going in with them.

06.00 hours

The shift commander, Inspector Ken Reeves, explained to the four uniformed police officers allocated to back up the RSPCA what was expected of them. 'Right, lads, this morning we are helping the RSPCA out with the arrest of an alleged dogfighter. The arrest at this stage is for cruelty to animals.' He explained that once they had gained entry they would search for any dogfighting-related evidence under section 32 of the Police and Criminal Evidence Act (PACE). 'Obviously if there are any dogs there, then these lads go first,' he said, gesturing at the two uniformed RSPCA inspectors. 'I don't want you lot hanging on the end of any pit bulls.'

'How many people are likely to be there?' asked a police officer.

'We've no idea,' responded Ian. 'He might have his wife there and possibly a Rastafarian called Winston Gold who we also suspect is into dogfighting.'

Inspector Reeves broke in: 'If you need any more back-up shout for it. I've got loads [of officers] on this morning. King's Cross [police] will be made aware you're going onto their ground.' The suspect's address was on the 'patch' technically covered by King's Cross police station. There were a few more questions, then the briefing wound up.

Dawn was breaking as the convoy of RSPCA vans and police cars sped through the empty streets to Papadopoulos's address. They parked in the tree-lined avenue and gathered outside a mansion block of flats. The sun was just beginning to glint through the trees, promising a hot day ahead.

Had any residents emerged for a peaceful early morning stroll, they would have been stunned by the spectacle confronting them. RSPCA Inspector Jon Storey headed the column of officers fully kitted out in protective equipment. He was wearing a crash helmet, leather gauntlets and carried a riot shield. He was also issued with a stun extinguisher. Nobody had any idea how many dogs to expect and there was no point in taking any chances. Jon would be the first officer through the door with the task of securing any dangerous dogs present.

06.30 hours
A police officer rang the entry buzzers and gained entry to the property. Sol-

Jon Storey headed the column of officers fully kitted out in protective equipment.

75

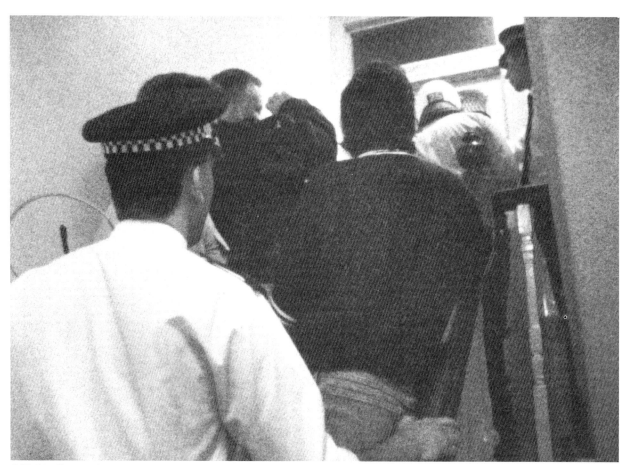

RSPCA officers and police armed with riot gear crowd the narrow staircase to Papadopoulos's flat.

emnly they tramped up the stairs to the third-floor flat, Jon in front. He banged on the door. A dog could be heard barking in response. A woman, sleepy and surprised, opened the door wearing a nightdress. It was Papadopoulos's mother.

The police officer behind Jon said, 'It's the police. Can we come in, love? We want a chat.'

She stepped aside ready to let them in.

'Where are the dogs?' asked Jon.

'In the living room,' replied the mother. It was safe to enter.

Papadopoulos stumbled out of his bedroom dressed in striped boxer shorts and a blue T-shirt. A police officer stepped forward and warned him he was under arrest. 'You've been arrested for an offence of cruelty to animals. Now

we have the power to search the flat for any articles involved in that offence.'

'How many dogs have you got here?' demanded Ian.

'Two. One's a Staff, and one's a pit bull,' replied Papadopoulos.

The officers split up and began a thorough search of the flat, while Papadopoulos stood, arms folded, grimly watching. He was a short, powerfully built man with a north London accent, whose mother's fractured English betrayed his Greek origins.

'What's going on?' she asked. 'Explain to me.'

'All right,' responded Ian. 'We believe your son has been involved with dog-fighting.'

She protested noisily.

'It's against the law,' continued Ian.

'I know now,' said Papadopoulos.

'This is because I took my puppy in at the weekend, innit?'

The police officers were working their way methodically through the property, searching for anything potentially incriminating. A collar and muzzle hanging on a rack behind the entrance door were examined and placed in one of the large plastic property bags the Metropolitan Police use to remove seized evidence.

Papadopoulos got agitated. 'Don't take that. That cost me a score, that did,' he shouted.

The officer replied calmly, 'You'll get it all back.'

'I hope so,' replied Papadopoulos sulkily. 'That's all my dog stuff.' The thick chain leads wouldn't have looked out of place in a shipbuilder's yard.

While police tried to calm the mother Jon Storey prepared to remove the dogs, and cautiously opened the door to the living room. As he and Bowe were busy securing them a police officer said encouragingly, 'Walkies!'

'Listen, if you start all that lot, they'll go for you,' warned Papadopoulos. 'Don't wind them up.' He was starting to lose his temper. 'This is the second time you've tried to do me for dog-fighting. Check your records. I won my case last year.'

Jon Storey emerged with the first dog, a light-coloured pit bull terrier, which Papadopoulos claimed was a Staffordshire bull terrier. A vet later confirmed it was an APBT. It was a powerful animal and strained on the lead, nearly pulling Jon off his feet. He took it downstairs, out to the van, and coaxed it into a secure carrying cage. Bowe brought out the second dog, a black pit bull terrier.

Ian, in the meantime, was getting a severe ear-bashing as he looked round the mother's room. She kept up a voluble torrent of abuse as he systematically searched wardrobes, drawers, and other furniture. Alan, working through Papadopoulos's bedroom, had already bagged a quan-

One of the pictures of Papadopoulos's dogs, which he claimed were only 'playing'.

tity of photographs and scrap-books. In the back bedroom Ian found some undeveloped films which he removed for processing.

Outside, on the pavement, Bowe was having difficulty getting the second pit bull into a carrying cage. Papadopoulos shouted out of the window, 'Don't be scared of her. Just pick her up. Stroke her.' But the dog continued to put up a spirited resistance. In the end Papadopoulos went down to calm the dog and get it into the van.

While he was there a friend who lived on the floor below stuck her head out of one of the other flat windows. 'Do me a favour,' shouted Papadopoulos. 'Phone Winston.'

'What's happening?' she demanded.

'They're nicking me for dogfighting,' he yelled back.

The woman, dressed in a blue towelling dressing-gown, rushed upstairs to Papadopoulos's flat, where his mother was getting more and more hysterical. 'Marie,' she shouted. 'I want you to telephone my solicitor because I can't stand it any more with these police officers.'

The search continued.

06.50 hours
Winston Gold turned up brandishing a mobile phone and screaming abuse. He claimed the films that had been removed for processing were his holiday snaps.

'If there's nothing on them you won't have paid for them to be developed and you can have them back,' said Ian jovially. 'I'm saving you money, aren't I?'

'Do you want to take some more, then?' said Gold sarcastically. 'I have some more actually.' He continued to be abusive and within minutes of his arrival was arrested for breach of the peace and taken away to be charged. Shortly after, Papadopoulos was also driven away in a police van.

The property seized included some live bullets, videos, undeveloped film, and an address book. There were also some pictures, showing dogs fighting, displayed in handsome frames. The two

men were taken to Holloway police station where the charge sergeant took down details of the arrests and logged the seized property. Gold was bailed but Papadopoulos was detained for interview.

The dogs had been driven straight to the RSPCA hospital where veterinary director David Grant was waiting to examine them.

08.00 hours
Jon Storey held the light-coloured pit bull terrier, called Ninja, firmly on the examining table while David Grant checked it over. The dog's face and body were riddled with scars. One ear was split and a tooth broken.

It took Grant only a few seconds to pronounce, 'Oh, this dog has been involved in fighting. No doubt about that. That's a relatively new wound there also. Probably only about ten days old.' Grant thought the dog looked thin. He placed it on the weighing scales and jotted down some notes.

Storey swapped over the dogs and lifted the other pit bull, Bess, onto the examination table. This was the one that had been most unmanageable earlier that morning.

'What's this one's temperament like?' asked Grant.

'I've had no problems,' said Storey, 'but John [Bowe] says she's a little bit ticklish. It's a matter of opinion. A personality clash. Doesn't like the back of the van – well, neither do I!'

There were a few scars on the dog's head but nothing serious. 'This one might be a breeding bitch. She's had pups recently by the look of things,' said Grant. 'She's in a bit better condition than the other one. I don't think she's been used for fighting.' The dog stood patiently while Grant completed the examination.

10.30 hours
Back at Holloway police station Alan Goddard and Ian Green prepared to interview Papadopoulos, who had sum-

moned a solicitor. Alan read the suspect his rights. The interview commenced at 10.37 a.m. Papadopoulos lolled in his chair looking bored.

Ian ran through what had happened in the park the previous Sunday (31 August), in response to which Papadopoulos repeated the story he had given hospital staff about his dog being attacked. The attack, he said, happened about midday.

'In that case,' asked Ian, 'why did you take so long to get it to the hospital?'

Papadopoulos claimed it had taken him a while to arrange transport.

'Didn't you think of phoning the hospital direct to get an ambulance there?' asked Ian.

'Well, we didn't think it was possible for the ambulance to come out,' replied Papadopoulos.

'What condition would you describe the dog as being in?'

Papadopoulos suppressed a yawn. 'She was crushed,' he said flatly.

Ian changed tack. 'Have you taken any other dogs to the hospital in similar situations where they have been attacked by other dogs in the park?'

'Once, yeah. Two years ago, I think.'

'What would you say if I put it to you that I believe that dog was attacked by another dog of a similar weight and size, possibly another American pit bull terrier?' said Ian.

Papadopoulos looked composed and shrugged. 'That's up to you to decide. I'm telling you what happened. If you want to make up whatever you want to make up, that's up to you.'

The interview dragged on. Papadopoulos stuck with the story that his dog had been attacked. The 'attack', he said, had lasted between two and five minutes.

Videos of dogfighting 'matches' had been among the property seized from Papadopoulos's flat earlier that morning. 'You've obviously got an interest in dogfighting, haven't you, otherwise you wouldn't have those videos,' commented Ian.

Papadopoulos protested that they were 'documentaries' about American pit bull terriers. These just happened to include some fighting footage.

'Tell me,' said Alan, 'what's the difference between a documentary dogfight and an organised dogfight?'

Papadopoulos thought and responded, 'The tape is legal. The fight is illegal.'

Alan asked Papadopoulos to describe what else was on the tapes.

'Weight-pulling, flirt pole, guard work ...'

'What's a flirt pole?' asked Alan carefully.

'It's an eight-foot stick where the dog chases it around, and it goes over obstacles,' replied Papadopoulos promptly. He insisted it was just a means of exercising a dog.

'I don't see people in the park with those exercising poodles and labradors,' interjected Alan. 'You know as well as I do that a flirt pole is a method used to bring up the reflexes of a dog prior to fighting.'

Papadopoulos feigned innocence. 'Really? Shows how much you know,' he sneered.

Later in the interview Ian asked why the other two dogs removed that morning and taken to the RSPCA hospital for examination also had scars.

Papadopoulos blamed one of the dog's poor condition on a problem with external mange. The scars he said came from them 'playing together'.

'They must be boisterous,' remarked Ian.

Papadopoulos claimed this was a Staffordshire bull terrier but a vet confirmed it was an American pit bull terrier.

79

Alan intervened: 'You allow them to play together to such an extent that they chew one another up and injure each other!'

Papadopoulos claimed they 'played' all over the place. When asked if he considered himself a responsible animal owner, Papadopoulos nodded.

'You're a responsible owner who's had a lot of unfortunate accidents,' said Alan sarcastically.

Later, the officers would discover that the unprocessed films removed from Papadopoulos's flat, which Gold claimed were holidays snaps, contained photographs of his dogs 'playing'. The dogs were snarling and biting each other.

'The injuries on the dog you took to the hospital were not consistent with playing or another dog getting hold of it for two minutes in the park,' said Alan.

Papadopoulos yawned again.

The interview dragged on. Why did his address book contain names and addresses of American magazines about organised dogfighting?

'To extend my knowledge of the breed,' replied Papadopoulos.

'What is it famous for?' asked Alan.

'Fighting,' said Papadopoulos.

'And is that the side of the dog that interests you most?' continued Alan.

Papadopoulos denied that, and claimed it was the breed's stamina that he most admired. He remained composed throughout the interview.

As the RSPCA officers brought the interview to an end Alan asked, 'Is there anything you wish to add?'

'Yes,' said Papadopoulos. 'When am I getting my dogs back?'

The interview had been recorded and Alan explained how Papadopoulos could have access to the tapes. It was concluded at 11.02 a.m.

11.56 hours

Just before midday Papadopoulos was brought before the station officer again and charged. The charge was read to him: 'You are charged that on or before 31 August 1991 within the Greater London area you did cause unnecessary suffering to a certain animal, namely an American pit bull terrier dog, by unreasonably omitting to provide proper and necessary care and attention to the said animal.

'That offence is contrary to section 1, subsection 1A of the Protection of Animals Act 1911.

'You do not have to say anything in answer to that charge but what you say may be given in evidence.'

Papadopoulos failed to turn up at the first hearing on 9 September. In the meantime the RSPCA entered five more charges. On 25 September 1991, Papadopoulos entered a plea of not guilty to all of them and jumped bail. In June 1992 he was re-arrested. A date has been set in the autumn for the trial.

Case Number SO/1306

Investigating Officer: Ian Green

Winston Gold meanwhile was also in hot water. He proved just as questionable a dog owner as Papadopoulos. Several weeks after Papadopoulos was charged an undernourished stray pit bull was taken to one of the RSPCA's hospitals suffering from a terrible skin condition. Staff there recognised the dog as one brought in previously by Gold. It was easy to identify because of a distinctive missing upper right tooth. The Blue Cross, another animal welfare charity providing veterinary treatment, also had records of the same dog being brought in for treatment. Again, by Gold. Gold was clearly allowing his dogs to get into a bad state, then expecting charities to patch them up for free.

David Grant examined Bugsy. He was appalled by its condition. Its skin was covered in open sores. 'This dog is so bad it's almost at the stage where it should be put to sleep. If he [Gold] hasn't had this dog treated then it's a cast-iron case of cruelty.'

The animal stood mournfully on the examination table, shivering. Grant stroked it gently. 'It's a nice dog really,' he remarked. 'It's just got a bad owner.' He took a skin scraping and went over to a microscope to analyse it. The dog's skin was crawling with eggs and lice. 'It's the result of indiscriminate breeding. It comes from the mother and is passed to the pups,' explained Grant. 'People don't give a damn. They just want to breed puppies for profit.'

By the end of Grant's examination there was enough evidence to proceed with a cruelty charge. Ian Green took on the task of tracking Gold down to interview him. That proved easier said than done. Gold moved around a lot and there were numerous addresses to check.

On 7 October Ian made a breakthrough. Backed up by three police officers he called at a house in Holloway where it was thought Gold might be staying. Inspector Jon Storey was also on hand. It was the third address to be visited that morning. There was no sign of the Rastafarian but some of his dogs were on the premises. An American pit bull terrier bitch, Suva, and nine puppies were found in the kitchen, all grossly undernourished. Arrangements were made to remove the dogs.

A friend of Gold's was in the house. 'The dogs aren't mine,' he said. 'I'm looking after them for Gold. You can't take them. I'll get into too much trouble.' He was clearly terrified: Gold, like Papadopoulos, had a reputation for violence.

'You'll get into more trouble if you leave them here. From me!' remarked Ian grimly.

The dogs were taken to the RSPCA hospital for examination, which confirmed that the emaciated animals had been badly neglected. The cruelty charges against Gold were mounting up but Ian still had to find him. He enlisted police assistance.

Gold was finally arrested for suspected cruelty to animals, bailed and ordered to return for interview by Ian Green. Following that interview he was served with twenty-one summonses including one under the new Dangerous Dogs legislation. Under interview Gold had claimed he had owners lined up for the puppies. Under the Dangerous Dogs legislation all APBTs must be neutered and it is an offence to offer for sale, or even give away, dogs of this type.

5 MAY 1992

The case was finally heard at Highbury Magistrates' Court. Gold cross-examined the witnesses for the prosecution himself, having sacked his own solicitor after he had advised Gold to plead guilty.

The case continued on 13 May when Gold presented the case for his own defence, its basis being that all the dogs were in fact owned by his family (he was separated from his wife) and he considered that, as he had left home, he was no longer responsible for the dogs' condition or welfare. However, the court was eventually satisfied that Gold was indeed responsible.

He was convicted on eleven counts. He was found guilty of causing suffering to the American pit bull breeding bitch, Suva (for which he was fined £20) as well as to her nine puppies (for which he was fined a total of £180). Gold was fined a further £200 for causing unnecessary suffering to the pit bull terrier, Bugsy. In addition to his conviction for cruelty, Gold was found guilty under the Dangerous Dogs Act for 'exposing puppies for sale' for which he was fined £100 and ordered to pay £500 in costs. Gold is banned from owning any dog for ten years.

COCK FIGHTING.

CONVICTION FOR 'COCKING'

The two inspectors knew it would be dangerous. They had been tipped off about a projected cockfight and were on their way to Hanworth, in Middlesex, to bust the fight. The cockfighters were violent men. The inspectors had taken the precaution of bringing along some 'muscle' – two strong volunteers. The RSPCA Secretary was there too.

The cockpit was opposite the Swan pub. The five had stationed themselves in the bar to keep a lookout when suddenly their cover was blown. A local, a man already with a conviction for 'cocking', recognised the inspectors. Assisted by his mates he waded in, fists flying. The five fought their way out of the pub and went to seek help. Accompanied by the village constable, they returned to the cockpit in order to arrest those responsible for the assault.

But the cockfighters were not going to give themselves up lightly. Another battle ensued. Retreating from a hail of blows and punches the inspectors sought refuge in the Brown Bear pub. Reinforcements were on the way. The Secretary had summoned assistance from a mobile police patrol.

Eventually, with their assistance, seven of the cockfighters were arrested and more were rounded up later. But the inspectors had taken quite a beating and a doctor was sent for to dress the wounds.

Inspector James Piper was particularly poorly. He was moved to St Thomas's Hospital in London, but despite intensive treatment died shortly after. A post-mortem was ordered, which showed he was suffering from tuberculosis and that, rather than the beating, was pinpointed as the cause of death. Although it was clear the injuries Piper sustained had contributed to his decline the cockfighters could not be charged with murder.

This incident happened in 1838. The 'mobile police' were six men from the Bow Street Patrol. Inspector Piper's name is prominent in the RSPCA's roll of honour for so courageously carrying out his duties. His death also had one practical outcome: it prompted the decision to put inspectors into uniform. Like today's SOU investigators the early inspectors were 'plain-clothes' officers and it was hoped that by issuing uniforms and warrant cards the inspectors would command more respect. As a practical measure they were also issued with truncheons for their own defence.

COCKFIGHTING

UNDERCOVER

Hard-gambling eighteenth-century 'sportsmen' enjoyed cockfighting as it provided a good outlet for heavy betting. Its support cut across all classes and the audience was likely to include aristocrats and nobles as well as ruffians and poor folk.

29 AUGUST 1991

On Thursday, 29 August, Norfolk Police Force released a statement advising that dawn raids earlier that morning had resulted in the arrest of two men suspected of organised cockfighting. During the raids, carried out by a squad of RSPCA undercover officers, uniformed RSPCA inspectors, and police officers from East Anglia, six fighting cocks were seized for veterinary examination along with a quantity of books and videos on cockfighting. The statement explained that the raids followed a long-running investigation by the RSPCA. Shortly after this Chief Inspector Mike Butcher received a death threat from one of two men arrested.

The resulting prosecution is still working its way through the courts and it is not possible, therefore, to provide further details until the case is concluded. However, the case provides a reminder that this barbaric sport is still going strong a century and a half after it was outlawed.

Cockfighting had been popular for centuries. In the twelfth century an annual 'treat' for the schoolboys of the City of London was being allowed to watch a cockfight, a 'diversion' held every Shrove Tuesday. By the reign of Edward III cockfighting ranked as an amusement fit for adults too and was a 'sport' that commanded royal support. Henry VIII added a cockpit at Whitehall, where James I was partial to watching it twice a week. It was briefly banned by the Puritans as an idle and useless pastime but before long cockfighting was again a popular 'entertainment'.

Sometimes the birds were primed beforehand with 'dutch courage'. An article in the *Gentleman's Magazine* in 1754 recommended that before a fight the bird should be fed millet seeds soaked in sherry and a few drops of vinegar. The practice has been revived in the twentieth century, with quail fed on alcohol-soaked grain to make them 'fighting drunk'.

Another pastime associated with Shrove Tuesday was cock-throwing in which the bird was tied to a stake and competitors took it in turns to aim sticks and stones at the terrified creature. Sometimes grease was put on its feathers to make the sticks shoot off and prolong the 'entertainment'. If the bird was too injured to stand, splints were applied to keep it erect until finally the cock became the prize of the 'marksman' who killed it. A variation was to bury the bird, leaving only the head visible, or imprison it in an earthenware container with just the head and tail protruding. The winner was the first person to break the jar.

A possible explanation for these 'sports' is that the cock was the national emblem of France and abusing it was one way of showing contempt for England's traditional enemy. But by the eighteenth century many Englishmen were ashamed of their countrymen's

brutality and opposition to cockfighting and other cruel sports grew. Hogarth went on the attack in his famous sequence of pictures *The Four Stages of Cruelty*, to convey his message that cruelty to animals corrupts mankind. The growing band of humanitarians found voice in the writings of poets such as William Blake. The opening lines of his 'Auguries of Innocence' are familiar to many:

> A robin redbreast in a cage
> Puts all heaven in a rage.

The same poem contains the following condemnation of cockfighting:

> The game cock clipped and armed
>   for fight
> Does the rising sun affright ...

Long after the 1835 Act made it illegal cockfighting remained a tremendous crowd-puller. One RSPCA inspector sent to Orton, Cumberland, in 1849 to stop a fight was driven off by a crowd of over 200 people. Although the RSPCA received plenty of tip-offs, the informants, often country clergymen, wanted to remain anonymous, afraid that the cockfighters might retaliate if they found out who had given them away. Evidence against offenders was therefore difficult to obtain as the rural supporters closed ranks against what was seen as the meddling efforts of 'townies' to interfere with their pleasures.

Cockfighting in the twentieth century still has a strong hold, particularly in rural areas. One of the reasons it lives on is the ease with which gamecocks can be concealed and transported to fight venues. Enthusiasts make every effort to keep the grisly business under wraps. They know that if detected they could face fines of up to £2,000 and/or six months in prison.

Cockfighting and dogfighting often go hand in hand. Those who derive pleasure from watching animals rip each other apart are not too fussy about where they find their 'sport'.

Cockfighting, like dogfighting, is associated with heavy gambling. Enthusiasts, who are liable to prosecution under the Gaming and Lottery Act if caught, study the 'form' of the birds, some of which may attract large bets. A fancied bird or its progeny can change hands for big money, the price depending on the kill rate and how many successful fights a bird has to its credit. Newspaper reports have documented some enthusiasts paying several hundred pounds for a game bird.

There are several varieties of game cock, most of them Asian in origin. Cocks destined for fighting are chosen by the breeders for strength, vigour and aggression. They are then specially trained to improve fitness by exercises like hopping on and off a swing perch to strengthen the leg muscles. Before a fight they may have their combs and wattles cut back (dubbed) to decrease the risk of injury and prevent an opponent's claws getting a hold.

The birds have natural spurs at the back of the lower leg. Although there is some naked spur fighting it is more usual to find the spurs trimmed so that vicious metal spurs can be fitted. These lethal devices are strapped on to increase the birds' maiming power. The 1952 Cockfighting Act makes it illegal to use any instrument or appliance designed or adapted for cockfighting, but spurs can be ordered from specialist magazines in America, where cockfighting is still legal in some states. Customs officers regularly intercept packages containing spurs and other paraphernalia.

The arena for a fight – the cockpit – is generally a makeshift enclosure created by partitions or pegging out wire meshing. Fights are known to have been held in this country in locations ranging from disused quarries to allotments and back gardens.

The fight usually starts by the handlers 'showing' the birds to each other. They deliberately antagonise the birds by thrusting them at each other and then hurl them into the air, whereupon the birds fly into each other in a frenzy of beating wings and the fight commences. They have been known to last more than an hour although a bloody clash can be over in just a few minutes.

The spurs inflict the most terrible damage and pain. Common injuries include punctured lungs, broken bones, gouged-out eyes and pierced flesh. Devotees defend their sport by claiming it is in the birds' nature to fight. But not under these conditions. And what is natural about fitting metal spurs? It is true that game cocks are territorial animals and will vigorously repel any intruders that enter their territory. But skirmishes are normally swiftly ended without a deadly outcome. The birds fight to determine a pecking order. Once that is sorted out the loser beats a hasty retreat and the dominant bird usually desists from further attack. But in a cockpit there is no escape route: the birds are forced to stay and fight on.

Even when the birds collapse from injury or exhaustion they are revived by their handlers. Revival methods include pouring water over their heads, pinching them or blowing on the back of the neck. The birds are then flung back into the arena to continue the conflict. It is even known for handlers to grab birds that have been punctured in the chest to force out any blood accumulating in the lungs; this is to prevent them drowning in their own blood so that the fighting can be prolonged for a few more minutes.

The fight normally ends only when one bird is dead or so injured that it cannot fight on. There is no mercy for the vanquished bird: its neck is normally wrung. All that remains of a once proud bird is a mutilated corpse and tattered bunch of feathers. Even the conqueror may not survive. The handlers are only interested in winners. And that means a bird fit enough to fight again. If its injuries make recovery unlikely the winner too is despatched without further ceremony.

In America winning birds which are seriously injured are sometimes entered in a 'Battle Royal'. A number of injured birds are placed together in a pit and whichever is left living at the end of the contest is declared the winner. A variant is a 'Blinker Derby' which is restricted to birds which have had an eye gouged out in a previous fight.

The furtive nature of cockfighting makes it extremely difficult to detect. It is not illegal to have gamebirds and many people breed them for showing purposes. Some breeders, however, use showing activities as a cover for their real interest – fighting. Ten men and a juvenile were caught red-handed in 1983 after a raid at Charlton in Hertfordshire. They included five members of a respectable Rare Breeds Society.

The arrests followed weeks of painstaking enquiries by the Special Operations Unit officers which led to a stakeout over an Easter weekend. When the inspectors, assisted by police officers, raided the suspected premises, a locked shed, they found a gory fight in progress. A makeshift cockpit had been constructed of straw bales, hardboard and sheeting, while the spectators sat on benches placed round the pit. One of the birds in the pit had blood dripping from its beak and a bruised and swollen neck; its right eye had been badly pecked and was closed up. Its adversary was also seriously injured. Two other birds with older injuries were found in the building and among the straw covering the floor of the pit, the top part of another bird's beak. Also discovered were a set of scales, a list of the birds' weights, and a video film of a fight in progress. At the subsequent hearing the men pleaded guilty and fines totalling £3,410 were imposed.

Two years later SOU officers were involved in another successful raid with police assistance, this time at some hunt kennels in Shropshire. There they found another cockpit with all the usual equipment plus many dead and injured birds. It was clear that a series of fights had been planned to last all day. Once again sizable fines were imposed at the subsequent court hearing.

SOU officers know that tracking down the people responsible for clandestine cockfighting is an uphill struggle, but it is an area of animal abuse assigned top priority.

'It would be wrong to assume that because relatively few cases of cockfighting have been discovered in recent years it is no longer a problem,' said Don Balfour. 'The small number of prosecutions merely shows how difficult it is to catch the criminals responsible. We are determined to stamp it out and will not hesitate to bring the people who organise these barbaric activities before the courts.'

A fighting cock seized during a raid on premises in Norfolk awaits examination by a vet.

Think again!

The trade

- According to British Government figures, around 185,000 exotic birds were imported into Britain in 1989.

- According to the Ministry of Agriculture, Fisheries and Food's figures, over 23,000 died within the first few weeks.

- According to several independent investigations, 400-600 out of every 1,000 birds caught die before being exported.

Almost all exotic birds are caught in the wild and then transported to countries around the world – the death rates are similar for Germany, Italy, Sweden and America.

There are several million birds traded on international markets every year. Hundreds of thousands die.

Are you going to support this trade when it involves the lives of so many innocent birds?

Trapped birds are jammed into tiny cages for long journeys.

Think again!

In captivity

Birds are social creatures. In the wild, parrots, for example, form permanent pair bonds and live in large flocks. Most of their time is spent either preening their partner or foraging for food. Without these activities, intense boredom can set in.

Without adequate attention, parrots are capable of human-like depression, with boredom and frustration causing a bird to pluck out its own feathers until it is denuded from the neck down.

- Can you provide the space all birds nee(

- Can you provide the time and commitment required to dedicate to the birds?

- Can you provide the expensive equipment needed to give birds the best possi(accommodation?

- All birds require a lot of care and att tion. They are living creatures and req(attention 365 days a year! Some parro live for more than 50 years.

- All birds do best in aviaries with th companionship of their own kind an(to fly and climb.

- A large aviary may cost hundreds pounds to build and equip.

The full dietary requirements of a entail much more than just a bowl

Several million wild-caught bi traded on international marke

The RSPCA campaigns for an end to the trade in wild birds.

CHAPTER TEN

THE WILD BIRD TRADE

Keeping tabs on the trade in wild birds is one of the Special Operations Unit's responsibilities and they are constantly on the alert for offences under the Wildlife and Countryside Act. Britain is very strict about the conservation of its native wildlife and this legislation makes it an offence to kill, injure, disturb or take any wild bird, its nest or eggs. The Act also makes it an offence to deal in wild birds or their eggs. There are certain exemptions to these restrictions but only when authorised by licence.

Despite these strict controls there are many so-called 'bird enthusiasts' willing to flout the laws either for their own satisfaction or for commercial gain. British finches, for example, are much in demand in certain foreign countries such as Malta and they are sometimes captured illegally and smuggled out of the country. Breeders sometimes cross wild birds with other species such as canaries, the attraction being that the resulting hybrids, called 'mules', make excellent singers.

There is also a black market for birds of prey such as peregrines, buzzards and kestrels. Unscrupulous dealers raid nests and snatch chicks to supply the demand. Some have sophisticated incubation facilities to hatch out the birds, which they then try to pass off as 'captive-bred'. However, true captive-bred birds are close-rung soon after hatching, and 'grow into' the rings, which provide a guarantee, when they are offered for sale, that they have been captive-bred. A common ploy used to pass off wild-

Birds are crammed into crates as many as fifty parrots or several hundred finches in a crate just three feet by eighteen inches.
photo: Environmental Investigation Agency

caught birds as captive-bred is to fit them with 'stretched' rings.

The undercover officers have tracked down and exposed many of these illegal dealers over the years. It often requires painstaking detective work and expert witnesses to prove an offence has been committed. If they are suspicious that birds have been taken illegally the SOU officers can get a warrant to search the premises. In one case they swooped on a London house and found three fluffy peregrine chicks, just a few days old and small enough to cradle in the palm of a hand. They were discovered in a back bedroom, where the dealer had built a 'nest' of towelling inside a plastic bucket and was hand feeding them. They had been snatched from the north-east of England. The case had a happy conclusion: the chicks were removed and later returned to the wild where they belonged.

89

The trade in birds is not just one-way. Birds are sometimes smuggled into as well as out of the country, using all sorts of ingenious methods. One successful SOU mission involved staking out Dover Ferryport over an Easter weekend. Vigilance paid off with the successful apprehension of a bird smuggler who was returning from Germany with an illicit cargo of over forty foreign birds concealed behind the door panels of his car and in the spare wheel.

The undercover officers work closely with the RSPCA's airports advisory officer at Heathrow, who is based at the City of London-run Quarantine Station. This is the reception point for wild birds coming into Britain. Many people feel it is wrong to protect our own wildlife yet happily exploit that of foreign countries. Pressure is building for a complete ban on the international trade in wild-caught birds. One of the most distressing things about it is the large number of birds that die in transit. Consignments with huge mortalities are not uncommon.

In 1991 for the first time the RSPCA, the Royal Society for the Protection of Birds, and the Environmental Investigation Agency joined forces to call for a halt to the import of wild birds into the European Community. It has been estimated that as many as 20 million birds are traded worldwide each year to supply the pet industry, for which the European Community is the world's largest market, the principal suppliers being Senegal, Tanzania, Argentina, Indonesia and Guyana. It is a trade littered with the corpses of the thousands of birds that die en route. For every bird that reaches a pet shop three others may have died during the journey between capture and sale. Undercover officers were assigned to obtain evidence for the campaign.

Crude trapping methods account for many deaths. Sometimes whole trees are felled to get at the nests, resulting in needless accelerated habitat destruction. In Argentina, for example, it has been estimated that over a period of nine years 100,000 trees were felled or damaged to obtain just one species of parrot chick. Trappers in Senegal use baited nets camouflaged with dust and straw. Live decoy birds are staked to the ground using string or wire, unable to escape because their wing feathers have been torn out, or hacked off to restrain flight. Once enough birds land the trapper springs the trap.

It is not surprising that large numbers of birds die through the shock of capture and handling. Many more die from the trauma of confinement in small cages and a change in diet. Since local trappers generally get only a pittance for the birds they collect, they pay little attention to their charges and simply collect more than needed in order to 'cover their losses'.

The journey to the holding stations and then on to the exporters' premises may take several days over rough terrain and in searing heat. The birds are sometimes loaded into car boots or strapped onto lorry roofs. Not unnaturally in these conditions, many die before ever reaching the airports for shipment abroad. Once there the suffering continues. They are crammed into crates – as many as fifty parrots or several hundred finches in a crate just three feet by eighteen inches by nine inches – and loaded into the tightly packed hold. On arrival huge numbers of birds die in quarantine, too stressed and weakened by the struggle to survive.

The misery, pain and suffering does not even stop once they reach the pet shops. Standards of care are often poor and unhygienic and many traders have no idea how to care for the birds themselves, let alone advise their customers. The birds, born to fly free in the wild, end up in tiny cages. They are social creatures yet many are kept for the rest of their lives in solitary confinement. Without adequate attention birds like parrots can succumb to depression. Boredom and frustration often cause a bird to pluck out all its own feathers.

For every bird that reaches a pet shop, three others may have died during the journey between capture and sale.

photo: Environmental Investigation Agency

So who are the villains in this trade? The consumer has to shoulder much of the blame. If there was no demand then the trade would wither. There are few species that cannot be captive-bred. If people insist on keeping birds then they should ensure they buy only purpose-bred birds. Some species have been pushed to the edge of extinction, and others have already disappeared.

The CITES regulations (Convention on International Trade in Endangered Species), designed to protect wildlife around the world, are not the answer. They identify species prohibited from trade or subject to controls. But not all countries are party to CITES. Furthermore the regulations are complex and easy to abuse, and are often flouted by ruthless traders whose only interest is profit. A further drawback is that they are reactive rather than precautionary. By the time it is realised population numbers have been reduced to danger levels, and the birds have been granted protection, it may be too late.

Organisations such as the RSPCA believe that the only effective solution is an end to the trade. Some progress has already been made towards this end. Many airlines have recognised the devastating welfare and environmental impact of the trade and over fifty now refuse to carry shipments of wild-caught birds. The European Parliament has voted to end imports into the European Community. The campaign is now focused on the other European political institutions.

Alarm bells are ringing in the exporting countries who are producing all sorts of specious arguments to justify continuation of the trade. The next chapter describes the role of the Special Operations Unit in investigating the claims of one major exporter that it was operating along model lines.

FACT: Millions of birds die every year due to the wild bird trade. Many die in brutal traps. Many die en route to airports. Still more die on planes to Europe <u>and</u> after they get here.

1 in 4 birds caught for Europe's pet shops end up in cages

CHAPTER ELEVEN

FROM JUNGLE TO CAGE

FRIDAY, 4 OCTOBER 1991, MIDNIGHT

The plane touched down in George-town, the capital of Guyana, just after midnight. It had been a long journey. The visit had been hurriedly arranged following an invitation from the Guyanese government. Like other bird-exporting countries, the Guyanese were alarmed by the growing clamour for an end to the trade in wild birds.

Guyana has a population of only 800,000. It is South America's second largest legal wild bird exporter, trading mainly in psittacines (parrots). The Guyanese authorities claimed that about 54,000 of their people were dependent, in some way, on the trade, and a ban would therefore cause tremendous economic hardship. It was also, they argued, unnecessary. The trade wasn't as cruel as the RSPCA and other organisations were suggesting. Properly regulated it caused no suffering or conservation problems. A quota system was in place to ensure wildlife resources were not dangerously depleted, and other controls had been introduced. It was unfair to keep campaigning for an end to the trade. Come and see for yourselves how we have established a model situation: that was the invitation.

The RSPCA decided to accept this offer to make a first-hand investigation. The team despatched was Frank Milner and Andy Foxcroft. Dave Currey, one of the EIA's principal investigators, was the third official member of the delegation, accompanied by cameraman Paul Berriff and sound recordist Keith

Rodgerson to film the investigation. They were met at the airport by a representative from the Guyanese Department of Agriculture and taken by taxi the short distance to their hotel in the centre of Georgetown.

SATURDAY, 5 OCTOBER

The streets of Georgetown were thronged with traders, the cries of stall-holders vying for business punctuating the noisy cacophony of car horns and revving motor-bikes. The pavements were lined with hawkers – large colourfully dressed women who sat patiently trying to sell chickens and other produce. Among the animals piled up on the pavements for sale were live iguanas, considered a delicacy in Guyana, brought fresh from the jungle. The animals were cruelly hobbled, their limbs tied behind their backs to prevent escape.

Left: These wretched parrots have been deprived of their flight feathers and face incarceration for the rest of their fifty-year lifespan.
photo: Environmental Investigation Agency

Below: An iguana with feet tied together awaits its fate.

The team were shortly to see how exotic birds were trapped. Arrangements had been made for them to accompany one of Guyana's main bird exporters, Lawrence van Sertima, into the jungle to visit a trapping station.

The journey started at Parika, a port about thirty minutes' drive from Georgetown. Guyana has some 85 per cent forest cover and there are few roads so access to the interior is generally by river or air. They would go most of the way by river-boat which is the local equivalent of a taxi. These vessels each carry about ten passengers and are functional rather than luxurious.

After the boat-trip came a bumpy two-hour journey overland to Charity, north-west of Georgetown on the Pomeroon River, from where they set off once more upriver. They hired two boats, powered by twin outboard engines, and sped along at a rapid pace, just seeming to skim the surface of the water. The river was about 500 yards wide, bounded by thick jungle broken at occasional intervals by small, straggling settlements with palm-thatched roofs.

16.00 hours

About fifty miles upriver they finally arrived at the trapping station. There, the trappers were happy to explain the methods they used. The most common, it turned out, was liming, which involved coating sticks with a natural gum and placing them in treetops under the flight path of targeted species, using two captive birds as decoys. When a flock of parrots approached, the decoy birds would be made to squawk and thus attract the wild birds to the glued perches. The investigators were told that once the birds alighted they would stick by the feet or wings. It was then a simple matter to grab them and cut off their flight feathers to prevent escape.

It sounded less than humane to the investigators. The birds would inevitably suffer considerable stress and trauma during capture and handling.

But van Sertima, burly and garrulous,

was scornful of criticism, especially about the use of a machete to cut the feathers. 'There is nothing cruel about that,' he protested. 'We're talking about an instrument that is sharp enough to shave with. And we are talking about people who use this for everything from cutting wood to cutting food, to taking a splinter out of a foot, to settling arguments.'

As van Sertima wielded one of the murderous-looking weapons the investigators hoped they would not be requiring any of his brand of first-aid.

Van Sertima was warming up to his role as spokesman for the virtues of Guyana's wildlife dealers. The charge that the birds would be distressed by handling was swiftly dismissed: 'If you treat the birds badly they're going to make a noise and chase off the other birds so you can't afford to rough them up or anything.'

And to make sure his trappers understood the need to treat the birds gently he made them hang onto them for several days before collection and payment. 'If a trapper could just grab a bird, run out quickly and pass it on to you, if the bird dies – say five days on – he doesn't care. But if he has to hold onto it for a while and see that his effort is wasted he will damn well learn,' reasoned van Sertima. He seemed proud of the training that he said was being passed down the chain to his agents and then on to the trappers. As a result mortality rates were minimal, he claimed.

Like all the dealers the investigators were to meet, van Sertima never missed an opportunity to expand upon the economic importance of the trade. If it were stopped many people would starve to death. That was the message he rammed home on every possible occasion.

Yet as the investigators asked more questions about the number of trappers dependent on catching birds for their livelihood, the figures did not add up. Van Sertima described himself as a 'medium-sized' dealer. He operated a network of six agents who in turn employed about 144 trappers who would catch on average about ten birds a week each. Further enquiries revealed that the catching season lasted about twenty-six weeks. A quick calculation showed that van Sertima's network could be expected to catch about 37,500 birds between them in a year (144 trappers x 10 birds each a week x 26 weeks).

And yet the declared number of birds exported from Guyana, in line with the government-imposed quota, was only 15–20,000 birds a year. Van Sertima's network alone caught more birds than the total export figure. And he was only one of seventeen active licensed exporters, all presumably employing large numbers of trappers catching birds at a similar rate. What explanation was there for this disparity? There were many possible answers.

Perhaps van Sertima was exaggerating the number of trappers involved in his keenness to stress the economic arguments for retaining the trade. Or maybe, despite claims to the contrary, there were massive mortality rates at the trapping and holding stages, with huge numbers of birds dying before reaching the exporters. A third possibility was that the official export figures were meaningless. Thousands more birds than officially acknowledged were being removed from the wild and shipped abroad. Whatever the truth of the matter it was clear that all was not as it seemed.

Frank questioned an Amerindian family closely about their lifestyle. Most trappers, like this family, come from the Amerindian community, who are self-sufficient and capable of living off the land, getting by on subsistence farming, hunting and fishing. This family had another sideline: making cane basket items. The trappers get minimal payment for their efforts: only about £1.50 for an Amazon parrot – less for smaller birds. Even in a very poor country like Guyana it could scarcely be called a get-rich-quick occupation.

As the visit wore on it became clear the opportunity they had been promised to watch trapping first-hand was not going to materialise. It was all talk.

'What do you feed the birds on once you've trapped them?' asked Dave Currey.

'Corn peas and fruit from the neighbourhood,' replied van Sertima.

'So there's no sudden shock in change of food?' persisted Dave.

This was the cue for another monologue on the sophisticated bird management systems employed. Dave listened sceptically. He had seen some of the primitive feeding methods in use in other countries. In Argentina, for example, baby parrots are brutally force-fed on mashed-up maize. Some suffocate during the process. Van Sertima said he lost few birds in the course of weaning them onto a diet of sunflower seeds, essential since the birds must be changed to food easily obtainable in the countries to which they are sent.

The light was beginning to fade as the visitors boarded the boats for the return journey. They had expected to see plenty of birds on the evening flight back to their roosts, but the skies remained curiously empty. Night had fallen by the time they got back to Charity so they made arrangements to stay at a local hotel and complete the journey to Georgetown in the morning.

The team were definitely feeling the effects of bumping about on the high-speed river-boats and potholed roads. Trapped birds would have to endure a similar journey by bus and river-boat to reach the exporters' premises in the capital and would inevitably undergo considerable stress as they were packed into carrying cages and jolted around. It was increasingly hard to believe van Sertima's claims of minimal mortality rates.

SUNDAY, 6 OCTOBER

The next morning van Sertima was anxious to assemble them all, at an early

Street traders in Georgetown display their line-up of birds and iguanas being sold daily for food.

hour, on the hotel verandah which would provide a perfect vantage-point to watch the daily fly-past of parrots en route to their feeding grounds. It was a disappointing spectacle. They only spotted about forty parrots in all. Van Sertima seemed genuinely surprised that so few birds had flown over and could offer no explanation.

One of conservationists' principal concerns about the wild bird trade is the impact on the overall population numbers of the exploited species. The investigators made a mental note to find out what studies had been done on the sustainability of the trade in Guyana. Later they discovered that there has been no research. Nobody knows how damaging the trade may be to the eco-system or how much it is depleting bird numbers. What is known is that some of the birds being taken, like the larger macaws, have a very slow reproduction rate.

Back in Georgetown the team spent the remainder of the day finding the exporters' premises, but it was not possible to get inside without prior appointments. Karen Pilgrim, Head of the Ministry of Agriculture's Wildlife Department, and the official responsible for the official itinerary, would make the necessary arrangements.

MONDAY, 7 OCTOBER

It was an early start – 4.00 a.m. with a long day ahead. Another wildlife dealer, Kurt Herzog, had been assigned to take them upriver to his holding premises. Karen Pilgrim joined the party. Herzog had a large holding station on the Demerara River beyond Linden where his trappers brought the birds to be sorted and 'stabilised'. They would be held there for a few weeks to 'settle down' before onward transport.

The station was called Land's End and was perched on the east bank of the river. Inside were between 200 and 250 parrots of assorted colours and plumage whose screeching filled the air. Herzog, a call bird clinging to his shoulder, had to shout to make himself heard as he showed them around. He was Swiss and spoke with a thick German accent. 'Two trips and you can get forty or fifty of the same kind with this net.'

Herzog, it appeared, used a different method of trapping – mist netting. Although the nets are costly, more birds can be caught using fewer catchers, but they are indiscriminate and trap any species that fly into their path. The nets, which according to Herzog do not harm the birds, are set near the roosts to catch the parrots on the evening flight home.

Frank, Andy and Dave gave close scrutiny to the conditions at the holding

station. The birds were housed in reasonable-sized purpose-built caging. But disease transfer would be easy. Contrary to Guyanese law there were a number of domestic poultry in the vicinity. This is forbidden, to avoid the risk of spreading poultry disease via the wild birds.

There was little flight room within the cages and many of the birds were

hovering together at the back of their cages. 'These parrots are displaying classic stress symptoms,' said Andy. 'They're all bunched up in the back of the cage looking very frightened. They're obviously quite scared of human presence.'

Herzog explained how he gave the parrots wooden sticks to chew on. 'It's good for their beaks.' There was precious little else for them to do in that barren environment.

News that the day before he had shipped out a consignment of 298 orange-winged macaws to Miami came as a surprise. Frank was annoyed because an aspect of the trade they particularly wanted to see was the method of packing and shipment for onward transport. The investigators already knew from figures supplied by the British government that there were high mortalities during and after transit. In 1988 22.42 per cent of the birds imported to the UK from Guyana were either dead on arrival or died in the thirty-five-day quarantine period. The figures for 1989 were not much better: a 20.16 per cent mortality rate.

Frank reminded Karen that they wanted to see everything for themselves and were not willing to be fobbed off by bland assurances from the exporters that all was well. He was even more annoyed when he discovered they had missed the only likely opportunity to inspect a shipment: there were no further exports scheduled prior to their return to England.

09.15 hours

They returned to the boats since Herzog wanted to take them even further upriver. As they travelled through thick rain-forest, Herzog was an informative guide and revealed that his principal trade was forestry. Now and then they passed another boat: a raft ferrying produce drifted by; they waved to some children paddling a canoe and watched an Indian pulling on the oars of a rowing boat. But most of the time they were

Above: A decoy parrot calls out from the treetops. Flanking the bird are the sticks smeared with glue. The decoy parrot's call will attract passing birds to alight on the sticks.

Below: Lawrence van Sertima, dealer in wild birds.

99

alone on the river. The journey was assuming epic proportions. On and on upriver. And in search of what?

Finally they reached the destination: Demerara River Falls. These were pretty but hardly worth a five-hour trip, especially as there was no sign of any birdlife. Indeed, throughout the river trip they had not spotted a single bird. The investigators did not attempt to hide their frustration.

TUESDAY, 8 OCTOBER, 08.30 HOURS

Lawrence van Sertima arrived at the hotel to collect everybody for a meeting at his home, attended also by Kurt Herzog. Relying on the exporters for an accurate view of the trade was obviously not the best way to pinpoint the facts. They had too much of a vested interest in its maintenance to paint an objective portrait.

Frank decided to put his foot down. Especially when it became clear that the next part of the official itinerary was a proposed flight over the rain-forest. The intention was apparently to demonstrate how sensitively the forest was being managed. But the investigators wanted to see birds not trees. Frank spelled this out. The two exporters were visibly annoyed by this refusal to conform with their plans, Herzog becoming very agitated and accusing them of wanting to kill off their livelihood. Frank retaliated that if they were unwilling to co-operate and let them pursue their own enquiries, then they would return to the UK and make a report to that effect.

Herzog calmed down and the team decided that the best way to achieve their objectives was by splitting up. Frank and Andy stayed on with the exporters and Karen Pilgrim, while Dave Currey set off with the camera crew to look around on their own. Dave had a hunch about the exporters' anxiety to keep them tied up with official excursions. Were they trying to keep them away from other areas? Was there

something to hide? They headed for the airport. Karen Pilgrim had said that there were no scheduled shipments. But maybe the government did not know the whole story.

At the airport the driver gained access to airside and drove to the cargo-handling area. He got out and struck up a conversation with one of the cargo handlers.

The driver reported that the handler had said they had just finished loading a consignment of birds onto a flight bound for Trinidad. Dave then went over to question the man for himself.

In the meantime the cargo handler had been joined by a taller official who denied any knowledge of bird shipments. 'I think if you want to get any information you should start at the Ministry of Agriculture,' he said curtly. Dave persisted but this official seemed defensive and was giving nothing away.

Dave gave up. Back in the car the team conferred among themselves. It was all very odd. Why would the first man make up a story about loading birds?

16.30 hours
Dave rendezvoused with Frank and Andy and related what had happened at the airport. They agreed that they would confront Karen Pilgrim the next day. The investigators were impressed by her sincerity and fervent belief that the system was working properly. But was the government being duped? Nobody would dispute that the authorities had taken tremendous steps to try and regulate the trade. But there are always unscrupulous individuals ready to buck the system.

Enforcement of the regulations was the key to the problem. The Wildlife Department, under Dr Pilgrim, was responsible for monitoring the trade. It was manned by capable, hardworking people, but it was desperately understaffed. The workload consisted almost entirely of the administration of the trade: collecting the export levies and supervising the paperwork. With no additional resources or personnel for independent investigation and policing, government officials were reliant on hearsay information, the principal source of which was the exporters who were unlikely to rock the boat by pointing out flaws in the system.

As the investigation progressed Frank, Dave and Andy began to piece together more and more indications that it was possible that the quotas were being routinely flouted. One source alleged that corruption was widespread. He claimed it was easy to bribe officials to look the other way while an illegal shipment of birds was smuggled out of the country. This achieved three things: avoiding the quota limits; evading the 20 per cent government levy; and bypassing the costly quarantine requirements. The same source also alleged it was easy to under-declare the number of birds contained in a consignment so that there could be many more packed than the number listed on the manifest.

Smuggling was both easy and lucrative. Even some pilots were on the take. The source claimed that birds were regularly smuggled to Miami, legal and illegal birds travelling on the same flight. Loading would be supervised by the captain. When the plane arrived at Miami airport, after dark, the captain would order the cargo doors to be opened before the handlers arrived. The illegal birds would then be transferred to the belly of the aircraft, out of sight. Once unloading was completed the captain would return to the plane, transfer the birds to a car, and drive out of the airport. A consignment of just thirty scarlet macaws smuggled in this way would be worth at least US $100,000.

The investigators knew this was just hearsay talk from one source. But it sounded plausible. And later enquiries to United States Wildlife Officers confirmed that this account of smuggling was perfectly credible. Another reputable source gave the same version of illegal birds being smuggled out at the same time as legal shipments. He also talked convincingly about smuggling by sea.

It has long been suspected that Guyana is used as a clearing house to 'launder' birds illegally taken from neighbouring countries. Brazil and Venezuela have both banned the export of their bird species, but policing their remote, unpopulated borders to intercept illegal traffic is virtually impossible. Venezuelan scientists studying the bird population there have estimated that between 65,000 and 75,000 psittacines are illegally exported each year from the Orinoco delta, many going via Guyana.

The team determined to press on with their enquiries and headed for one of the streets in Georgetown where the bird trappers plied their trade direct to the public. They quickly spotted a trader with exotic birds for sale. He had dozens of birds crammed into ramshackle containers: some in hessian sacks, others in wicker baskets or wire cages. Two birds perched perilously on a pole slung across his shoulder. A macaw huddled on top of one of the cages. There was no danger of any of the birds getting away: they had all had their flight feathers clipped.

The dealer had dozens of birds crammed into ramshackle containers.

A machete has been used to cut off the flight feathers of these wild parrots.

When Frank asked him how he caught the birds the trader said he used gum or nets. The team already knew about these methods, but they had also heard about others. Larger macaws, for instance, are sometimes caught by lassoing. A call bird is tied to the branch of a tree while the trapper builds a hide a few feet away. When a macaw, attracted by the decoy bird, lands, the trapper swiftly lassos it with a noose on the end of a pole. The flight feathers are promptly clipped before it is lowered to the ground into the arms of a waiting accomplice. In some regions young birds are taken from their nests, which can sometimes only be reached by felling trees. And in other parts of the country the birds are smoked out of the trees.

Dave pointed to a big blue macaw. 'How much for this one?' he asked.

'Four thousand [Guyanese] dollars,' replied the trader. Twenty pounds sterling.

Roughly handling the bird he stretched out the wings to show off the plumage. The bird screeched anxiously.

'Can we take it out of the country? Is it easy?' asked Dave.

The trader looked hopeful, anticipating a sale. 'Yes, yes – you could take it anywhere.' He hauled out another bird to show off, which prompted more anguished squawking.

Another small cage contained about a dozen small monkeys, clinging to each other for comfort. The trader banged on the cage to stir them up. The monkeys huddled together, petrified. The trader turned, smiled benignly for the camera, and shoved some bananas through the wire mesh. The large macaw was also given a banana.

As they chatted a man approached and introduced himself. He was another wildlife dealer. No need for the team to introduce themselves: he already knew who they were and why they were there. Word had obviously spread like wildfire among the exporters that the investigators were in Guyana.

WEDNESDAY, 9 OCTOBER

The investigators set out to find more

street traders selling parrots in order to glean more information about ways round the quota. Then they proceeded to the Ministry of Agriculture building to confer with Karen Pilgrim and tell her about their suspicions concerning smuggling. She felt it was impossible for an illegal consignment to have gone through the system. 'We will look into it right away,' she promised and set out with them for the airport.

En route they stopped to visit some of the exporters' quarantine stations. All the exporters profess to put their birds through a four-week quarantine period. However, it is not a strictly isolated quarantine as birds are coming and going all the time, and is seen more as a stabilising period when the birds 'settle down' and receive any medication required prior to export.

The first station was like an enormous aircraft hangar and contained row upon row of cages holding dozens of different species of birds. There seemed to be an enormous number of birds on the premises. Yet Karen Pilgrim said that this particular exporter did not have a very high quota.

'If there are a whole lot more premises like these it just shows the scale of the trade,' remarked Dave.

A blue and gold macaw, the owner's tame pet, provided a brief distraction. According to their guide it liked playing football and answered to the name of Goalie. But Goalie was in no humour to show off her skills. Despite insistent coaxing from the guide she refused either to play or to talk.

The mood grew more sombre as they paraded up and down the assembly line of cages, raised off the ground at eye level. 'This is a factory – a wildlife factory,' muttered Dave. 'The ethical question is whether or not the modern world should have wildlife factories like this.'

'To be fair the conditions here are a damn sight better than any I have seen in exporting countries before,' said Andy. He noted that although the cages were a little rusty at least they were

Dozens of parrots await their fate at Jean Lall's holding station near Georgetown.

properly raised for easy sweeping out. The overall standards of hygiene were reasonable.

'Even so, I reckon you've only got to show the public buying these birds one bird being caught – it doesn't even have to die – and they will realise that the bird they've got was once free.

'They won't want it. It's as simple as that.'

Dave nodded. 'The conditions here are totally different to the way wild parrots live. They've got nothing to chew on, their diet has been changed and they've got nothing to do. They normally fly in pairs and mate for life. They have a fifty-year life span. I wouldn't like to be incarcerated in a cage like this for the rest of my life, that's for sure.'

12.30 hours
The team moved on to visit another exporter's quarantine station, called 'The Friendship Holding Station'. The cages here were smaller and more densely packed with birds. The owner

A trapper climbs into a tree carrying limed sticks with which to trap parrots and other birds.

claimed to be a 'medium-sized' exporter, who employed about twenty main trappers using the gum method. All the birds were caught locally.

'Have you got many here compared to normal times?' asked Dave.

'No,' replied the owner. 'We don't like to keep too many birds. When we keep a few they live better, you know.' Despite what he said it looked like a huge number of birds on the premises.

'Which countries do you send the birds to?' asked Frank.

England, Holland and America, was the response. European countries were prepared to pay higher prices for the birds, he confided. 'You make a few dollars more in Europe.'

'When's your next shipment?' asked Dave.

'We don't know with the airline problem.'

This was encouraging confirmation that the airlines' embargo was beginning to bite. Over fifty international airlines now refuse to carry wild birds, a direct acknowledgment of the problems involved in their transport. The trader confirmed that all routes out of Guyana were now closed with the exception of two flights a week to Miami.

'So how much is the airline embargo affecting your business?' pressed Dave.

'A lot, a lot.'

14.30 hours

At Georgetown airport, true to her promise, Karen Pilgrim was anxious to check out the allegation of an illegal consignment. The investigators followed her to the blue painted shack that housed the duty quarantine officer. The birds have to be taken to the Airport Quarantine Station at least four hours prior to departure. This is to provide enough time to inspect and count the birds, and remove any sick ones. The quarantine officer handed over the previous day's paperwork. There was no reference to any shipment. The tall official who had denied any birds being loaded the day before was on duty in the cargo shed, some 200 yards away. Frank and Karen questioned him closely.

'It's the same answer as I gave that chap yesterday.' He pointed at Dave Currey. 'I told him that nothing had gone out.'

17.30 hours

Van Sertima had arranged another opportunity for them to see trappers at work, and they headed out of Georgetown towards the bush. It was still light when they met up with the trappers, who arrived on bicycles. One had the two decoy birds tied to a pole slung over the bike's handlebars.

The trappers selected a suitable spot. One then climbed a nearby tree to build a hide while his accomplice prepared the liming sticks. Thick gum from the Batabali tree sap with a consistency like latex was wrapped around the tip ends of several long thin sticks. These were then placed in the top branches of the tree the first trapper was hiding in, protruding so as to provide an inviting-

looking roost. The first decoy, known as the call bird, was fastened on to another stick and placed among the gummed branches at the top of the tree. The trapper kept the teaser bird, secured in a mesh cage, beside him in the hide.

As dusk fell parrots could be spotted on the flight home to their evening roosts. For some this would be their last flight of freedom. The trapper in the hide made the teaser bird start squawking by poking his hand inside the cage. The screech set off the call bird at the top of the tree and, attracted by the commotion, other birds came to investigate. The first bird caught was a flycatcher. This was of no value to the trappers so it was pulled off the gum and released at once. No attempt was made to remove the gum from its feet.

'I have no doubt at all that that bird would have stuck to the next branch it landed on and remained stuck until death,' said Frank afterwards.

The next bird caught was an orange-winged Amazon parrot. The trapper hauled in the branch, cut off the bird's flight feathers with scissors, and lowered it to the ground in a sack. Its piteous squawking as it struggled to escape alarmed other parrots roosting nearby. They took off in a panic and circled the trees, screeching loudly. Within a relatively short period four more orange-winged Amazons were caught.

When they reached the ground they were roughly shaken out of the sacks to be cleaned up. Cooking oil was used to soften and remove the gum and once the birds were cleaned up they were transferred to a wicker cage. The man-handling involved as the trapper dabbed at their feet and wings to pull off the gum was obviously distressing for the birds, who made frantic attempts to escape. But their frenzied wing-beating got them nowhere.

One bird inside the cage was still badly gummed, its wing stuck to its legs. The trapper hauled it out again to apply more cooking oil. As the latch was opened another bird managed to claw

The last flight of freedom, as this parrot becomes stuck to one of the limed sticks.

its way out of the cage, but the escape attempt was short-lived. Deprived of flight it could not get far.

As night fell the trappers continued their work by torchlight to the piteous screeching of the captured birds and the call bird, still tied to its stick at the top of the tree. After about two hours they decided to call it a day, retrieved the call bird and loaded the cage of birds onto one of the bicycles and set off for home along the rough track.

The team were appalled by what they had seen, whilst Lawrence van Sertima, who clearly could see nothing wrong with this method of capture, seemed disappointed at their reaction.

THURSDAY, 10 OCTOBER

The investigators' last full day in Guyana and Karen Pilgrim had arranged for them to visit more exporters' premises. It was obvious that they were expected everywhere they went: all the exporters were on their best behaviour, ultra co-operative, and anxious to cast the trade in a favourable light.

The first stop was the premises of Jean Lall, Guyana's largest wildlife dealer, with twenty-five years' experience in the bird exporting business.

The most disturbing sight was a number of scarlet macaws, one of the most endangered species in the world.

She took them inside a vast warehouse to inspect some of the stock. The din from the birds, of every variety imaginable, was deafening, too noisy for speech. The most disturbing sight was a collection of scarlet macaws, one of the most endangered species in the world. They counted fifty-one. It is on Appendix 1 of the CITES regulations and international trade in the birds has been banned since 1987. However, it was not against Guyanese law to own endangered birds. Mrs Lall claimed she got the macaws before the ban on trade and had kept them ever since. That meant they must have spent several years in captivity.

The failure to prohibit ownership provides an obvious loophole. Andy pointed out there was a lucrative illegal trade in endangered species. Dealers could ship some out and replenish their stock without the government ever knowing.

'How many scarlet macaws have you got?' asked Dave.

Mrs Lall was unsure. 'Some flew away and I don't know how many are left. Between about fifty-eight and sixty.'

'How many birds have you got in total?' asked Frank.

Mrs Lall estimated over 1,000.

'And how many do you export a year?'

Mrs Lall replied, 'I don't know, I don't keep track of every bird.' She paused and then volunteered, 'About seven or eight thousand.'

She was vague about many aspects of the trade including the source of the birds. Most came, she thought, from the north-west region. She used 'hundreds' of trappers and her son travelled to the small towns to buy the birds. This system, whereby 'collectors' regularly visit villages on a fixed day to buy birds from the trappers is quite common. Like the other dealers visited, Mrs Lall was also feeling the pinch from the effects of the airlines' embargo and talked about the need to find another way to ship the birds out.

As they toured the conveyor belts of cages the investigators were awed and depressed by the scale of her operation. Like some of the other exporters they had visited, Mrs Lall dealt in mammals as well as birds. She shipped out about 300–400 monkeys a year, mostly to Japan. For what purpose? As pets? 'I don't really know what they're for,' she confessed.

In a smaller room Dave and Andy spotted an ocelot in a tiny cage, its floor made from wire. Convenient for easy cleaning but hardly ideal for the cat. 'Imagine having to walk on wire all the time,' said Dave. 'Its feet are used to walking through the jungle. The animal

must be suffering.' He was equally appalled by the tiny cramped cage and voiced what they were all thinking: 'I believe in about fifty years' time we'll look back on places like these and view them in the same way that nowadays we view slavery.'

At the end of the tour of holding stations the team compared notes. There were no horror stories. All the premises visited had been in reasonable condition with reasonable sanitation and hygiene. What had made the most impact was the sheer number of birds involved. It was difficult to equate the scale of the exporting operations they had seen with the officially quoted figures.

They were also concerned that there were no laws to prevent Guyanese dealers removing some of the rarest birds in the world from the wild. One trader told them he had offered one of his trappers an outboard motor, about the equivalent of three years' wages, to catch 'a small blue macaw'. The bird he was after was possibly a Lear's macaw, an extremely endangered species of which there may be only 100 left in the wild. He saw nothing wrong in remov-

ing these birds from their natural habitat. He told the tale because he thought it amusing that his trapper returned, saying he had seen such a bird but had not bothered to catch it, because it was so small that he had not thought it could possibly be valuable.

FRIDAY, 11 OCTOBER

On the last morning there was just time for a final wander round the streets of Georgetown before driving to the airport for the long flight home. It had been a fruitful visit. They had talked to government officials and traders, visited and inspected exporters' premises, and seen first-hand many aspects of the trade.

There was no disputing that the Guyanese authorities were taking the trade very seriously, and had set up a system of regulations that on paper sounded impressive. But they had also heard enough from non-official sources to suggest that the system was riddled with loopholes and open to abuse. The very existence of a legal trade provided cover for illegal activities, including exploitation of the wildlife of neighbouring countries that have banned the trade.

The complacent assumption put forward by many of the traders that plenty of forest equates with plenty of birds was unproven. The habitat of wild birds is coming under increasing pressure as a result of commercial logging activities. Coupled with continuing exploitation through trapping, the conservation consequences could be disastrous.

Then there were the welfare problems. Trapping methods were barbaric and there were strong indications of heavy mortalities during holding and transport.

Guyana was deluding itself that it had a 'model situation'. Certainly it was better than some of the worst exporting countries but it was none the less far from acceptable. The investigators would report to that effect when they reached the UK, convinced that the traffic in wild birds was causing enormous suffering. The campaign for a ban on the trade would continue.

At Kurt Herzog's holding station, parrots bunch together in a typical response to fear.

Case Number: SO/6914
Investigating Team: Chief Superintendent Frank Milner; Inspector Alan Goddard; Colin Booty (RSPCA Wildlife Unit)

CHAPTER TWELVE

BEHIND BARS

During the autumn of 1991 the RSPCA received a request for help from the Hellenic Animal Welfare Society in Athens, who were concerned about the condition of two zoos in Greece and asked if the RSPCA could send an observer to investigate the problems. The RSPCA agreed and sent a team to Athens to compile a report on the Greek zoos.

26 NOVEMBER 1991

Carol McBeth, a veterinary nurse with the Hellenic Animal Welfare Society, met the team at the Holiday Inn hotel

to brief them before setting out to visit a zoo in Athens. She had arranged for them to visit the New Philadelphia Zoo in the city and later in the week a zoo at Florino in the north of the country. It was mid-morning when the team arrived at New Philadelphia. The zoo was set amid large gardens behind a football stadium in the north of the city, surrounded by a twelve-foot-high white-washed wall. The zoo did not charge admission fees, so no one noticed the team as they walked through the entrance.

The first thing they saw was a large desert-like enclosure filled to capacity

A large desert-like enclosure filled to capacity with an assortment of waterfowl, goats and other animals.

109

with an assortment of waterfowl, goats, tortoises and cockerels. Colin Booty estimated there must be about a hundred animals in the compound. The area, about forty feet square, consisted of soft sandy soil with a large oval pond in the middle that had barely a couple of inches of water in it. Alan Goddard could scarcely believe there was so little water in the pond. Carol McBeth, who was accompanying the team, said it was a vast amount compared with its usual depth. She had never seen any water in the enclosure before.

Some of the goats came up to the fence, all very hungry. There was no vegetation in the enclosure nor any sign of food. Everywhere was very dry apart from one corner of the compound where a hosepipe had been left on and where a couple of ducks were attempting to drink from a small puddle. Plastic supermarket carriers bags were scattered around the compound. As Colin Booty explained how goats were notorious for eating anything, one of them came up to the fence and started chewing one of the multicoloured bags. Suddenly they saw a goat with overgrown hooves trying to walk across the enclosure. It looked like a rocking horse

with turned-up feet: all four of its hooves were between six and ten inches long. The team then spotted another three goats with the same problem. Evidently little attention had been paid to the goats for some months. The team spent a further five minutes making notes and taking photographs before moving on to the next enclosure.

Two large brown bears were crammed into a small, damp, miserable-looking cage about fourteen feet wide, which Colin declared the worst bear enclosure he had ever seen. A large pile of stale loaves stood outside its peeling green railings through which the bears were attempting to claw the food into the cage. Colin Booty was horrified. 'These bears should have a varied diet consisting of fruits, grains and vegetables. Bears are intelligent, inquisitive animals which like foraging and exploring. There is absolutely nothing in that cell for them at all. Once they've eaten up the bread they'll go absolutely berserk.'

When asked, Carol did not know where the bears had come from, but pointed out that brown bears live wild in the north of the country. Colin was now trying to peer through the two-foot-

All four of its hooves were between six and ten inches long.

Left: A pile of stale bread is all that these bears are given to eat.

Centre: Two large brown bears were crammed into a small, damp, miserable-looking cage.

Below: Another prison-cell housing a lone wolf.

square opening that led into the bears' quarters but it was difficult to see into the black chasm. What little information could be gleaned indicated there was no straw at all for bedding material. He then noticed about a dozen sharp pieces of jagged wire hanging down into the cage. 'When it rains the water will run down the wire into the cage,' said Colin.

There was no pool for the bears to paddle in. Even the drinking trough, a small marble sink, was almost empty.

In the next enclosure two tigers basked in the warm November sunshine. There was little in the enclosure to keep them amused, not even a pool to wallow in during the unbearable summer heat. Frank Milner declared that such animals should be kept in confinement only in a safari park and not imprisoned in tiny cages like these.

Just around the corner from the tiger enclosure was another 'prison cell' housing a lone wolf from where the smell of urine was almost overpowering. The wolf was walking around in circles in its small box-like cage which measured ten feet by eight feet. Frank Milner, who was busy photographing the animals, suggested the wolf should not be on its own since it was a pack animal and should live with a pack. The animal continued to walk round in

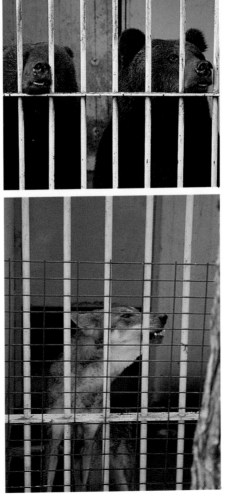

circles, stopping to urinate on each circuit. Colin shook his head and remarked that this was the sign of a behavioural problem.

In the middle of the next compound a lion was stretched out in the sunshine. The enclosure appeared much better than the previous prison cell, with a lot more room for the lion to move around but few facilities for him to play on. Colin spotted two trees in the enclosure with rusting metal spikes hanging down from their trunks which would certainly injure the lion if he decided to stretch himself on the trees. Adjacent to the lion's cage was an enclosure housing four ponies, thus placing a predator next to its prey which would be against UK standards.

Next stop was the leopard enclosure where the animal was continually pacing up and down the cage, bored and frustrated. Colin suggested the leopard could do with a much bigger enclosure with somewhere to climb instead of its present featureless cage. The team spent a few more minutes watching the leopard before moving off to the other side of the zoo where the monkey cages were situated.

The monkeys and baboons were housed in wire cages which had been crudely patched up. Their occupants had obviously been trying to escape. One of the monkeys was attached to a ten-foot length of chain which was severely restricting its movements and which could hang it if it were to fall off its perch. Carol McBeth pointed out to the visiting RSPCA team that the monkey had constantly been escaping from the cage, hence the chain.

Outside the monkey's cage were two small troughs. One contained water and the other a mixture of bread and apples. Colin thought the troughs were placed outside the cages to make life easier for the keepers who could water and feed them without going inside. They also washed down the enclosures by squirting a hosepipe through the cages from the outside. The team watched as the monkey began his battle to eat lunch. His food was quickly being raided by half a dozen pigeons who obviously came and visited at every mealtime. Within ten minutes all the food that had been placed in the trough had disappeared. During that time the monkey had only managed to eat half an apple.

The animal was continually pacing up and down the cage, bored and frustrated.

As soon as this was consumed the monkey, still hungry, picked up a deflated aluminised balloon that was lying in the bottom of the cage and started eating it.

After a further thirty-minute stroll around the zoo the team left, utterly depressed at what they had seen.

27 NOVEMBER

The following morning the team flew from Athens to Thessaloniki in the north of the country. Although Carol McBeth had not visited the zoo herself, she had heard that Florino zoo, on the northern border of Greece with Yugoslavia, was in a poor state. The team arrived at Thessaloniki just after 8.00 a.m. and set off in two hire cars to visit the zoo, situated some 120 miles to the north-west.

It was late morning when they arrived in the little town of Florino, which looked miserable and drab in the overcast weather. After about ten minutes the delegation found the zoo tucked behind a large imposing property on a hillside at the back of the town. The building, once a private house, was now being used as an agricultural training college. Its previous occupants had started the zoo with a private collection of animals which had remained there ever since. The three RSPCA officers accompanied by Carol McBeth parked in the grounds of the training college and walked round the back of the building in search of the zoo.

The first thing they came across was a large tiger in a very small cage. Alan Goddard couldn't believe his eyes. 'It's a tiger in a budgie cage,' he shouted. The tiger was pacing up and down the twelve-foot length of its cage, the smallest cage they had ever seen for a big cat. It was not a good start. In the enclosure next to the tiger a couple of lions were also pacing up and down their cage, which seemed marginally bigger. Suddenly another two smaller lions appeared from the sleeping quarters and they all came up to the railings to watch

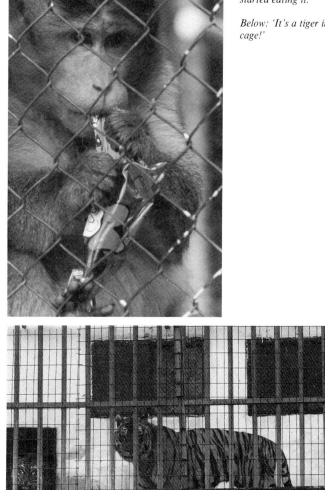

Left: The monkey picked up a deflated aluminised balloon and started eating it.

Below: 'It's a tiger in a budgie cage!'

their visitors. Keith Rodgerson, the film crew sound man, was too busy recording the angry comments of the RSPCA team to notice the effect his fluffy gun microphone was having on the lions. As Keith walked along the side of the cage, holding his microphone, attached to the top of a four-foot-long boom, the lions followed. Then they started to growl. Keith looked up from the flashing red lights on his digital tape recorder and

realised what was causing the lions to make all the noise. For the next ten minutes he literally played a cat and mouse game with the microphone by running up and down the outside of the enclosure with the lions, on the inside, in hot pursuit. Colin thought it was probably the most interesting adventure the lions had had for years.

Behind the tiger and lions' cages was a grassy hillside area of about three acres containing rocks and a few trees which would have provided an ideal enclosure for the cats rather than their empty cages. The team could not understand why this had not been done, but concluded it had to be put down to a lack of both money and imagination.

They moved on to another small enclosure containing several wolves, with a paddock only a few feet away, a classic example of what not to do when keeping animals. It was the same situation they had found in Athens, predators next to their prey. The interior of the wolves' cage was awash with mud and water, rainwater draining directly into the cage making it a quagmire. The wolves were covered in thick brown mud and looked as though they had been in a mud-wrestling competition.

The bear enclosure was the next stop, and this certainly looked a much better situation for the inhabitants. The enclosure was on two levels and included a pool on the top level for paddling as well as rocky outcrops for the bears to climb onto. A run led down to a bear pit situated on a lower level. Although the enclosure was by far the most spacious of any they had seen during the tour of both zoos, it still left a lot to be desired. Astonishingly the public were able to walk up to the single set of railings surrounding the enclosure and put their arms directly through to the bears, as Colin demonstrated for the cameras. The bottom of the bear pit was covered with a thick layer of rotting, decaying food. It looked as though the keepers threw the bears' food over the railings into the pit and did not bother to clean it out. As the team watched, one of the bears came looking for food and started slithering around on the slimy mess of orange peel as though it was on a skating rink.

The zoo at Florino was much smaller than the one in Athens and after about an hour the investigating team were nearing the end of their inspection. Situated on the hillside below the car park stretched an area of poorly built wire enclosures housing a selection of birds of prey. Each bird was confined to a small area about twelve feet square and eight feet in height, often not large enough for it to flap its wings. The wire which was holding the aviary together was in poor condition and the birds could easily injure themselves on some of the rusty ends protruding into their enclosures. The close proximity of the public footpath seemed to unsettle the birds and make them very nervous. Each small aviary contained one bird, some of whom were attempting to fly. They kept taking off from their single perches at the back of the enclosures, flew forward, then immediately collided with the wire meshing at the front of the aviary. Some of the eagles had damaged wings through repeatedly coming into

contact with the wire. Once again the birds' food had just been pushed through the wire mesh and no attempt had been made to clean out the aviaries which, like the bear pit, had resulted in slimy piles of rotting food everywhere.

It was now nearing 2.00 p.m. and the team were rapidly running out of time. They had to make the 120-mile road journey back to Thessaloniki before catching the evening flight to Athens. As they walked out of the zoo they discussed what they had seen and agreed that the overwhelming impression was one of filth, dilapidation, decay and lack of concern. The staff seemed to know nothing about keeping animals and were probably scared to enter the enclosures. As the team walked back to their vehicles they passed two of the keepers at work: they were sweeping the footpath.

28 NOVEMBER

The following morning Carol McBeth, an interpreter and the RSPCA team were back at the New Philadelphia Zoo in Athens. They had arranged a meeting with the local mayor to discuss the zoo's condition and to establish if they could offer help and advice.

The mayor, Gzeiflias Pantlais, who had been in office ten months, opened the discussion by declaring that he was aware of the situation and now had some money to improve the cages and start a veterinary clinic inside the zoo, although a vet already visited the zoo each day. The team were surprised that a vet could visit the zoo daily and yet not notice the condition of the animals. They brought up the matter of the goats with the overgrown feet but were told that the animals had arrived in that condition and that the vet had been unable to do anything about it. When told that a harder surface underfoot would wear down the hooves naturally, the mayor changed the subject. He promised the team he would be expanding the bear cages and adding a pool. Frank Milner said the RSPCA could provide advice and supply drawings and plans of what ideal enclosures should look like, both for the bears and for the other animals, as well as veterinary advice for the proposed zoo clinic.

After a brief discussion on feeding, when the team were assured that the bears were fed vegetables, fruit and fresh meat every day, the mayor and his entourage then explained that time had run out and they would have to dash off to an election meeting.

The team were sceptical as to the mayor's sincerity and promises of better conditions and saw few grounds for optimism. Their visit clearly demonstrated the sort of problems found in zoos in Europe and highlighted the need for some form of European legislation and licensing system. The team then made arrangements to keep in touch with Carol McBeth and the Hellenic Animal Welfare Society and hoped that with a bit more persuasion the mayor might improve conditions at the zoo.

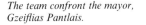

The team confront the mayor, Gzeiflias Pantlais.

THE FIGHT CONTINUES

★★★★ TODAY Tuesday

...anned in Britain since January, but our calves still fa...
...ate misery to satisfy the appetites of European gourm...

FOR THE SAKE OF A LITTLE TENDERNESS

by RUSSELL JENKINS

THE velvety head...

sardines for more than 30 hours."

In Britain, the 1975 Transit Of Animals Order states that livestock can not go for longer than 12 hours without food or... 24...

LIVING DEATH: The calf bleats in agony in the cage wh...

wheel of the cattle wagon had done his best. Stan, a middle-aged York-shireman, said the heat-wave had meant that only 160 calves had been packed into an area usu-ally taken up by 200 to give them more space.

"We aren't all savages," he said. "If I had been going any further into a would have gone obviously lairage, because you cannot mix milk on the wagon."

This was just one jour-ney The RSPCA says hundreds of thousands of animals suffer the same

the exporter. But Diana Jones of the RSPCA says: "What makes this har-rowing story into a tra-gedy is that it is happening all the time.

"We have files inches thick, accumulated over 15 years, recording simi-lar — and worse — trans-European journeys.

"Reports of cattle hurled around inside lor-ries and breaking their legs is common. Vast transporters have been photographed with the limbs of sheep jammed through the slats.

The four months that Paul Berriff and his camera team spent with the RSPCA gave them a glimpse into the Special Operations Unit's undercover activities. But the footage they obtained only tells part of the story of the unit's work. This chapter outlines some of the other areas of animal abuse the officers have been investigating.

Perhaps one of the most stomach-turning investigations of recent years was infiltrating Spanish abattoirs to check slaughterhouse standards, prompted by pressure on the British government to begin exporting live animals to Spain. The Spanish government claimed its abattoirs complied with European humane standards. In just three days in November 1990 a team of four inspectors uncovered the sickening truth.

They found goats strung up by their rear legs to have their throats slit while fully conscious. The animals' bleating could still be heard while they bled to death. They witnessed cattle and horses stabbed with a dagger (*puntilla*) to sever the spinal cord and render them immobile. This method paralysed the animals but did not render them unconscious. In some cases the slaughtermen had to stab the animals four or five times before they collapsed. One white horse was still blinking and clearly conscious while it was shackled, strung up and bled out. The abattoir's vet was asked why the EC regulation captive bolt gun was not being used. He replied: 'We had a gun but it broke many months ago. With the *puntilla* we only miss about 5 per cent of the animals.'

117

The veal crate system of production has been banned in Britain. Sadly, the rest of Europe hasn't followed suit.

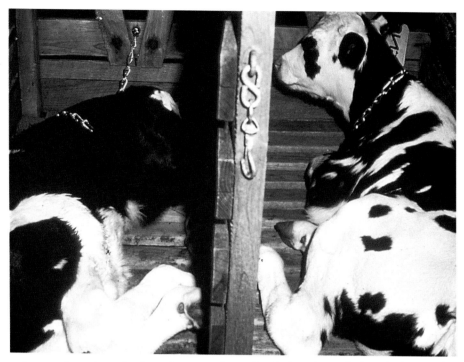

In another abattoir they discovered electrical tongs (an approved method of stunning) used incorrectly either by applying them in the wrong place or for too short a time. The result was that many animals regained consciousness before being shackled and stuck. The evidence they gathered was forwarded to the European Commission as part of a formal complaint. The Spanish authorities were severely reprimanded and told to put their slaughterhouses in order. It also helped to strengthen the British government's hand in resisting calls for live exports to Spain.

Another investigation welcomed by the British government was that exposing the horrendous trade in calves shipped abroad to be reared in crates. Veal crates have been banned in Britain since the beginning of 1990 but they are still legal in other European countries. The crates are two foot by five foot wooden pens in which the calves are locked when they are still tiny – just one to three weeks old. They are kept inside twenty-four hours a day until they are ready for slaughter. Imagine a young animal imprisoned in darkness for months on end: it has no bedding, no room to exercise or turn around, and can barely stand on the slatted floor. Its diet consists of reconstituted dried milk to keep its flesh pale and tender as demanded by European gourmets.

Despite the ban in Britain, thousands of British calves are shipped abroad to be reared by this brutal method. The undercover investigators have trailed lorries carrying one-week-old calves to rearing units in Holland. They also monitored huge shipments of veal leaving Holland to be re-exported back into Britain. A survey by a TV programme on the trade showed that a shocking 80 per cent of Britain's top 100 hotels and restaurants sell Dutch veal. This evidence was used to alert consumers to boycott European veal and help the British government to apply pressure on the European Council of Agricultural Ministers for a Community-wide ban on the crates.

That campaign continues. Flicking back through the pages of history it is encouraging to find other campaigns,

spearheaded by the SOU, that have already been won. For instance the campaign to end the tortoise trade. In the late 1970s SOU officers played an important role gathering evidence to highlight the stress and suffering caused by the trade. Thousands of tortoises were imported into Britain each year. But their chances of surviving in the cold, damp climate were poor. Studies indicated a mortality rate in excess of 80 per cent for the first year in captivity. There were also fears about the impact the trade was having on tortoise numbers in the wild.

The tortoises would be brought from North Africa and the Mediterranean, in semi-refrigerated lorries to keep them torpid. They were often shipped in unsuitable crates and arrived with broken shells or other injuries. Many died en route. The evidence obtained by the SOU officers from inspecting consignments in this country and monitoring conditions abroad helped to rouse public outrage and outlaw the trade.

The appalling conditions in which

dealers are willing to transport animals of all shapes and sizes for commercial gain is all too familiar to the SOU investigators. Puppy farming is an area for concern. Not only are puppies often bred in shocking conditions in unlicensed establishments, but many also endure terrible journeys to the pet shops. The SOU investigators have uncovered puppies crammed into car boots to be driven up the motorways or shoved into tea chests for transport by rail. The public buying these animals is creating the demand to continue churning out production-line puppies. RSPCA advice is only to buy from reputable breeders where you can see the puppies with the mother.

One problem that raised its head in the 1980s was the export of breeds such as alsatians for use as guard dogs abroad. Unscrupulous dealers snapped up unwanted animals, claiming they would be trained as security dogs. Then they just crated them up and shipped them out to countries such as Nigeria where crime is rife. The dealers were selling them as cheap burglar alarms

This wretched cow is clearly unfit for travel: the reality of casualty slaughter.

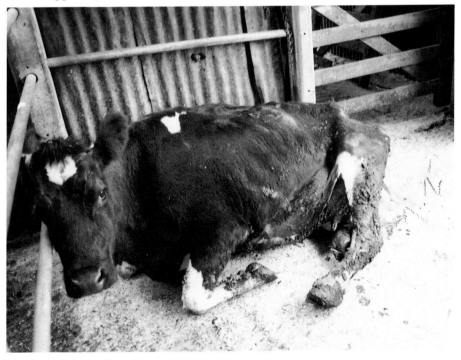

and reports surfaced of the dogs being kept chained up all day in hot temperatures and terrible conditions. The trade was stamped out by making life difficult for the dealers. SOU officers intercepted consignments and prosecuted the exporters for transit offences.

Nigeria was also the destination for another traffic in misery – the export of 'day old' chicks. In the early 1980s the SOU officers kept regular checks on the consignments bound for Lagos. Their observations brought results in 1983 when officers discovered, in one consignment of 30,000 chicks at Gatwick airport, 3,500 that were already dead or dying. A further 1,500 had to be humanely destroyed. The Special Operations Unit prosecuted the exporters responsible and the company had fines and costs imposed totalling £7,500.

Poultry in transit has always been a problem area. When birds are removed from a controlled environment and loaded onto lorries, exposed to the elements, for transport to processing plants, distress and suffering are almost inevitable. The birds are already fragile after continuous confinement in tiny cages. Brittle and broken bones are common. Many have lost their feathers and are ill equipped to withstand extremes of heat or cold. Extremely long journeys are not uncommon. One successful prosecution involved poultry transported from southern Ireland to north Yorkshire where the birds endured a journey of sixty-eight hours without food or water. The driver was fined £400.

The SOU officers also keep a close watch on conditions inside intensive rearing units. A long stake-out was needed to prove a case against a farmer responsible for a unit where some 21,000 poultry were caged. The law requires regular inspection. The investigators were able to prove the farmer spent just over nine minutes in a twenty-four-hour period inspecting the stock. This was patently negligent. Sometimes they have found the most appalling conditions inside battery units. In one case they discovered broken cages, rotting uncollected eggs, and dead or dying birds.

Rabbits raised for slaughter often also get a raw deal and the unit has carried out several successful investigations into this problem. It tends to be a 'cottage industry' with part-time breeders looking for an extra money-spinner. One transporter may be responsible for picking up rabbits from dozens of different far-flung locations. As a result the first rabbits loaded may spend many hours on board before reaching the slaughterhouse. Extensive surveillance and subterfuge was necessary to prove the case against one collector who allowed rabbits to spend twenty-nine hours in transit without food or water.

The fate of worn-out racing greyhounds, in demand at Spanish racetracks to entertain tourists, has also attracted the attention of the unit. Disturbing reports that the dogs are kept in miserable conditions and rumours that some end up in research laboratories are being checked out.

Casualty slaughter is yet another area for concern. Sick or injured livestock should be put down on site or taken to the nearest abattoir for immediate destruction. Because meat from animals not slaughtered in approved abattoirs cannot be offered for human consumption, farmers favour having the animals removed in order to get more money. Providing the animal is fit to travel and properly conveyed this is legally acceptable. But that doesn't always happen, as one horrific investigation revealed.

SOU officers suspected one haulier was transporting sick animals for slaughter many more miles than necessary, bypassing nearer abattoirs in order to reach one where he was guaranteed a better price. It took many weeks of distressing observations to prove their case, in the course of which they had to watch animals clearly unfit to travel enduring terrible journeys and sickening

Poultry birds are already fragile from continuous confinement in tiny cages and may have lost all their feathers. Transit conditions for them can be particularly cruel.

treatment. But their patience paid off and resulted in a conviction against the haulier and the owner of a Barnsley slaughterhouse.

While people are prepared to ship animals in disgraceful conditions in order to make a profit, monitoring the transport of animals has to remain a top priority for the unit. But as the preceding chapters have shown there are many other calls on their time.

RSPCA inspectors, whether unifor-med or undercover, must be one of the few groups in society who would be happy to discover their jobs no longer needed doing. If there was no more animal abuse, no more cruelty, and no more exploitation they could hand in their ID cards and find work elsewhere. But sadly that is not the case. The mistreatment of animals seems to escalate rather than diminish and while such cruelty exists the RSPCA will do all in its power to combat it.

The only food this calf will be given during its short life is reconstituted dried milk.

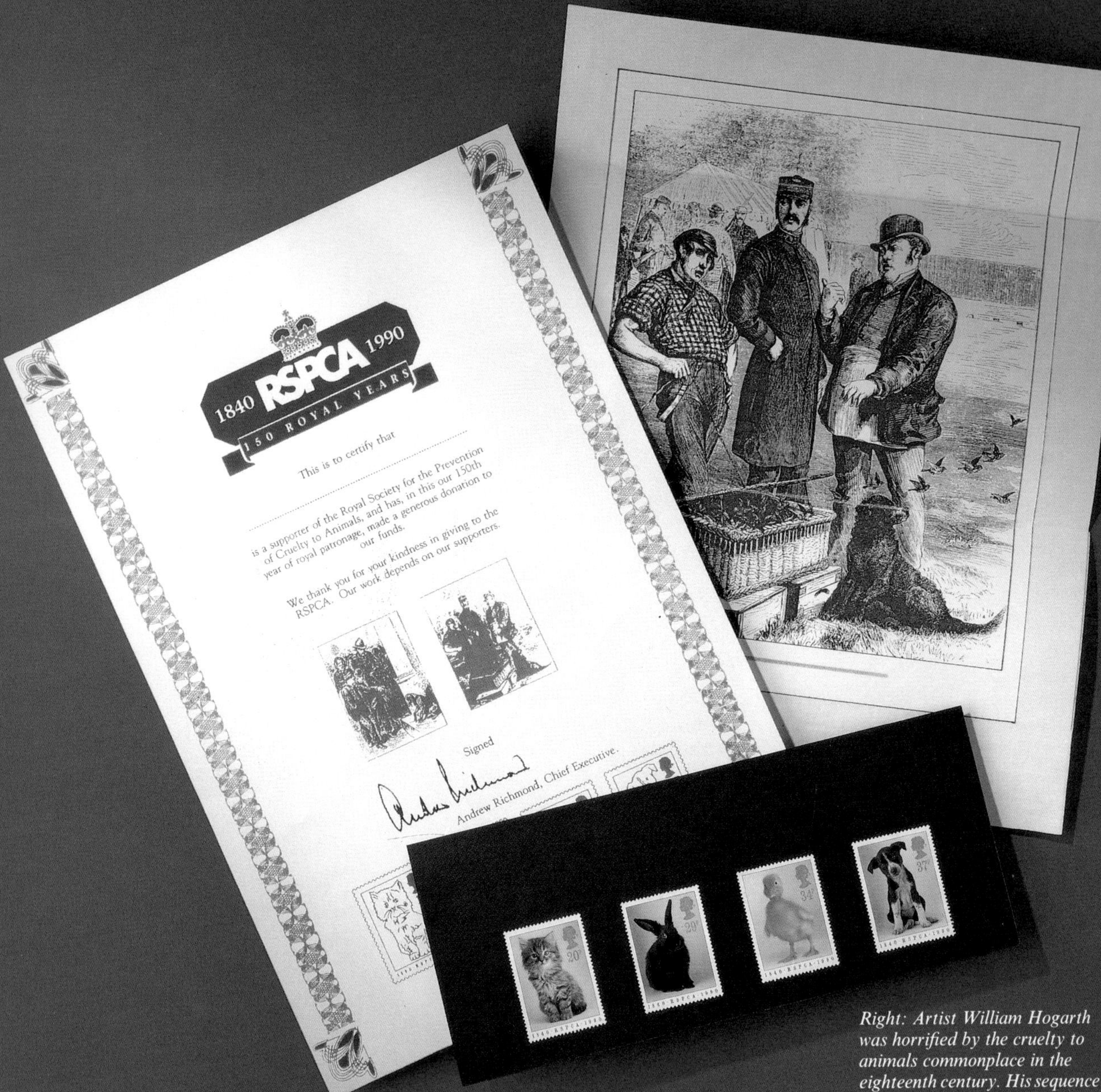

1840 RSPCA 1990
150 ROYAL YEARS
This is to certify that
is a supporter of the Royal Society for the Prevention of Cruelty to Animals, and has, in this our 150th year of royal patronage, made a generous donation to our funds.
We thank you for your kindness in giving to the RSPCA. Our work depends on our supporters.
Signed
Andrew Richmond, Chief Executive.

Above: When the RSPCA celebrated its 150th royal anniversary in 1990, this commemorative material was produced to mark the occasion.

Right: Artist William Hogarth was horrified by the cruelty to animals commonplace in the eighteenth century. His sequence of pictures, 'The Four Stages of Cruelty' (1751) conveyed the message that cruelty to animals led to cruelty to humans. In this picture, the Second Stage, a coachman is shown hammering the head of his fallen horse, while a drover beats a sheep that has collapsed. In the background, other cruelties can be seen, including a bull tormented by a mob.

CHAPTER FOURTEEN

HISTORY OF THE RSPCA

One midsummer eve in the early part of the 19th century, a group of men met at a London coffee-house to debate an urgent issue. From their discussions grew the world's oldest and largest animal welfare organisation – the Royal Society for the Prevention of Cruelty to Animals.

At that time the idea that animals needed protecting was still a radical concept. Cruelty to animals was commonplace. Contemporary accounts document how it was not unusual for overworked horses to be beaten to death. Slaughterhouse conditions were appalling. Animals were tossed into underground cellars to lie broken and bleeding for days at a time until despatched by the butcher's knife. Calves were strung up and slowly bled to death with their mouths bound up to hush the moans. Cats were skinned for their fur while still alive. And cruel sports like bull-baiting and cockfighting were popular entertainments.

In the eighteenth century, most people took a callous attitude towards animals. Only an enlightened few worked to improve conditions. One such was Sir William Pulteney who in 1800 brought in a Bill to outlaw bull-baiting, a cruel and rowdy affair but one much enjoyed by the masses. The proposed ban ran up against the prevailing view that it was a man's right to do as he pleased with his own property. And property included animals. Furthermore, if the sports of the poor were to be banned, why not also those of the rich such as shooting and hunting which were equally cruel? The Bill was fiercely contested. Even *The Times* went on the attack. 'Whatever meddles with the private personal disposition of a man's time or property is tyranny direct,' thundered the paper. The Bill was defeated. Two further attempts to reintroduce it also failed.

The next attempt at reform came in 1809 when Lord Erskine, a former Lord Chancellor and one of the most eminent lawyers of the day, presented a Bill to prevent malicious or wanton cruelty to animals. The Edinburgh-born Erskine seems to have been quite a character who owned a menagerie of animals including dogs, a goose and two leeches.

It is reported that while out walking one day on Hampstead Heath he encountered a carter unmercifully beating a horse.

When Erskine remonstrated with him the man replied, 'Can't I do what I like with my own?'

'Yes,' responded Erskine, 'and so can I – this stick is my own.' He then gave the man a thorough thrashing.

Although Erskine's advocacy skills had netted him a fortune at the Bar he failed to persuade his fellow parliamentarians of the case for reform. His Bill was greeted with derision and

A rider callously flogs his donkey. It was not unusual for horses and pack animals to be literally beaten to death.

although it did make some progress, was eventually thrown out. However, attitudes were starting to change, not least in the press. This time *The Times* gave its blessing to the idea of 'a system of rights and privileges even for the mute and unconscious part of creation.'

The next move came in May 1821 when Richard Martin presented a Bill to prevent the ill-treatment of horses. It was kicked out but Martin was back the following year with another attempt which he extended to include cattle. The Bill made it an offence for anybody in charge of these animals to be found wantonly beating, abusing or ill-treating them. Martin would have liked to broaden it still further by including cats, dogs and other animals, but he was pragmatic enough to know that that would invite certain defeat. Even so there was still strong opposition. What next? scoffed one member. Laws to prevent boiling lobsters or eating live oysters?

However, the Bill was eventually passed by both Houses and received the Royal Assent on 22 July 1822. Lord Erskine, who steered it successfully through the House of Lords, must have been pleased. The first animal protection law was now on the statute book and Richard Martin had earned himself a new nickname: 'Humanity Dick'. In another tribute he was referred to as 'Thou Wilberforce of hacks!' Offenders could be brought before the magistrates and if found guilty faced a minimum fine of ten shillings or maximum penalty of two months' imprisonment.

Richard Martin, 1754–1835, was the Irish MP responsible for the first animal protection law.

HUMANITY DICK

Richard Martin was an Irish barrister and MP for Galway. Educated at Harrow and Cambridge, he had a privileged upbringing and was heir to a 200,000-acre estate. In his youth he had earned a formidable reputation as a duellist, but there was a softer side to his character. He was adored by his tenants and among many kindly deeds provided for homeless children in his own castle. He was associated with other humanitarian causes including Catholic emancipation and the abolition of capital punishment for forgery. Martin was also an advocate of free legal aid for the poor.

In a famous case, legend has it that when it looked as though the magistrates might acquit a costermonger of ill-treating a donkey he decided to force their hand. He had the animal brought into court so that they could see for themselves the wounds inflicted. It is a colourful tale but hard to substantiate. However, perhaps there is some basis to the legend because a popular song at the time contained the following lines:

If I had a donkey wot
  wouldn't go,
D'ye think I'd wallop
  him? No, no, no!
But gentle means I'd try
  d'ye see,
Because I hate all
  cruelty.
If all had been like me,
  in fact,
There'd ha' been no
  occasion for Martin's
  Act.

Martin's kindly disposition was again in evidence when in some of the cases he paid the fines himself, having no wish to penalise poor employees.

In 1826 there was a General Election in which Martin was successfully re-elected for County Galway but the campaign was evidently a rowdy affair. Critics accused his supporters of attacking opponents and rigging the voting. Although nobody suggested Martin had personally condoned these malpractices, he was unseated on petition.

There was further misfortune when Martin ran into money problems. His estates were heavily mortgaged and the creditors were baying for payment. Martin escaped to exile in France where his concern for animal welfare never diminished. With his death in Boulogne in 1834 the animal welfare cause lost a courageous champion.

Many prosecutions under the 1822 Act were brought by Martin himself. This depicts the legendary trial of Bill Burns, a costermonger prosecuted for cruelty to a donkey. Martin had the donkey brought into court to show Magistrates the wounds.

Martin personally threw himself into enforcing the new law. He prosecuted one of the first cases at the Guildhall on 11 August 1822 against two men for savagely beating tethered horses at Smithfields Meat Market. When one of the defendants announced he was a butcher by trade Martin replied: 'Yes, I perceive that. A horse butcher.' The men were fined twenty shillings each.

Richard Martin's attempts at reform did not end with his milestone Act. During the next four years he threw his energies into promoting measures to end bull- and bear-baiting and dog-fighting, and to improve conditions in knackers' yards. He also sought to widen the 1822 Act to include other domestic animals. Unfortunately all were defeated.

However, the law at last recognised that animals had some rights. But laws are meaningless without enforcement and even a man of Martin's energy

could not enforce the new law single-handed. But who would help to implement the Act?

The Reverend Arthur Broome, vicar of the Parish of St Mary's, Bromley St Leonard, in the East End of London, had already made one attempt in 1822 to form an organisation to support its enforcement. When that failed to make headway he personally paid the cost of employing a man named Wheeler to watch for offences against the Act. As a result of his vigilance sixty-three offenders, most from Smithfields Market, were brought before the magistrates in the first six months of 1824.

But the Reverend Broome was determined to make a second attempt to achieve his aim. Thus on the evening of 16 June 1824 a group of worthy men made their way to Old Slaughter's Coffee House in St Martin's Lane, London, a favourite meeting place for painters and sculptors. But the company, which included several MPs, clergymen and other distinguished gentlemen, had not come to swop idle chat about art. They had been summoned to a meeting by Reverend Broome to discuss starting a society 'for the purpose of preventing cruelty to animals'.

Among the twenty-one people gathered was William Wilberforce, well known for his fight to end the slave trade. Richard Martin, the MP responsible for winning the first successful animal protection law, just two years earlier, was also present. Fowell Buxton MP, brother-in-law of the prison reformer Elizabeth Fry, took the chair.

The minutes of the 1824 meeting record that they decided to appoint two committees to further the work of this newly founded society. One was 'to superintend the publication of tracts, sermons, and similar modes of influencing public opinion'. The other was 'to adopt measures for inspecting the markets and streets of the metropolis, the slaughterhouses, the conduct of coachmen, etc.' The newly formed society took over the cost of employing Wheeler's services and in 1825 appointed an assistant, Charles Teasdell. These men were the forerunners of today's RSPCA inspectorate.

Over the years there has been continuing debate about the best approach to tackling cruelty. Whether to concentrate on education or punishment, or, to put it another way, propaganda or

prosecution? At the inaugural meeting Richard Martin himself stressed it should not be just a prosecuting society, but rather one whose prime aim should be 'to alter the moral feelings of the country'. Wisely the founders decided to pursue a twin-track policy.

Today it is accepted that the inspectorate fulfils both an educational and a law-enforcement role. Publicity about cases brought to court can deter prospective offenders. Often the mere presence of an inspector makes people think twice before committing an offence. So it was too in the early days. During its first year inspectors appointed by the society successfully prosecuted in 149 cases of cruelty to animals.

However the infant society was soon experiencing grave money problems. Within two years of the founding meeting the society had to dispense with the services of paid inspectors. (Wheeler was obviously more than a hireling because he continued to work in a voluntary capacity. That labour of love was to be rewarded in 1832 when he was presented with the society's silver medal in recognition of his services.)

In 1826 the Reverend Arthur Broome was held responsible for the society's debts and imprisoned. The committee was by then on the verge of winding things up. Fortunately a much-needed cash boost arrived in the shape of a legacy from a well-known thriller writer, Mrs Ann Radcliffe, who left £100, which enabled the society to continue and released Broome from prison.

Following Broome's resignation in 1828, the society's next Secretary was a man with a reputation for eccentricity. Lewis Gompertz was a prolific inventor and a devout vegetarian. He felt so strongly that man had no right to use animals simply for his own benefit that he refused even to ride in a horse-drawn carriage. Like Broome he too loaned the society money that was never repaid.

By April of that year the society was on a more even financial footing and the committee was able to report that all

William Wilberforce, best known for his fight to end the slave trade, was one of the RSPCA's founder members.

former debts had been liquidated. However this proved only a temporary reprieve: by 1832 lack of funds was forcing economies. At that time two full-time inspectors were employed on a wage of ten shillings a week and it was decided to dispense with their services. Gompertz fell out with other members of the committee over this decision. He also disagreed with a proposal to conduct the society on purely Christian principles, taking the view that people's religious beliefs had no bearing so long as their hearts were in the right place when it came to animals.

Although in the long term Gompertz was proved correct about the need for full-time inspectors he lost the argument and resigned that year. He went on to found the Animal's Friend Society which for some years rivalled the original parent body.

The decision to stop employing permanent inspectors did not mean the society abandoned its law-enforcement role. Several members of the committee took on these duties and prosecuted the most flagrant cases of cruelty. They also decided to employ inspectors for specific tasks. That year, for example, the committee made a short-term appointment for a man to deal with the ill-treatment of horses on Blackheath.

The legal framework for animal protection was being added to all the time. The next Bill to reach the statute book after Martin's Act was the 1835 Protection of Animals Act which was piloted through the Commons by Joseph Pease, a Quaker MP and member of the society's committee. It met with remarkably little opposition. This was attributed by some to the fact that the Bill was sponsored by a society which had recently been honoured by receiving the patronage of the future Queen of England. The Bill increased the scope of Martin's Act by including bulls and domestic animals. It also banned baiting and cockfighting and laid down a system for licensing slaughterhouses. All horses and cattle brought to slaughterhouses had to be killed within three days, and in the interim must be fed daily. The Act also made it an offence to use premises to fight a bull (or any other animal), offenders being faced with a fine of £5 for every day they kept or used such places.

But progress was piecemeal. The Act for instance ignored the plight of dogs used as beasts of burden. Joseph Pease confessed he had not included a ban on using dogs as draught animals because he thought it would be subject to ridicule. The users of dog-drawn vehicles ignored arguments that dogs' soft paws ill equipped them for pulling heavy

THE FOUNDER OF THE RSPCA

Little is known about Arthur Broome, but of his generous and devoted service there can be no doubt. Records show he was born in 1780 to a family from Devon. He went to Balliol College in 1798 and graduated three years later. In 1803 he was ordained and spent several years as a curate in Kent before coming to London in 1820.

When, at the first meeting of the society, Broome was appointed Honorary Secretary, he resigned his living in order to devote himself full time to the work of the society, paying many of its debts. In 1826 he was thrown into prison for the society's debts of £80, from which he was rescued by a timely legacy. Even then the society's financial state was such that it was only able to repay him £10; the remaining £70 was never refunded.

He resigned as Secretary of the society in 1828 and although he continued to serve on the committee, there is no record of his attending meetings between then and his death in Birmingham in 1837. He was buried in an unmarked grave in what is now Birmingham Cathedral churchyard. But as chroniclers have noted there could be no more fitting memorial than the success of the society he founded.

A RUNNING BATTLE

Bull-running was often used as a warm-up to the main spectacle of baiting. The bull would be chased through the streets and fields, goaded by a crowd wielding cudgels and other weapons. The town of Stamford was a stronghold of bull-running. The citizens were determined to maintain their 600-year-old 'right' to indulge in this annual event even though it had been declared illegal by Joseph Pease's Act of 1835. The streets were blocked off and the run took place as usual in November 1836 with much attendant cruelty and riotous behaviour.

The SPCA helped to bring a successful prosecution of some of the residents but despite this the townsfolk made plans to repeat the event the following year. Over 200 special constables were sworn in to

Smithfield Market.(Death of) This Print is Pub.^d in Commemoration of Smithfield Market, & Dedicated to the Rt. Hon. the Lord Mayor, & Corporation of the City of London, with my best wishes to the inhabitance of Copenhagen-fields & Islington. — N.B. The nighest Police court Clarkenwell !!! J.L.Marks Long Lane Smithfield.

prevent the run but they proved ineffective and unable to stop it.

In 1838 the Home Secretary cracked down and drafted in the 14th Light Dragoons and a dozen trusted police officers to keep order.

Despite their presence the mob stole a bull and started the usual attack. The next year a bull was again smuggled into the town and a mob estimated at over 4,000 strong engaged in a pitched battle with the cavalry. The Battle of Stamford was, however, eventually won after the town was ordered to foot the bill for the hire of outside forces. The mayor promised that if the Home Secretary would refrain from sending in troops he would guarantee no more bull-running.

---

loads on hard roads. Dogs had the advantage of being cheaper to run than horses and their drivers were exempt from tolls. Like horses they were flogged unmercifully to pull their loads at full gallop, so that, for example, they could make the journey from Brighton to Portsmouth in a day and return the next. Nearly twenty years were to elapse before dog-drawn carts were finally outlawed in 1854.

By 1838 the society's funds were looking healthier and the committee reverted to a policy of employing permanent inspectors. Two were taken on, who wore metal badges as identification and were called constables. These inspectors were London-based but would be despatched to various parts of the country for temporary duty from time to time, bringing prosecutions where they could, the theory being that this should deter other potential cruelty offenders. It was an economical use of resources when money was scarce and men were few.

Inspectors' pay was topped up with a proportion of the fines imposed in successful prosecutions. This, however, was a controversial practice since magistrates disliked 'paid informers' and the system was open to abuse. In 1840 the society banned inspectors from accepting money resulting from convictions. Yet it remained common for some time after for police officers to receive two

Dogs used as draught animals were flogged unmercifully to pull their loads at full gallop.

shillings from the RSPCA for every successful case concerning cruelty to animals they brought to court.

That year the society received a tremendous boost: the prestige of royal endorsement.

In the meantime the inspectorate was going from strength to strength, by 1841 having a complement of five inspectors on pay of a guinea a week. The society had its roots firmly in London. As like-minded people outside the capital proved anxious to establish similar organisations the committee tried to help out by sending gifts of literature and grants of money, and sometimes they loaned inspectors for short periods. The first formal auxiliary society was formed in Liverpool. in 1841, following several earlier abortive attempts to establish organisations for 'suppressing cruelty' in that city. By 1842 Brighton,

Bristol, Bath, Coventry and Scarborough were all requesting inspectors. Supporters were asked to contribute £20 a year for the maintenance of 'their' inspector. This was the beginning of the national network of local branches familiar today.

The inspectorate was now benefiting from the RSPCA's growing prosperity. In 1851 it was decided to double the strength from five to ten constables, but due to the unpopularity of the job only eight posts were filled. The committee was determined to get its money's worth from its officers. In December 1850 the constables had to explain in person why they had obtained so few convictions. A year later the constable with the fewest convictions was dismissed.

By 1878 the society was employing forty-eight inspectors and by 1886 the number had risen to eighty. Not surprisingly, given the society's emphasis on temperance, a quarter were tee-totallers! Their success rate in the courts was impressive. In 1849 the RSPCA could pride itself on a lower failure rate than the police.

The number of prosecutions roughly doubled each decade between 1830 and 1900, so that during the 1890s the RSPCA conducted some 71,657 prosecutions, and moved into the twentieth century with a force of 120.

The society's influence was also spreading overseas. As early as 1834 a member of the committee had gone to Paris to advise on founding a French society. A German society was started in Munich in 1841 and others followed in rapid succession in the Netherlands, Belgium and other European countries.

Developments in America were to have the most far-reaching influence in another humanitarian endeavour: the prevention of cruelty to children. An American diplomat, Henry Bergh, passing through London in 1865 had visited the then Secretary of the RSPCA, John Colam. Inspired by that meeting he returned to the States, which at that time had no anti-cruelty laws, and founded the first SPCA in New York the following year.

Several years later Bergh was approached by a New York charity worker who asked if he could help to relieve the suffering of a 'little animal' at the hands of a brutal woman. Bergh promised to assist and then discovered the animal in question was a child. He remained true to his promise and the woman was prosecuted for cruelty to an animal. The success of this case precipitated a flood of similar requests for help, which led to the hasty formation of a separate society for the prevention of cruelty to children.

On hearing of this development the RSPCA decided a similar organisation should be started in Britain. In 1884 Lord Shaftesbury, helped by Dr Barnardo and Cardinal Manning, formed what was to become the NSPCC. John

Queen Victoria took an active interest in the work of the Society throughout her reign.

Colam became a committee member of this 'kindred organisation' and the RSPCA offered the boardroom of its Jermyn Street headquarters for meetings. So much for the taunts that people are concerned about cruelty to animals at the expense of humans. The links between child and animal welfare have remained close ever since.

From its beginnings the RSPCA had worked closely with children. Education was seen as the key to preventing future cruelty. Hence the founding decision to establish a committee 'to superintend the publication of tracts and sermons'. As early as 1845 the RSPCA had gained the co-operation of the National Schools Society to distribute society material and give lessons on the importance of kindness to animals. They also distributed leaflets to the Ragged Schools and workhouses. A thousand children were invited to the society's annual meeting in 1860. The penny buns dished out to all attending may have been intended to stimulate their appetite for animal welfare!

131

A ROYAL PATRON

Princess Victoria had been approached some time in 1835 with a request to honour the society by becoming a lady patroness, to which she 'readily acceded'. Two years later Victoria ascended the throne and in 1840 granted the society permission to use the royal prefix. The Queen's endorsement conferred respectability and the prestige of her association did much to help animal welfare, which it now became fashionable to support. Dickens, like many other eminent figures of his age, was a member of the society. Charles Darwin was another supporter. He marked the RSPCA's Jubilee Year by offering a prize of £50 to the first inventor of a humane method of keeping down rabbits.

During her long reign Victoria took a keen interest in the work of the society. In 1874 when the society was celebrating its jubilee she sent a donation of 100 guineas and a letter requesting the President of the RSPCA to: 'Give expression publicly of Her Majesty's warm interest in the success of the efforts being made here and abroad for the purpose of diminishing cruelties practised on dumb animals.'

Little escaped Her Majesty's observant eye. When by royal command a medal was prepared for presentation to those who had helped the society the design was sent for her approval. She returned it with the comment that the artists had omitted to include a cat. This must be rectified and she included a sketch of the cat to be added.

Her own jubilee took place in 1887 and there were many events to celebrate the occasion. Despite a punishing round of official duties she still made time to attend the RSPCA's Annual Meeting and Prize-giving. In her address she stated: 'Amongst other marks of the spread of enlightenment amongst my subjects, I notice, in particular, with real pleasure, the growth of more humane feelings towards the lower animals. No civilisation is complete which does not include the dumb and defenceless of God's creatures within the sphere of charity and mercy.'

In the last quarter of the century the national junior membership movement grew out of a body known as the 'Wood Green Band of Mercy for Promoting Kindness to Animals'. This was founded by Mrs Catherine Smithies and aimed at encouraging the young to work

hard for the good of animals. The children listened to stories with an animal welfare message, sang hymns and recited poems. More bands sprang up and in 1883 the movement became formally affiliated to the RSPCA. It published a monthly journal called *Band of Mercy*, the forerunner of today's RSPCA children's magazine.

Essay-writing competitions were another popular way of spreading the animal welfare message. These were enormously popular and in their heyday attracted thousands of entries: in 1924 the number of entries from London schools alone was 253,000. The prize-giving became an annual occasion attended by thousands of children and their parents. It was often held at Crystal Palace and notables, such as the Prince and Princess of Wales, would be invited to present the prizes, which were generally complete sets of the works of well-known novelists, Dickens or Scott, for example.

As the twentieth century dawned, the RSPCA's missionary zeal had gained

Left: Mrs Catherine Smithies founded the Wood Green Band of Mercy. This encouraged the young to promote kindness to animals and grew into a nationwide movement.

Below: 11 May 1907. HRH the Prince and Princess of Wales present certificates and prizes to the winners of an RSPCA essay-writing competition at Alexandra Palace. There were 274,699 entries.

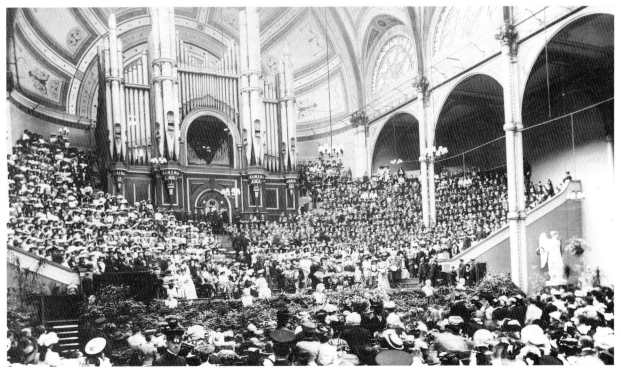

During the First World War, over £250,000 was raised for the RSPCA's Sick and Wounded Horse Fund. It paid to equip thirteen hospitals and to provide 180 horse-drawn ambulances, bandages and other supplies.

thousands of new young converts through the Bands of Mercy; more animal protection laws had been added to the statute book; the nucleus of today's network of animal homes and shelters was evolving: much had been achieved but there was still much to be done.

There is no space here to detail the many campaigns already won or still to be fought: the crusade against vivisection, the quest for humane killing and slaughtering methods, the horrors of the trade in worn-out horses and the plight of pit ponies deserve a book of their own. The same is true about the struggle to win rights for birds, provide protection for performing animals, tackle hunting, and many other welfare issues. The RSPCA's work to help animals during the two world wars that scarred the twentieth century is equally fascinating. Once again the inspectorate was to the fore helping animals in time of trouble as well as peace. (The bibliography lists some of the excellent books on these subjects which have been consulted in preparing this brief summary of the RSPCA's early years.)

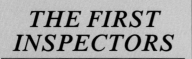

THE FIRST INSPECTORS

What kind of men were these forerunners of today's inspectorate? Many were former police officers. A recruitment advertisement from 1856 required familiarity with police court practices and 'an ability for conducting prosecutions'. By then the constables were equipped with uniforms: frock coats, dark green trousers, and hats similar to the police.

The 1856 rule book shows they had to submit a written report of each day's activities to the superintendent, who assigned the duties for their nine-hour day. The terms of employment were very strict and constables were liable to dismissal for 'unfitness, neglect of duty or misconduct'. Drink was frowned upon and the merest hint of intoxication while on duty could result in instant dismissal. Several constables fell foul of this rule.

THE LAST ENGLISH BULLFIGHT

In 1870, a bullfight was staged in the Agricultural Hall, London, organised as part of a general celebration of Spanish 'culture'. The promoters promised there would be no

A spread from the RSPCA's official journal. According to a poll conducted by the Spanish Ministry of Culture, 53.5 per cent of Spaniards are opposed to bull-fighting.

bloodshed. The bulls were reportedly young and docile while the matadors were old and lethargic, and the crowd soon grew bored of the tame antics and started howling for blood. The matadors tried to liven things up by peppering the bulls with spears and spikes. They succeeded in enraging the bulls and also John Colam, the current Secretary of the RSPCA, who leapt into the ring

and, with the help of some of the society's inspectors, succeeded in stopping the fight.

This brave move was hugely unpopular with the bloodthirsty crowd and provoked some rough resistance. Afterwards Colam was offered a reward by the society but he directed that the money should go to a pension fund for ageing inspectors.

Campaign *RSPCA*

Firebull fiestas
These fiestas take place along the Mediterranean coast. The one held in Segorbe, near Valencia is typical. A ball of pitch or tar is fixed to the end of a bull's horns and ignited. The bull is then driven through the town shedding bits of burning tar. Sparks burn its eyes, head, neck and shoulders in the process.

In other fiestas, spears and darts are used. At the Toro de San Juan fiesta, held in Coria each June, a bull is chased through the streets for some hours whilst long metal darts are blown at it. The bull ends its run in the town square where banderillas and other sharp objects are jabbed into it before being shot.

In other parts of the country 'fiestas' involve cockerels being hacked to death, chickens having their heads ripped off, bull spearing, cow beating and goats being thrown from buildings. In the Zamora village of Manganeses de la Polverosa a goat is paraded and thrown from the church bell tower, although in response to national and international pressure the falling animal is now caught in a tarpaulin.

Banning bullfighting "would be like banning the changing of the guard".

Cultural torture

Every year in Europe, 30,000 bulls are tortured and killed in the name of sport and tradition. Few die swiftly. With world attention already focusing on the Olympics in Barcelona, the RSPCA is determined that attention also be drawn to a far less glorious sport ... bullfighting. *Yolanda Brooks reports ...*

Banning bullfighting, in the recent words of one Spanish government official "would be like banning the changing of the guard in London. It would attack the very heart of the Spanish people. We couldn't allow it."

Furthermore, pro-bullfighters say that international pressure from foreign animal welfare groups and MEPs to ban the blood sport is unacceptable interference rep-resentative of cultural imperialism. But the real reason for the continued existence of the blood sport could be money. Overall ticket sales for bullfights in Spain are worth approximately £170 million and have created a handful of matador millionaires.

Each year an estimated 20 million spec-tators attend bullfights in Spain. Attendance figures are substantially boosted by tourists in holiday areas.

Death in the ring
The cruelty extends far beyond what the spectators see in the ring. It begins during the selection for the 'feisty' bulls known as bravos. The bulls are provoked with wooden poles and the ones that react are destined for the bullring. This is where the real torture begins.

Before confrontation with the matador, the bull is housed in a dark box. When it enters the ring the matador's assistants, called toreadors, use red capes in a series of passes to confuse and exhaust the bull. Picadors on horseback use lances to pierce its neck and shoulder muscles. The bull's neck is also

speared with 3ft-long metal-tipped band-erilleras which remain embedded. With its weakened muscles the bull cannot lift its head and appears as if it is about to charge.

At this point the matador enters for this most unequal of battles. The RSPCA's chief veterinary officer David Wilkins, who has witnessed several bullfights says: "It has been claimed that these bulls have been trained to be hyper-aggressive and their one intention on entering the bullring is to charge and kill whoever is in sight.

"In my opinion, the length of time that the bull spends in the ring, together with the injuries done to it, are sufficient for its natural aggression to be replaced by bewilderment and for it to experience both pain and terror."

Once the matador has finished the 'preening' rituals, he will stab the bull with a slightly curved sword, hoping to hit an important blood vessel or the heart. In one bullfight in Sant Feliu de Guixols, Mr Wilkins saw a novice matador make five attempts to kill a bull. The novice then tried to cut the spinal cord and six attempts were made to place the sword in the right spot. The bull was still stumbling on its knees before someone came and put it out of its misery.

Plight of the horses
The suffering of the bull has been well documented, but the plight of the horses sometimes ridden by the picadors is less well known. The horses are often injured during

the bouts and many are just stitched up and sent into the ring again.

In the same stadium, Mr Wilkins saw horses which were sent back into the ring before their wounds had healed. "One of the horses I examined was lame, yet it was still used in the ring. These horses were just expendable and treated with utter callousness," he said.

Bullfights are also traditional in Portugal. Here the wounded bull is not killed in the arena where the fight is conducted on horseback, but slaughtered afterwards in accordance with a law introduced about 50 years ago. In the south of France, Spanish-style bullfighting occurs in areas where it is traditional and efforts have been made in recent years to increase the audience for bullfights.

Blood fiestas
In Spain, bulls are not the only animals tortured for entertainment, others are used in the blood fiestas. Some of these celebrate religious festivals such as saints' days, some celebrate local superstitions and events, and not all involve cruelty.

The Spanish animal welfare organisation, the Federacion Espanola De Sociedades Protectoras De Animales Y Plantas has listed over 100 blood fiestas involving cruelty that take place throughout Spain. But there may be many more.

But despite international condemnation, the Spanish government has shown a reluctance to end these cruel practices, although it is hoped that a draft national animal protection law tabled in the autumn will be adopted this year. In the meantime five regions within Spain have made positive steps and introduced some animal welfare legislation. In Catalonia – the first to do so – the law bans most fiestas and restricts the places where bullfights can be held.

This summer the RSPCA will be working to promote change within Spain supporting Spanish animal welfare groups. There is already considerable support within the country for the banning of blood fiestas and bullfights – a poll conducted by the Spanish Ministry of Culture showed 53.5 per cent of Spaniards opposed bullfighting. RSPCA will be working on a campaign highlighting the cruelty involved in and bullfighting with other animal organisations.

Although the European Community will not legislate on this subject, the European Parliament's all-party Intergroup on Animal Welfare has recently tabled a motion calling on countries where so-called 'tradit-ional events involving cruelty take place to introduce laws banning the use of animals.

You can help! Turn to Action Line on page 29

A blood fiesta participant holds aloft his 'prize'

Animal Life

Cruelty to animals? These were used on our inspectors.

One chilly November evening Bob Phillips' answered a knock on his front door.

Seconds later, he was fighting off a vicious attack by a man armed with a large spanner.

The reason for the assault? He was an RSPCA Inspector.

His assailant? A dog-owner whose house he had visited earlier that day investigating a cruelty complaint.

Although he did escape injury this time, Bob Phillips knows full well that it could happen again.

Because he is not the first of our Inspectors to be attacked.

And, sadly, he's not likely to be the last.

It's the job of an RSPCA Inspector to respond to reports of cruelty to animals.

While making determined efforts to prevent cruelty in the first place.

When an Inspector follows up a report of ill-treatment, he has no idea of what he's likely to face.

Relief? Guilt? Anger?

Will he get verbal abuse or, as in Inspector Jim Smith's' case, a shotgun thrust into his ribs?

Our Officers never know. They're not psychic, they're human.

And they've been assaulted with a variety of weapons that would not be out of place in Scotland Yard's infamous Black Museum.

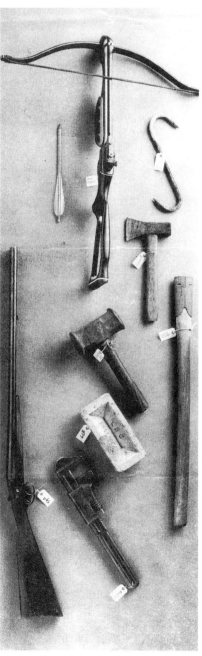

Yet they carry on because their first duty is to animals.

Rabbits that have been stabbed. Cats that have been maimed. Dogs that have been starved or beaten to death.

Last year the RSPCA received over a million calls for help.

Unfortunately we only have 287 Inspectors. We need to increase that number to 300.

But, like most things in life, it will take money. A lot of it.

The total cost of training, equipping and keeping one new Inspector on the road for the first year is £31,088.

After that it costs us £7 an hour to keep him, or her, on active duty.

We do our best, it's true, but we could do far more.

We could investigate more cases, protect more animals, prevent more deaths.

We need your help. Please fill in the coupon.

Because we need to show those people who mistreat, torture and kill animals that we too have a weapon.

A very powerful one.

Your support.

THE RSPCA TODAY

Sadly there is still a desperate need for the RSPCA's services. True, many advances have been made. Some of the horrors of the Victorian age have been stamped out, and there are now many laws providing greater protection. However, the passage of time has brought new threats and ways of exploiting animals. Factory farming, transgenic animals, long-distance transport, risks from pollution...the list goes on. The problems are formidable.

How does the RSPCA meet this enormous challenge? The answer is only through the generosity and support of caring people. The RSPCA is a charity, entirely reliant on voluntary donations, a fact sometimes forgotten. Possibly, because the RSPCA has been around for so long, it has become part of the fabric of our society. People take it for granted. Some think it is a state-funded service like the police, an impression perhaps created by the uniformed inspectorate. Complainants are occasionally heard demanding, like a disgruntled tax-payer, why the RSPCA does not give an even better service. The answer is simple: the RSPCA does the very best it can with the limited resources at its disposal. It copes with an enormous workload in the face of almost overwhelming odds.

The first point to make clear is that the RSPCA cares for *all* animals. It is a champion and watchdog for every living species. The RSPCA's work with pet animals is often what comes first to mind, however. It looks after thousands of abused and abandoned cats, dogs and

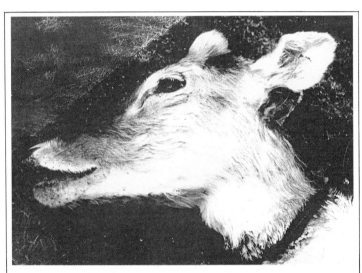

Killed by a legal loophole.

When an animal gets caught in a snare a strong, slim wire draws tight around its body.

The animal realises that it's trapped and panics.

It thrashes and strains against the dead weight of the snare's anchor stake.

The more it struggles, the tighter the snare becomes.

Eventually it will die.

Most snares are laid for rabbits and foxes.

But a snare is just a piece of twisted wire, it cannot tell the difference between its intended prey and other animals.

Dogs, cats, badgers, hedgehogs and even deer are regularly caught in snares.

It is illegal to deliberately trap any of these animals, but the trappers escape prosecution because they are allegedly only trying to trap "vermin".

The snare is, quite simply, a loophole in the law.

But from 14th February all that could change.

On that date a Private Member's Bill aimed at protecting our wildlife from hunters and trappers comes before Parliament.

It needs the support of 100 MPs to progress.

You can help make your MP one of them.

Phone the RSPCA now on 0800 400 478 and we will send you an action pack.

Because the law needs tightening, not the snares.

Support the Bill to protect our wildlife. (RSPCA)

other companion animals every year. But the society works with equal energy to help wildlife. For example the RSPCA's recent project to save North Sea seals decimated by a deadly virus. Or the all too frequent clean-up operations needed to help oil spill victims. Farm animals are another major concern. The society is constantly striving to improve the conditions in which livestock are kept. And last, but not least, the RSPCA campaigns for improvements in the treatment of animals used for experimental purposes. The society's work in this area recently hit the headlines when it stepped in to help rehome hundreds of beagles destined for research laboratories.

How, then, does the RSPCA achieve its declared aims of preventing cruelty and promoting kindness? The contribution of the Special Operations Unit has already been well documented. The work of their colleagues, the uniformed inspectorate, is examined in the next chapter. If inspectors are the 'fire-fight-ers' then the branches are the 'pump-primers': the thousands of voluntary workers who make up their membership are the backbone of the society.

There are 207 branches located in towns and villages throughout England and Wales, each of which is separately registered with the Charity Commissioners. The members generously devote their time, money and energy to animal welfare activities. Many branches run their own charity shops, animal homes, clinics, or welfare centres, and help to find new owners for thousands of unwanted animals every year. Others assist the needy with veterinary bills or organise cheap neutering schemes to prevent the production of unwanted pets. Members also play a vital role at grass-roots level mobilising support for RSPCA campaigns and helping to spread the animal welfare message.

In addition to the fifty branch-run animal homes, thirty-four clinics and twenty-four animal welfare centres, the RSPCA operates six headquarters-run

This fox was held captive and then stabbed to death.

animal homes and six clinics, and three centrally funded national animal hospitals. The hospitals, two in London and one in Birmingham, provide modern surgical and clinical facilities plus emergency ambulance services. A dog shot with a crossbow bolt, and another doused in fuel and set on fire, were two recent casualties benefiting from their life-saving services. Open twenty-four hours a day, the hospitals provide subsidised care for animals that might otherwise go untreated. Although cats and dogs account for the bulk of animals passing through the RSPCA's homes, they come in all shapes and sizes. Finding a new owner for a pot-bellied pig or a python may sound a tall order – but it is all in a day's work for the RSPCA.

Who is in charge of all this work? The RSPCA's governing body is made up of a council of twenty-five voluntary, unpaid members. Fifteen are elected by the national membership and ten by branch committees to represent the regions. Up to three more members may be co-opted by the council for their specialist knowledge. The council determines the policies, which, on issues ranging from support for dog registration to opposition to hunting, are spelled out in a manual available on request.

Overall responsibility for running the RSPCA, and implementing council policies, lies with the Director General who is based at the society's headquarters in Horsham. This is also home to the RSPCA's technical departments which provide the scientific evidence and intellectual weight the RSPCA depends upon to make its voice heard and respected.

The Farm Animals Department campaigns against any farming methods which cause unacceptable distress. Examples are plentiful: hens kept in battery cages too small to let them stretch their wings, or pigs forced to give birth in farrowing crates that restrict movement. Winning a ban in the UK on the crate system for rearing calves was a recent breakthrough. Legislation to phase out sow stalls in which the animals can be tethered and chained is another victory.

It is the charity's proud claim that almost every piece of animal welfare legislation enacted has been passed largely as a result of pressure from the RSPCA. The Parliamentary Department works closely with MPs of all parties to win new, or extend existing animal protection laws. However, there is little cause for celebration if the cruelty is merely transferred to another location, which is what has happened, for instance, with veal production. Consumers have been horrified to discover that British calves can be exported for rearing in crates on the continent where the practice has not been banned. Other

Left: A man from Bath smashed one puppy's head in with a club hammer. When his girlfriend walked out on him a week later, he killed the other three the same way after she refused to come back. An inspector obtained a confession and stood over Mr D as he dug the puppies up from their garden grave. He was sentenced to four months in prison and banned for life from keeping a cat or dog.

Below: One of the sheep found by RSPCA inspectors in a field near Taunton. Several were in this pitiful condition, while others nearby lay dead and dying, pecked at by carrion crows. The company responsible was fined £2,000.

examples abound of cruelty permitted in Europe that would be prosecuted in Britain.

That is why the RSPCA also devotes considerable energy to lobbying for European reforms. The society was a founder member of, and is the driving force behind, Eurogroup for Animal Welfare, which is an alliance of animal welfare groups across the Community. As the influence of the European Community increases the RSPCA's campaigns will inevitably focus more and more on the European political institutions. Wildlife protection is another area where European, rather than domestic, legislation will bring the most benefits.

Campaigns against the fur trade and the import of wild birds are two issues on which the RSPCA's Wildlife Department has been to the fore. The department's concerns extend to the protection of animals in captivity as well as in the wild: conditions for exotic animals in zoos and circuses are closely monitored.

Scientific research and reports are important but the RSPCA's technical staff are not just a bunch of 'boffins'. Wildlife Officers frequently roll up their sleeves and help out with problems such as cleaning oiled birds or saving seals. When the Kuwaiti government wanted help with Gulf War wildlife victims an RSPCA Wildlife Officer led the mercy mission, using sophisticated cleaning techniques pioneered at the RSPCA's Wildlife Field Unit in Somerset. This provides a hospital facility for treating and rearing wild animals, with the aim of teaching them to fend for themselves so they can be returned to the wild. Plans are already under way to build a similar facility in Norfolk.

The plight of laboratory animals raises passions faster than almost any other issue. The RSPCA's ultimate aim is an end to the need for any animal experimentation. It is totally opposed to all experiments or procedures which cause pain, suffering or distress. The mission of the RSPCA's Research Animals Department is to implement

A dog shot through with a crossbow bolt.

the three Rs. That is, to achieve: a *reduction* in the number of animals used for experiments; a *refinement* of scientific procedures to alleviate suffering; and the *replacement* of experimental animals with other techniques such as tissue culture or computer modelling.

Throughout the RSPCA's history, education has been a powerful weapon in the fight against cruelty. The Education Department promotes animal welfare issues at both the school and adult levels of the education system, their Education Officers spreading the message throughout England and Wales. Targeting the young ensures the RSPCA's aims will be taken to heart by future generations and a thriving junior membership scheme is one sign of the popularity of the RSPCA's work with youngsters. Many take advantage of projects like organised 'animal treks' or courses at the RSPCA's wildlife sanctuary and field centre in Sussex.

The influence of the RSPCA ranges far and wide. Through its International Department it provides practical aid such as veterinary drugs and equipment, professional advice and support to over 150 affiliated societies. The Inter-

This baby seal was one of the victims of the virus that decimated the North Sea seal populations towards the end of the last decade.

national Department also lobbies foreign governments to take action to end cruelties perpetrated on their soil.

The growth of the RSPCA from a handful of reformers to a national institution with a worldwide reputation is cause for pride. But there is no cause for complacency. There is still much to be done. Throughout the years the RSPCA has remained steadfast in its protection and defence of animals from exploitation and abuse. As it heads towards the twenty-first century there are new cruelties to combat and campaigns to be won. Only with the continuing support of a generous public can the RSPCA hope to meet the challenges.

Right: From time to time the RSPCA inspectorate seconds staff to help train the workforce of overseas animal welfare societies.

Below: The RSPCA is trying to promote the better care of draught animals on the Indian sub-continent.

CHAPTER SIXTEEN

THE THIN BLUE LINE

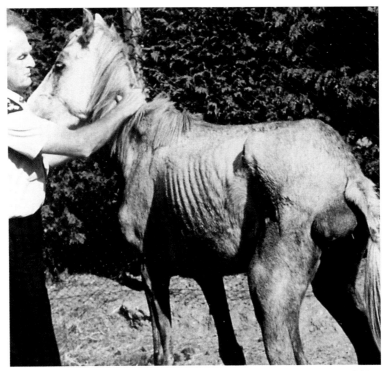

This emaciated grey horse was starved by a callous owner.

In the early hours of the morning a storm is raging. Inside the house all is quiet, the occupants long since gone to bed. Suddenly a telephone-call shatters the silence. A sleepy inspector grabs the phone and listens intently to the voice on the other end. 'Right, got that. I'm on my way,' she mutters, sliding out of bed. Her husband turns over and goes back to sleep.

The inspector dresses quickly and stealthily leaves the house. Inside the van she consults a map, then drives off into the fury of the storm. The rain lashing down makes it hard to see, even with the windscreen wipers on fast speed. Soon she is on a deserted country road. At last the headlights pick out the forlorn shape of an animal huddled beside the road: a badger, unconscious and bleeding profusely. The inspector parks, opens the van and spreads out a blanket. Gently she lifts the animal into the back of the van, carefully secures it, then retraces her route. She remembers passing a telephone-box.

Five minutes later she is in the kiosk fumbling for change. The RSPCA Duty Officer answers promptly.

'Right, I've got the badger. It's in a

143

Right: The RSPCA's seven-month inspectorate training course involves learning mountain rescue techniques.

photo: Tamara Gray

Below: An inspector tends to a horse so weak from neglect that it is unable even to lift its head.

bad way. Can you ring the veterinary surgeon?'

The officer replies, 'Okay, I'll tell him to open up for you.'

The vet is already waiting when she pulls into the practice car park. 'Hit by a car,' she explains tersely. 'We got an anonymous call reporting the location.'

Together they carry the badger into the surgery. The vet decides to operate immediately. Forty-five minutes later it is all over, the badger made comfortable in one of the holding cages. Only time will tell whether the animal will pull through. The inspector makes her weary way home.

There is nothing special about a call-out like that. RSPCA inspectors are on stand-by every hour of the day or night to help animals in distress. It may be a traffic accident, or it could be an animal used as a punch-bag by some mindless drunk after the pubs have shut.

Whatever the call RSPCA inspectors must be ready to use all their skills to do what seems best for the animal involved. That is why the training an inspector receives – an intensive seven-month course – is so important. The competition for the job is intense and new inspectors are selected from hundreds of applicants from all walks of life. Some may have already worked with animals, perhaps as an ambulance driver, farm-hand or kennel-maid. For others it is all new. They may be fresh out of the forces or turning their backs on a lucrative career. What unites them is an overriding commitment to animal welfare. Given the RSPCA's law-enforcement role (it is the biggest private prosecution agency in the land) it is not surprising that a large part of the training concentrates on legal matters.

But the job of an RSPCA inspector is not just about prosecuting people for cruelty. The priority is to prevent it. A good inspector is a bit like a social worker. People not pets cause problems, so you have to know how to handle them. They may be pensioners, unable to fend for themselves, let alone their

pets. A friendly word of advice may do the trick, or the inspector may call in the social services to help out. Or perhaps the children look poorly. Bad pet owners can also make poor parents. Indeed there is a growing body of research that suggests animal abuse and child abuse often go hand in hand. As already noted, the NSPCC sprang from the roots of the animal welfare movement and the links between child and animal welfare have remained close. An inspector concerned about the occupants of any premises visited while investigating a complaint will tip off the appropriate authorities.

Obviously the inspectors have to learn practical animal handling skills. An irate swan snagged on fishing tackle may not take too kindly to being caught even if it is for its own good. Since animals have an uncanny knack of getting stranded in all kinds of difficult places the inspectors learn a variety of rescue skills: tree-climbing, mountain rescue and boat-handling are just some of the specialist courses they attend. When suspended over the side of a cliff with a sheer drop 200 feet to the rocky shore below, it helps to know how to abseil. Studying is alternated with field postings. Trainees spend twelve weeks 'shadowing' an experienced inspector – six weeks in a rural station and six in a city.

After graduating, the new inspectors could be posted anywhere in the country. But even that intensive training cannot fully prepare an inspector for the terrible cruelty they will then confront as their daily routine. A collie hanging by its neck from a tree in a cemetery. The dog had been beaten and burned before being strung up to die. Puppies clubbed to death then flushed down the sewer. A sore-infested horse starved for three months and scarcely able to stand. A cat doused in petrol by two schoolboys and set on fire, or a fox held captive and stabbed to death.

Those cases were chosen at random from the RSPCA's cruelty files. Sadly

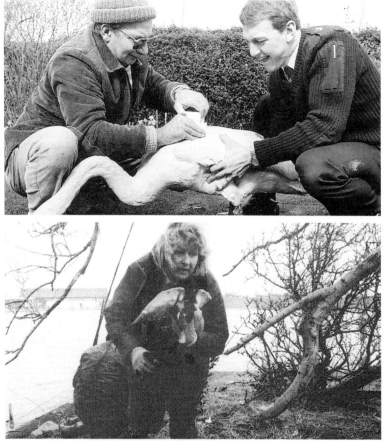

Top: Inspector Alan Fisher binds up a swan's broken wing.
photo: *Lynn News*

Centre: Inspector Janet Brassington rescues an oil-covered mallard from an island at Portishead's seafront lake.
photo: Barry Stewart, *Bristol Evening Post*

Bottom: This dog was beaten and burned before being strung up to die.

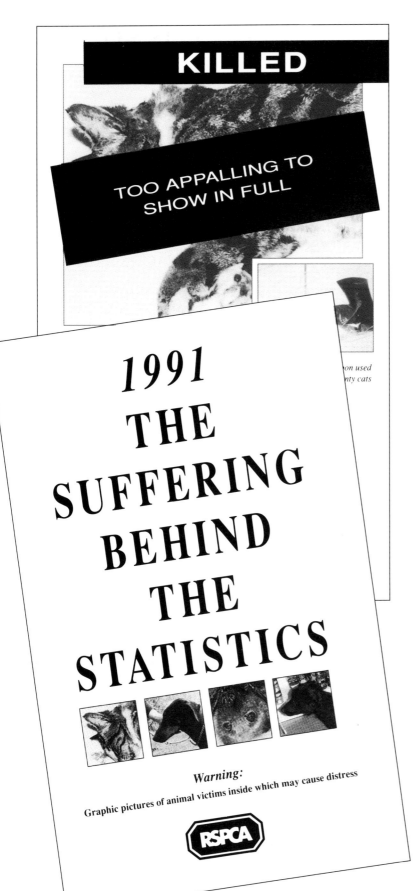

KILLED

TOO APPALLING TO SHOW IN FULL

...on used
...ty cats

1991
THE
SUFFERING
BEHIND
THE
STATISTICS

Warning:
Graphic pictures of animal victims inside which may cause distress

RSPCA

they are not isolated incidents.

People are sometimes surprised by the size of the force confronting this tidal wave of animal abuse. Truly the thin blue line, with fewer than 300 inspectors to cover the whole of England and Wales. The RSPCA is therefore really at full stretch trying to cope with over a million phone-calls for assistance every year. The public are the RSPCA's eyes and ears. Inspectors rely on them to report animals in difficulty. So what happens when somebody makes a call for help?

For operational purposes the RSPCA is divided up into ten regions under the direction of a regional manager. Within the region there may be three or more group communication centres (GCCs) to which the first call for help is directed. These centres are the control base for a group of between five and eleven inspectors under a chief inspector or superintendent. Each inspector has his or her own patch to patrol and works on a rota to provide day and night cover all year long.

The GCC operator will log the details of the call and then pass it on to the appropriate inspector. Their vans are fitted with two-way radios so they can be contacted immediately. If the call is urgent the inspector will respond at once, racing to the scene of a cow drowning in a slurry pit or a beached seal. They can also summon help from the other emergency services. Less urgent calls are handled as soon as they can be fitted into a hectic schedule.

Every effort is made to report back to the original informant on any action taken. Even anonymous calls must be investigated. The RSPCA cannot ignore a complaint. In all cases complaints are dealt with in strict confidence, names never being divulged without permission.

In serious cases of animal abuse the RSPCA may decide to prosecute. Not because the society enjoys 'punishing' people, although prosecutions can serve as a deterrent to other offenders, but primarily to get a ban stopping the defendant from keeping animals. That way animals at risk can be removed and the offender prevented from causing further suffering.

Such cases may require the inspector to employ some sleuthing skills since suspects usually attempt to cover up their wrongdoing. They will have to be interviewed, statements taken, witnesses found, and corroborating evidence obtained. The inspector will almost certainly need veterinary assistance to substantiate a charge that suffering has been caused. Once all the facts have been assembled the 'case' will be reported to RSPCA headquarters for further action.

It is then assigned to one of the four specially trained legal chief superintendents who will decide whether or not to prosecute. If they sanction a prosecution then the inspector who originated the case is instructed to 'lay information' with the local magistrates' clerk who will then issue a summons. A local solicitor will be briefed and instructed to act on the RSPCA's behalf. When the case comes to court the inspector will probably be called as one of the witnesses.

There are dozens of animal protection laws but the principal weapon for tackling cruelty cases is the 1911 Protection of Animals Act which prohibits all kinds of ill-treatment of animals. Anyone, whether the owner or not, who permits an animal to suffer unnecessarily can be held to have acted unlawfully and is subject to punishment. The maximum penalties under this legislation are a £2,000 fine and/or up to six months in prison. In some of the most horrific cruelty cases, like bludgeoning a dog to death, or torturing a cat, some observers believe offenders get off lightly.

One of the most frustrating omissions in the 1911 Act is the exclusion of wild animals. The Act only applies to captive or domestic animals. There is therefore nothing to stop someone from using a wild animal, for example a hedgehog, as

a football. After kicking it about a bit they can then beat it to death with a broom. And if anybody protests – no problem. They will get off scot-free. That case is not fictitious. The RSPCA prosecuted the offender but the case was thrown out by the courts because the creature was not regarded as captive, and was consequently not legally protected.

The RSPCA is working continuously to change, amend or improve animal welfare legislation and threw its weight behind a private member's bill earlier this year (1992) to win greater protection for Britain's wild mammals.

The Wild Mammals (Protection) Bill, introduced by MP Kevin McNamara, sought to make it an offence to cause unnecessary suffering to a wild mammal. Fox-hunting, hare-coursing, stag-hunting and the snaring and baiting of wild mammals would have been banned by the bill. The RSPCA published a series of powerful newspaper advertisements with stark slogans conveying the horrors of hunting: 'Huntsmen would never kill a stag in cold blood. They prefer it warm,' and 'Hunts start at eleven because a fox runs better after it has digested its breakfast. Two hours later they rip out its digestive system.'

Left: A leaflet from the 1991 campaign details the case of two young men from Worcester who over two months snatched twenty pet cats off the streets, took them to wasteland and killed them with axes and iron bars. Both were given six months detention.

In the eighteenth century, foxes had to be imported from the continent when numbers dropped too low for the sport to continue. In the present day, many hunts maintain artificial earths to ensure a sufficient supply of foxes for hunting through the season.

Thousands of people rang a special hotline number to obtain action packs supporting the campaign and a survey showed that eighty per cent of the population were opposed to fox-hunting. The pro-field sports lobby also moved into top gear to rally opposition to the bill which they described as an attack on traditional country pursuits. There was massive media coverage of the arguments on both sides in the run-up to February 14 when the Bill came before Parliament.

MPs were allowed a free vote and campaign supporters almost won the day. Sadly, however, the Bill was defeated by just twelve votes: 187 MPs voted against with 175 in favour. The RSPCA has vowed it will continue in its efforts to win greater protection for wild mammals and believes it is not a question of if, but when hunting will be banned.

In the interim the society has to work within the limitations of existing legislation, a fact not always appreciated by the public. A common complaint concerns stray animals. Why will the RSPCA not come and pick up a dog seen roaming the streets? The simple answer is that the law prevents it. Finders are required to take a stray to the police, or local authority dog warden, where it can be formally reported and recorded. Only once the legal formalities are completed can the animal be signed over to the RSPCA's care. The RSPCA does not set out to be unhelpful or unco-operative, but like everybody else it has to abide by the law.

Inspectors do not just wait for complaints to come in. As the name suggests their role is to go out and see for themselves that all is well. They regularly visit and 'inspect' any establishment where animals are kept, from pet shops to zoos, and breeding to boarding kennels. They can be seen on duty at pet shows or market days; indeed they are liable to appear anywhere animals are to be found.

A considerable part of inspectors' time is spent in the familiar white vans, racing from one call to another. Inside the van they carry the tools of the trade, which include different-sized carrying cages for transporting animals, since it is obviously important to keep animals secure when on the move. One unfortunate inspector got caught out by a contortionist python which escaped and slithered behind the door panels. It was several days before it re-emerged.

Apart from obvious items like ropes there are more esoteric pieces of equipment like graspers and swan-hooks, which do as their names imply. Graspers are used to capture and hold an animal. They can be extended by adding rods to pluck an animal to safety from a considerable height. Unexpected items are the riot shield and crash helmet with which inspectors are now issued, a necessary response to the growing problem of dangerous dogs. They provide vital protection on police raids where inspectors can be called in to remove any dangerous animals that may be present.

Any inspector will agree that the worst part of the job is putting down an animal. It may be an injured animal that needs to be put out of its misery, or it could be a vicious dog that must be destroyed. Whatever the cause no inspector likes having to destroy animals, but they are trained and equipped to do so humanely and efficiently.

To sum up, an RSPCA inspector has to be a jack-of-all-trades: a strange mixture of police officer, veterinary nurse, lawyer, animal psychologist and counsellor. In between juggling their direct animal welfare responsibilities they are also expected to work closely with other staff and volunteers to promote fund-raising, campaigns and other concerns. Inspectors need almost superhuman qualities if they are to achieve the RSPCA's objectives – to prevent cruelty and promote kindness to all animals.

GETTING INVOLVED

WORKLOAD

This book has lifted the lid on the under-cover activities of the RSPCA, and has also provided a brief sketch of the charity's day-to-day workload. The enormous demands are spelled out in the figures below.

In 1991 the RSPCA's inspectorate received 1,156,696 telephone calls for assistance.

They investigated 86,531 complaints.

They obtained 2,718 convictions.

They inspected 16,225 establishments.

And they rescued 2,605 animals ranging from cats stuck up trees to sheep stranded on cliff faces.

The animal homes, hospitals and clinics were equally busy. In 1991 they handled 202,804 cases requiring treatment and found new homes for 95,037 unwanted animals; 93,054 animals had to be humanely destroyed.

JOINING THE BATTLE AGAINST CRUELTY

Fighting cruelty and promoting kindness is a full-time battle and the RSPCA needs all the recruits it can get to help in this work. For anybody interested there are a number of ways to get involved.

You can become an annual or life-time member of the society. It costs £15 a year for individual membership, £20 for joint (husband and wife) and £9 for affiliated membership (which carries no voting rights). Further details can be obtained from the Membership Department at RSPCA headquarters.

Or how about joining your local branch? Volunteers are always needed to help with fund-raising and other practical activities. Contact the Branches Department at headquarters to find out the Secretary of your nearest branch.

Young people aged between seven and seventeen can join the RSPCA's junior membership scheme which costs just £4.50 a year. Members get sent a badge, certificate and passbook, plus magazine six times a year. They also get the opportunity to take part in practical activities like Animal Trek holidays and other projects.

REPORTING CRUELTY

Of course one of the most important ways to help the RSPCA is by reporting suspected cases of cruelty. You should also contact the RSPCA immediately to

This badger is unable to defend itself against the terriers because it is being held immobile by its tail.

enlist help for animals in trouble. The telephone number of the nearest inspectorate centre can be found in the telephone directory under Royal Society for the Prevention of Cruelty to Animals. The Appendix gives further information on how the RSPCA is structured plus details of regional branches.

If you see or learn of cases of cruelty there are certain things you can do which will help to ensure a better chance of stopping it and bringing the culprits responsible to justice. First, if the cruelty is something that can be ended immediately, for example a horse or dog being beaten unmercifully before your eyes, then try to stop it. But only intervene if it is safe to do so. The type of person liable to mistreat an animal in this way is also perfectly capable of turning on humans. A camera will seldom be readily to hand but if you do have one available then start snapping. Photographs are very useful evidence.

Say your suspicions are aroused by something like men spotted digging in the countryside with terriers in attendance. It crosses your mind they might be badger-diggers. Get down as much useful evidence as possible. For instance

if there are cars parked nearby make a note of the registration numbers. The more detective work you can do at the initial stages the more chance an inspector has to follow up successfully.

When you do phone the RSPCA be ready to give as much of the following information as you have available:

- **your name, address and telephone number (all complaints are treated in strict confidence but this information is needed for record purposes and enables the inspector to inform you of the result of an investigation);**
- **the name and address of the subject of the complaint;**
- **the date, time and place of the offence;**
- **the names and addresses of any other witnesses.**

You should then give a detailed factual account of what you have seen and say if you are prepared to testify in a court of law.

Some people are frightened of getting involved in legal proceedings but hopefully anybody who feels strongly enough to report a case is also prepared to do everything needed to set the matter right and bring the offender to justice.

PUTTING THE MESSAGE ACROSS

One of the easiest ways to help the RSPCA is by supporting its campaigns and helping to spread the message. If politicians are convinced that enough people care about something they will take notice. Whether at local, national or European level, no elected representative readily ignores public opinion.

The simplest way of making your views heard is by writing a letter. You may think you are unable to express yourself well enough, or you will not be taken seriously. Nonsense! Every letter that goes unwritten is an opportunity missed. The fact is that, as all newspaper editors and elected officials know, very few people bother to put pen to paper. So when they do get a letter it leaves an impression. It is assumed to represent the views of the proverbial silent majority.

The following guidelines should help to ensure your letter achieves maximum impact.

1. **Remember the golden rule, KISS, which stands for keep it short and simple. Long rambling letters are more likely to be thrown away than a clear, concise one.**
2. **Make your letter personal. No matter how much reference material you use, put it into your own words. A personally written letter has much more impact than a mass-produced copy.**
3. **Be polite. However incensed you are by the recipient's apparent indifference or opposition to date do not get abusive. Even politicians have feelings.**
4. **Spell out what you want the recipients to do. For example there may be some legislation you want them to back or an Early Day Motion to sign. Give them full details.**
5. **Request an answer to your letter. Ask for a detailed statement of opinions and how the recipient intends to deal with the matter. As your elected representatives they owe you a reply.**
6. **Lastly, when a representative takes action it is worth writing again. Either to thank them or express disappointment if they have failed to back the cause.**

The above guidelines also apply if you are writing to a newspaper. Your views could have even more impact because they will be seen by the publication's many other readers. Do remember that animals have no say in determining what happens to them. Your voice could make the difference.

In 1991 the RSPCA stepped in to help rehome hundreds of beagles from the bankrupt Perrycroft breeding establishment in Worcestershire. The beagles were destined for research laboratories in Europe.

photo: Tamara Gray

Join the

RSPCA

*Caring, campaigning
and committed to
animal welfare*

PUBLICATIONS

The RSPCA produces a wide range of posters, leaflets, booklets and other material on animal welfare subjects. Want to find out how to care for your pets? Why the RSPCA opposes snaring? Where to buy 'cruelty-free' cosmetics? You can obtain a leaflet listing all the material on subjects like these, and others, produced by the RSPCA from the Publications Department at headquarters.

REMEMBER THE RSPCA

Last year's bill for the fight against cruelty was £33 million. Every penny of that sum has to be raised from the donations of caring people.

There are a variety of ways you can donate money to the RSPCA to help fund its vital work. One of the newest is payroll giving. Anybody who receives their salary or wages under PAYE can sign up to donate in this way. The competition for charitable donations is getting harder and harder, yet for the RSPCA the need is greater and greater. Continuous committed giving is even more important than occasional gifts.

Another way you can help is by remembering the RSPCA in your will. Legacies are a vital lifeline, with approximately £18 million reaching the RSPCA through wills in 1991. The society has an information pack and leaflet providing information on how to make a will. Copies can be obtained from the Legacy Officer at headquarters.

The address for any headquarters correspondence is: RSPCA, Causeway, Horsham, Sussex RH12 1HG.

The RSPCA Regional Structure: Who Does What

REGIONAL HEADQUARTERS

Every one of the RSPCA's ten regions in England and Wales has a strategically placed regional headquarters, which is the focal point for overall supervision and administration of RSPCA services, inspectorate and branches in the region.

INSPECTORS

The RSPCA inspectorate is the largest non-government law enforcement agency in the country. Its expertise in animal welfare legislation is acknowledged by the police, who often call in the RSPCA inspectors on animal-related cases. The inspectorate staff also offer help and advice on all animal welfare matters.

BRANCHES

There are 207 branches of the RSPCA located throughout England and Wales, all staffed by volunteers who devote their time and energy to running animal homes, clinics and welfare centres, operating rescue and re-homing programmes and fund-raising by flag days, special events and charity shops.

GROUP COMMUNICATION CENTRES

Every region is divided into groups, each one of which has a GCC, the first point of contact for people wanting RSPCA help with an animal welfare problem.

The GCC acts as a central 'clearing house' for calls and makes the most efficient use of resources by making radio contact with the RSPCA officer on duty nearest to the incident or advising the caller on where to get veterinary help, or the assistance of other emergency services. GCCs are staffed from 9.00 a.m. to 6.00 p.m. after which calls are re-routed to the RHQ. During the night and at weekends emergency calls are handled by officers on duty within the regions.

EDUCATION OFFICERS

The Education Officer team provides a specialist educational service within each region and for the national Society. Each makes a specific contribution to the Education Department: producing resources for teachers and pupils, liaising with Local Education Authorities and professional bodies and co-ordinating Junior Membership activities.

ANIMAL WELFARE ESTABLISHMENTS

Hospital: Veterinary treatment for both in- and out-patients with a 24-hour emergency service.
Clinic: Veterinary treatment for out-patients. Often open for limited periods – check on opening hours before visiting.
Animal Welfare Centre: Lay advice on the care of animals and facilities for humane destruction.
Home or Shelter: Provision of accommodation for stray or unwanted animals awaiting re-homing, or cruelty victims whose owners are awaiting prosecution.

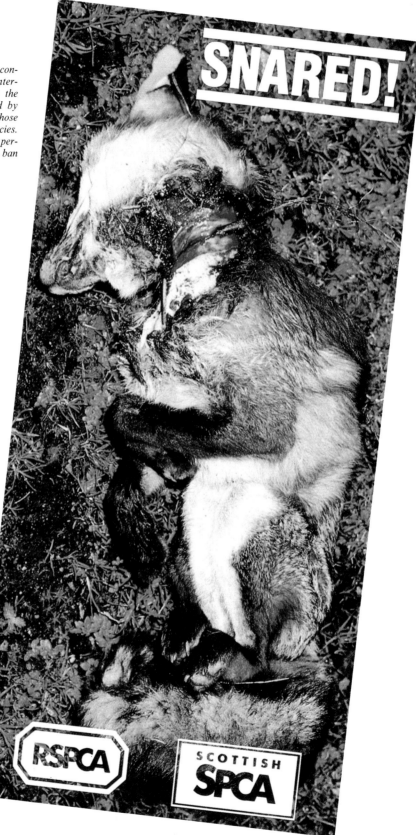

A leaflet from the RSPCA in conjunction with its Scottish counterpart, the SSPCA, detailing the indiscriminate injuries caused by snares. Only a third of those animals caught are 'target' species. Campaigning continues to persuade the Government to ban snares.

Contacting the RSPCA

REGION 1: *THE SOUTH-WEST*

RSPCA Regional Headquarters
Blackhat Lane
Bakers Hill
Exeter EX2 9TA
Tel: 0392 55114
Fax: 0392 218983

Region 1: Group 1
Group Communication Centre:
TRURO
Tel: 0872 223023

Region 1: Group 2
Group Communication Centre:
EXETER
Tel: 0392 55125

Region 1: Group 3
Group Communication Centre:
YEOVIL
Tel: 0935 29096

Region 1: Group 4
Group Communication Centre:
BRISTOL
Tel: 0272 351111

REGION 2: *THE SOUTH CENTRAL*

RSPCA Regional Headquarters
3 Church Close
Andover
Hampshire SP10 1DP
Tel: 0264 323982
Fax: 0264 351764

Region 2: Group 1
Group Communication Centre:
ANDOVER
Tel: 0264 354111

Region 2: Group 2
Group Communication Centre:
READING
Tel: 0734 352066

Region 2: Group 3
Group Communication Centre:
SOUTHAMPTON
Tel: 0703 231440

Region 2: Group 4
Group Communication Centre:
GUILDFORD
Tel: 0483 450282

REGION 3: *THE SOUTH-EAST*

RSPCA Regional Headquarters
93a Week Street
Maidstone
Kent ME14 1QX
Tel: 0622 693675
Fax: 0622 693677

Region 3: Group 1
Group Communication Centre:
BILLINGSHURST
Tel: 0403 784823

Region 3: Group 2
Group Communication Centre:
MAIDSTONE
Tel: 0622 675855

Region 3: Group 3
Group Communication Centre:
CHELMSFORD
Tel: 0245 422202

REGION 4: *THE EAST*

RSPCA Regional Headquarters
Station Road
Thorney
Peterborough
Cambridgeshire PE6 0QE
Tel: 0733 270046
Fax: 0733 270075

Region 4: Group 1
Group Communication Centre:
LINCOLN
Tel: 0522 539977

Region 4: Group 2
Group Communication Centre:
PETERBOROUGH
Tel: 0733 270046

Region 4: Group 3
Group Communication Centre:
NORWICH
Tel: 0603 765500

Region 4: Group 4
Group Communication Centre:
IPSWICH
Tel: 0473 240300

REGION 5: *THE EAST MIDLANDS*

RSPCA Regional Headquarters
190 Scudamore Road
Leicester LE3 1UQ
Tel: 0533 311688
Fax: 0533 320137

Region 5: Group 1
Group Communication Centre:
ILKESTON
Tel: 0602 441114

Region 5: Group 2
Group Communication Centre:
LEICESTER
Tel: 0533 313588

Region 5: Group 3
Group Communication Centre:
OXFORD
Tel: 0865 873006

Region 5: Group 4
Group Communication Centre:
LETCHWORTH
Tel: 0462 482607

REGION 6: *THE WEST MIDLANDS*

RSPCA Regional Headquarters
Wellington Road
Donnington
Telford
Shropshire TF2 8HQ
Tel: 0952 677118
Fax: 0952 677420

Region 6: Group 1
Group Communication Centre:
STAFFORD
Tel: 0785 46642

Region 6: Group 2
Group Communication Centre:
TELFORD
Tel: 0952 677118

Region 6: Group 3
Group Communication Centre:
WORCESTER
Tel: 0905 26504

Region 6: Group 4
Group Communication Centre:
STONELEIGH
Tel: 0203 696713

Region 6: Group 5
Group Communication Centre:
BIRMINGHAM
Tel: 021 428 2242

REGION 7: *THE NORTH-WEST*

RSPCA Regional Headquarters
256–258 Bury New Road
Whitefield
Manchester M25 6QN
Tel: 061 767 9283
Fax: 061 767 9342

Region 7: Group 1
Group Communication Centre:
CHESTER
Tel: 0244 341232

Region 7: Group 2
Group Communication Centre:
MANCHESTER
Tel: 061 767 9281

Region 7: Group 3
Group Communication Centre:
LIVERPOOL
Tel: 051 264 7496

Region 7: Group 4
Group Communication Centre:
PRESTON
Tel: 0772 881570

Region 7: Group 5
Group Communication Centre:
KENDAL
Tel: 0539 729012

REGION 8: *THE NORTH-EAST*

RSPCA Regional Headquarters
66 Armley Road
Leeds LS12 2EJ
Tel: 0532 342102
Fax: 0532 446053

Region 8: Group 1
Group Communication Centre:
BARNSLEY
Tel: 0226 748650

Region 8: Group 2
Group Communication Centre: LEEDS
Tel: 0532 342144

Region 8: Group 3
Group Communication Centre: YORK
Tel: 0904 639991

Region 8: Group 4
Group Communication Centre:
MIDDLESBROUGH
Tel: 0642 224641

Region 8: Group 5
Group Communication Centre:
NEWCASTLE UPON TYNE
Tel: 091 496 0848

REGION 9: *WALES*

RSPCA Welsh Headquarters
Villiers House, Charter Court
Phoenix Way, Llansamlet
Swansea SA7 9EH
Tel: 0792 310449
Fax: 0792 310450

Region 9: Group 1
Group Communication Centre:
LLANDUDNO
Tel: 0492 860897

Region 9: Group 2
Group Communication Centre:
SWANSEA
Tel: 0792 310445

Region 9: Group 3
Group Communication Centre:
NEWPORT
Tel: 0633 821834

REGION 10: *LONDON*

RSPCA Regional Headquarters
20 Station Road
South Norwood
London SE25 5AJ
Tel: 081 653 3420
Fax: 081 653 2358

Region 10: Groups 1–4
London Communications Centre
Tel: 081 653 3420